THE

THE RETREAT

ADAM
LITTLER

WP
WELLFIELD
PUBLISHING

WELLFIELD
PUBLISHING

First published in the United Kingdom in 2025
by Wellfield Publishing

Print ISBN 978-1-9192928-0-9
Ebook ISBN 978-1-9192928-1-6

Cover design by Victoria Davies

Cover images © Shutterstock

Printed and bound in Great Britain by Lightning Source LLC

I

To Mum

PROLOGUE

This was not supposed to happen. It wasn't the plan – it was not what they were there to do.

The body looked so strange, lying there on the floor. It was sprawled awkwardly, with limbs outstretched at different angles. His mouth was hanging slightly open, as though he was in the middle of a sentence.

As though he still had something to say.

But that was his problem; he always had something to say. That was what led to him ending up in this mess. This horrific, unsightly mess.

It was too late now. What would happen next?

The silence in the room was deafening. The kind that only comes once the yelling stops and the blood has been spilled. The kind that suffocates a person, rather than being peaceful. Engulfs your thoughts, rather than eases them.

They stared at him, hands trembling whilst standing alone with his body. Two people, one heartbeat – thumping quickly enough for the pair of them. What to do?

Murder wasn't the intention. Or maybe it was. But not like this. This was reckless. A spur of the moment reaction to the venom he had spewed from his poisoned tongue. His words began to echo inside the room, inside their mind, taunting and cruel.

Deliberate or not, he was dead now. That wasn't going to change. It didn't matter anymore.

What did matter, was what followed next. There were people who could help – they always had. But they needed to be found quickly. Discreetly. They would know what to do. Hopefully they would understand – they would have to.

This wasn't the justice they craved. Nor was it the revenge any normal person would want. Not really. But why did it feel right?

Perhaps it was about control, and taking it back from a man who stole it from so many.

The only question that really remained now, was how far must someone go to keep it?

CHAPTER ONE

Gareth

Gareth had been dreading it all week. But, after driving for what seemed like an age through a winding, anonymous corridor of fields and trees, he had finally arrived. He sighed as he pulled into the car park of *Wellderness Adventure*, the location of the 'Compulsory Team Building Trip', and cursed the pot-holed minefield he had just inflicted on the suspension of his aging Ford Focus.

He had been pondering since Monday how to get out of being there. It was difficult to remember how many of his grandparents had 'died' since he'd started this job, and he had concluded he couldn't risk claiming to have a fifth funeral to attend – particularly on a weekend.

Unless it was his.

'Smile, Gareth. It might never happen!' his line manager, Theo, had said to him last week, as he had been reading the email sent from Claire in HR, notifying him of the weekend's arrangements.

Theo didn't understand the depth of the turmoil, which festered behind Gareth's visible disgruntlement. How could he? Sure, he was one of HomeHubs's longest-suffering employees, but Theo and the CEO, Benjamin, had known each other through their parents' friendship long before that. Theo toed the company line. Anything for an easy life. He ignored the arduous bullshit that came with the place, completely desensitised to the constant micromanagement and unethical treatment Benjamin inflicted on his staff.

Gareth had wished Benjamin dead, many times. He had even fantasised about doing it himself, in a violent sequence of action scenes from the Deadpool playbook.

But he had bills to pay, so he needed the job, and until he found something else – which was proving to be exhaustingly difficult, he was stuck in a gruelling, continuous cycle of workplace misery.

He assessed his surroundings through his car's windscreen. Rural North Wales. For a place that was only around half an hour to forty-five minutes' drive away from the built-up townscape he called home, it really did scream 'wilderness'. As he sat there, alone, he absorbed the varied tones of green from the overgrown grassland, and trees which pierced the clouds, sights which made for the perfect setting to experience peaceful seclusion. It was a shame the group he was joining would not complement such tranquillity. If only he was in such a place under alternative circumstances.

After a few more moments of contemplation, he reluctantly opened the driver's side door, slowly getting out of the car. He took in a lungful of fresh air, and noticed that even without the Ford's protective bubble, beyond the delicate breeze, only silence surrounded him.

The woodland retreat was a few miles from the 'town centre' of Pontfechan – which was more of a quaint, olde-worlde hamlet, with little activity of note, when he had passed through earlier – and it showed. Pontfechan sat within the boundary of Llangollen, according to the address Claire's email had provided, but Gareth assumed that was more to do with electoral wards and historic parish boundaries than helping out-of-towners to find their way.

Further down the car park, there was a battered old pickup sitting beside a white Mazda convertible with its top down; both were caked in dirt. He didn't recognise either vehicle from work. There also was no sign of the vehicles' owners.

First here, for a change, he thought. Despite his reluctance to be there, he daren't have been late; the mere thought of the scene his boss would have created over such a *sin* made his stomach tighten.

Just beyond the car park, was a wooden structure. It didn't look quite as luxurious as some of the log cabins Gareth had previously seen advertised online – there would be no 'glamping' this weekend. He walked around to the back of his car, opening the boot to gather his belongings, before shuddering, as he heard the unmistakable roar of one of Benjamin's seemingly endless fleet. The bright yellow Lambo – a stupid choice for the terrain. It rolled into view, and Gareth could see Benjamin and Francesca, his girlfriend and HomeHub marketing manager, in the two front seats. Benjamin locked eyes with his, and gave him the usual scornful, condescending look he always did, whilst Francesca was too distracted by her mobile phone – pouting in front of a selfie.

'Oh, you're early. Well done,' sneered Benjamin as he climbed out of his car, brushing his hair back with his fingers. 'Surprised the motor got you here at all, let alone before everyone else.'

Ah, yes. The one about 'the motor' again. Perhaps if you paid me more...

It was regrettable that Benjamin's car hadn't disappeared down one of the potholes.

'Hiya, Gaz,' said Francesca, actually giving him the time of day – a rarity. 'Benny, can you get my bags please.'

Gareth watched her as she made her way from the car park, over towards the cabin which stood parallel with the car park. She looked like someone who was about to enter a reality TV show, set before a more tropical backdrop. She strutted along in her designer minidress, high heels and oversized sunglasses – an outfit which probably cost more than Gareth's car. Her elegantly preened chestnut hair fluttered as the air brushed past her.

'Gareth, can you get these,' said Benjamin, pointing an elbow towards a Louis Vuitton suitcase and matching holdall, without looking up from his phone screen.

He didn't give Gareth opportunity to decline, instead stomping off in the same direction as Francesca, snarling to himself about having 'no bloody phone reception'.

Gareth sighed. *What did his last slave die of?*

He pulled his own rucksack over his shoulder and locked the car. The sound of a couple of other vehicles approached, as they pulled into the car park behind him, their tyres crunching over the gravel. Turning around, he saw it was a couple of the sales team, Billy and Matthew. With everyone else beginning to arrive, there was no going back. He was stuck.

He struggled towards the cabin, overloaded with luggage like an exhausted mule. He heard heavy footfall scraping along the gravel up ahead. A burly man, who Gareth guessed was around sixty, dressed in khaki workpants and a faded black sweatshirt, was lugging freshly chopped logs of wood towards an existing pile which sat against the cabin wall.

The man glanced at him briefly, before shaking his head. He placed the remaining logs with the others and looked back at Gareth.

'Packed for all weathers, have you?' he said, in a deep, baritone voice which echoed.

Gareth smiled, continuing to try and keep hold of the luggage.

'Something like that.'

'Aye, well the forecast had a bit of rain when I checked last night.'

The man's attention returned to the logs, and Gareth continued onwards.

'All right, Gaz?' bellowed Billy from behind him. The unnecessarily high volume of his Kentish accent scratched at Gareth's eardrums. 'Did I see Ben going down here?'

'Yeah, up here somewhere,' replied Gareth, still struggling to walk at any pace as Billy and Matthew caught up with him.

'Nice one,' said Billy, before rushing ahead.

'They all yours?' asked Matthew with a chuckle, gesturing to the bags Gareth was carrying.

'Francesca's.'

'Thought so,' said Matthew, reaching out to the one closest to him. 'Here, I'll take this one for you.'

Gareth nodded. 'Thanks.'

'Looking forward to this?' asked Matthew.

'Can't wait,' said Gareth sardonically. 'Two days of corporate bollocks and stupid games in the middle of nowhere… what's not to look forward to?'

Matthew smiled to himself. 'It won't be that bad, mate.'

Gareth looked around, taking in the building he had seen from the car park and realised beyond it were two more cabins, both made of the same, wooden outers. They were wider, though, with small, decked areas to the front, and were fitted with long, dusty windows. The lights were on inside the middle building, and Gareth could see people inside.

Let the weekend from hell commence.

CHAPTER TWO

Jodie

'Is that the place, there?' asked Tara, looking up from the map on her phone.

Jodie signalled the left indicator as she turned down yet another a narrow entry. What greeted her was less a road, and more of a broken-down dirt track. But they hadn't seen anything resembling a point of interest for a while.

'I bloody hope so,' she said.

'It's going to be fab, this,' said Tara. 'Do you reckon the lads have actually brought any beers?'

'I've got no idea. Probably.' Jodie was too busy trying to manoeuvre the car safely down the lane, before they came to a small bridge, which took them juddering over a stream below.

'Well, they aren't having any of ours.'

A weekend of team-building activities was definitely something Jodie could get behind – even if it did involve physical exercise, which she tended to avoid at all costs. She wasn't, however, fully on board with Tara's plans to get sloshed in the evening. She loved working with her in the finance team, and had grown close to her as a friend away from the office, but the trip was a perfect opportunity to catch Benjamin's eye. *That* was more important than drinking alcohol and making a show of herself.

She worked hard. She had ambition. She wanted progression and success, and whilst that may require stealing an idea or throwing a colleague into the fire every now and again, it was just the nature of things. One does not climb the food chain by settling for the scraps, after all. You had to be ruthless, and play the game well, to succeed.

The fact she was utterly besotted by Benjamin's confident, outspoken and charismatic presence, was simply an additional source of motivation.

It was no coincidence that he was attending on the same weekend as her. She had helped Claire from HR to plan the team building trips, and had made sure to influence the make-up of the groups to suit her agenda.

As for that spoiled bitch Francesca, well, she was an unavoidable compromise, to ensure they got Benjamin there. She would just have to mitigate against her. But for Christ's sake, surely he was smart enough to see through the ditzy bimbo act? The simpering 'you would not belee-ave the number of likes my new Loubs have got, Benny', as she shared her attempts at an upper middle-class lifestyle through the filtered lens of Instagram. It made Jodie's blood boil.

'Well, here we are,' she said.

'Let's go, it's time to par-tay!' replied Tara, doing a little dance with her arms, before opening the passenger side door.

As she stood and took in her surroundings, Jodie was struck by just how quiet everything was. She could smell the clean floral air as she inhaled deeply, and felt her lungs thanking her for it.

They dragged their wheeled cases over towards the wood-cladded buildings, unsure where exactly to go, but they found five of the group inside the second hut along.

Tara stepped in through the open door first, announcing her arrival with a confident 'hiya!' before Jodie followed behind. She saw Matthew and Billy from the sales team loitering by the door. Inside the cabin reminded her of the type of places she would go to on school trips, to learn about insects and collect leaves. Here though, there were no indecipherable pieces of artwork from children pinned to the walls – instead it was quite minimalistic and lacked décor of any kind.

She spotted Gareth sat alone on a plastic seat at one of the long cafeteria-style tables, with his usual sullen expression, and Francesca was taking photographs on her phone – seemingly of her surroundings, rather than herself. Jodie scowled as she took a good look at her outfit, which was in no way fit for the occasion. Did she think she was going on Love Island, or something?

Finally, she saw Benjamin.

He was speaking on the phone, pacing up and down between the banks of tables. She could tell it was a work call. The man never stopped. Whoever was on the other line was receiving a thorough grilling. His paces slowed, developing into a swagger, as she guessed he had begun to win the argument. The confidence he displayed was just so attractive to her. Her eyes met his, just for an instant, and she felt her heart flutter uncontrollably. Even wearing simple waterproofs and walking boots, he was a good-looking guy, and his scruffy, just-out-of-bed hair gave a slightly rugged edge to his boyish charm.

Suddenly, a lady began waving a plate in front of Jodie. 'Do you want a bacon sandwich, hun?'

It took her aback, momentarily, but she smiled as she took one, and said 'thanks.'

'I'm Ceri, the camp manager,' said the lady. 'Strapping young fella over there is Bryn, our ranger'. She pointed over to an older gentleman, who clearly spent a lot of time outdoors. He had the gruff look of a proper working man, with the dirty mahogany skin tone to go with it.

Jodie was surprised that Ceri was working in such a place. She was a mature woman, but she clearly took pride in her appearance, and compared to Bryn, she looked very glamourous. The bleached blonde hair and fancy manicure made Jodie think she would be more at home in a hair salon. She just couldn't imagine her risking those pristine nails in the grubbiness of manual labour, or trying to navigate her way through the muddy woodland in high heels.

'Morning, girls,' said Benjamin, walking back into the centre of the group. 'Bloody phoneline and wi-fi is useless.'

'I'm *awfully* sorry, we're in a bit of a black hole for any kind of signal here,' said Ceri, clearly put out by Benjamin's complaint.

'Mnhorming, Nhenjamin,' said Jodie, almost choking on a mouthful of sandwich in her attempt to intercept any more comments from her boss. The last thing she needed was for him to grow annoyed and leave.

'Erm, yes,' he replied, raising an eyebrow. He too, took a sandwich from Ceri's plate, but did not thank her, or even acknowledge her in any way. 'Are we waiting on anyone, Jodie?'

She looked around the group, quickly completing a muted headcount.

'Just one more. Steffan, from the warehouse.'

'Okay,' he replied, before bringing his face towards her ear and whispering, 'I'll go and do some actual work while we're waiting'. The sensation of his breath touching her skin as he spoke left her tingling.

As he drifted back across the room, to try and make another phone call, Jodie just stared. She took another bite of her sandwich, without taking her unblinking eyes from his behind.

God, I love you.

CHAPTER THREE

Steffan

Steffan stared out of the passenger side window, as the satnav barked directions in its monotone voice. He saw sheep in the fields, minding their own business in the peaceful simplicity of the land around them. They were supposed to have arrived a few minutes ago, and now he was late. He despised being late. Promptness and organisation had been instilled within him during his time in the armed forces.

He was looking forward to the trip, even though the people he would meet there were strangers. He hadn't got to know many people at work beyond those on his shift, and such circumstances may have been daunting for another man, but he had plenty of experience of being in close-knit environments with unfamiliar faces.

There was a strange divide between the office and warehouse staff. Steffan understood it. It was prevalent in all walks of life. Like how the Army and the RAF hated each other. But his warehouse supervisor, Dan, seemed to enjoy feeding the hostility downwards when addressing his staff, as though his role positioned him on a middle-ground.

'I'm guessing you've not heard the news,' Dan had begun with a smirk, on Monday. He waddled down the aisle towards Steffan, before resting his laptop on the underside of his forearm. 'Says here, you're in the first group to go on a team building trip to some wilderness place on the weekend. Only you from over here though, I'm afraid.'

'Sounds good,' replied Steffan. He was being genuine, but he also knew that offering anything other than a positive reaction would only provoke and feed the type of condescending 'banter' people often received from Dan. He was, what Steffan would have called on camp, a JAFFA: Just Another Fat Fucking Arsehole.

Dan had soon skulked off, clearly disappointed at not receiving the rise he was after, mumbling that he would 'print the details off'.

Despite his supervisor, Steffan quite liked his job at HomeHub. It was physical work, rushing around the warehouse all day. It kept him busy. The shifts weren't always ideal – having to get out of bed at half-past four and cycling in for a six 'til two, or the waiting around all morning for a two 'til ten. But it was a job. A job he had struggled to find, after being dismissed from the forces before an eighteen-month stint at Her Majesty's pleasure.

Life had been tough over the last few years. Tough on him. He knew that he hadn't helped matters, by getting caught after breaking and entering a pensioner's bungalow. But the country hadn't helped him to re-integrate into life on Civvy Street, either. He had lost count of the number of times he had found himself in the middle of a scuffle outside the pub, after someone who had sunk one too many had then fancied their chances against 'the big man from the army'.

He had wondered, initially, if it was his fault, for failing a drugs test when he was back at Catterick. Perhaps he would have had it easier back in the real world had he completed his service honourably. But he wasn't an anomaly. He went online, saw the posts about homeless veterans with squeaky clean records and holes in their limbs, or those suffering from PTSD, whilst migrants enjoyed the luxuries of comfortable housing and easily attained benefits.

A reward, almost, for the suffering they had endured in their home countries.

He didn't resent people who had sought refuge – he had helped, even fought with, citizens of war-torn countries, and had nothing but sympathy for most of them. But it wasn't the point. After all, British troops often returned home from similar – and sometimes the same – environments. Why were they not rewarded for their suffering? Why were they left to fend for themselves, through all the nightmares and flashbacks?

HomeHub had given him a fresh start. He'd heard from an old friend on his parents' estate, how they were always taking on warehouse staff. An asylum for the local degenerates, somewhat, with crap pay for mindless work – but that was better than no pay and a dependence on food banks. And now, he was around six months in. He had kept his head down, and nose clean.

Whilst he had been more willing to attend the trip than Dan seemingly would have liked, getting there turned out to be a struggle. After being let down by his father, who had been called out to work at short notice, his mother had reluctantly agreed to drive him to the outskirts of Llangollen.

'Bloody hell,' she said. 'It's about time you got yourself driving, Steff. You're nearly thirty-five.'

He knew she was right. It would make life easier, but he liked riding his bicycle. It kept him in shape, after almost a decade of military service, his body was used to the routine of being pushed.

'You don't mind giving me a lift places, though, do you Mam?'

'No, course not, my love,' she said, with a forced smile.

When they eventually arrived, twenty minutes late, he gave her a kiss on the cheek, and hopped out of the car, with an old army-issued daysack he had managed to keep hold of. He waved at her, and waited until she was out of sight, before taking a deep breath and turning towards the camp.

The world around him was silent, except for the crunch of gravel beneath his feet, and the faint trickling of water from what he guessed was a nearby stream. It felt as though the echoes of civilisation were further away than he had realised. The camp lay before him like a forgotten relic, nestled deep in the North Walian countryside. He continued to the timber cabins, constructed in a clearing which blended into the surrounding woodland. There was no sign of any life at first, a place still and almost unsettling, as the countless trees around him stood like sentinels, staring down at him as he marched on in search of company.

A rustling took him by surprise. As he turned sharply, a grey squirrel jumped out of some overgrown brush before scurrying into the woods and out of sight.

'Get a grip, you wally,' he muttered to himself with a shake of the head.

'Steffan, you're here. Thank God,' said a voice laced with relief.

He looked up to see a girl he thought he recognised from work, stood on the decking outside the cabins. 'Sorry I'm late,' he said.

'Don't worry,' she said. 'You're here now. I'm Jodie, by the way. In case you didn't know.'

He smiled, before following her inside, relieved his lateness hadn't caused him any problems.

CHAPTER FOUR

Gareth

'All here, are we?' asked Bryn, shooting a look at his colleague, Ceri, as he spoke.

She smiled, and gently brought her hands together in a silent clapping motion. 'Okay, everybody,' she said. 'First things first, I'd like to officially welcome you all to *Pren y Glowr*, or 'The Miner's Wood', for those of you who don't speak Welsh.'

'Who *does* speak Welsh, nowadays?' chirped Billy, which Ceri did not dignify with an answer.

'The name of the place dates back to the early eighteenth century, when – as the story says – a local man named William Edwards had returned home to Pontfechan from working on the colliery to find his wife, Maria, in the company of the village constable. In his rage, William slashed Maria's throat, and fled, after a struggle with the other man.'

'Jesus,' muttered Gareth.

'I know,' she said quietly, before pausing. 'He was found later that evening, hanging from one of the tree branches in this very wood.'

'Serves him right,' whispered Francesca.

'What are you talking about?' snapped Benjamin. 'His whore wife had embarked on an adulterous escapade… why shouldn't he defend his own honour?'

‘Maybe he didn’t satisfy her needs,’ Francesca retorted.

‘But anyway,’ said Ceri, cutting them off. ‘It’s a far happier place now, being home to Wellderness Retreat. And on that note, we ask you to hand in any mobile phones during the daytime – you need to switch off from the outside world to truly embrace the wellness element of this weekend. Then, we’re going to gather together as a group and do a quick icebreaker.’

There was a stunned silence, as everybody processed what Ceri had just announced.

‘Nobody said anything about giving our phones in,’ said Tara.

‘What if there’s an emergency?’ asked Matthew.

‘Good question, but don’t worry,’ said Ceri with a grin. ‘There’s not much mobile phone reception anyway, but we have a landline in the office for that purpose.’

‘Guys, just hand them in,’ said Jodie, taking charge and collecting everybody’s phones. As he passed his own over, Gareth noticed Benjamin had slinked away momentarily – there wasn’t a chance *he* would be ‘switching himself off from the outside world’; how else would he harass suppliers and other employees, spoiling their weekend?

‘Thanks, love,’ said Ceri, taking the phones from Jodie. ‘Right… let’s get going with the icebreaker, shall we?’

Gareth stifled a groan. He hated these types of activities. He hated how corporate-types always seemed to love them, because it serves as an invitation to fellate their own ego, with an admiring – or at least obligated – audience.

‘I know what you’re thinking,’ continued Ceri, ‘you all know each other already – you’re all friends…’

I wouldn’t go that far.

‘But, it will give Bryn and I a chance to familiarise ourselves with the group, and more importantly, you may even discover something new about the people you’re standing next to.’

‘So, what are we doing then?’ asked Billy. Ceri smiled at him, but Gareth spotted her nostrils flaring, ever so slightly, as she did so.

‘What I would like everyone to do, is take a pencil and a piece of card from the table behind you, write down something interesting about yourself, and pop it into the lovely bag that Bryn is holding, before we mix them up.’

Gareth looked over at Bryn, who lifted and displayed a little velvet bag, which reminded him of the one used in the F.A. Cup draw.

‘Can it be anything?’ asked Jodie, who’s face portrayed the concerned look of somebody who was taking the activity far too seriously.

‘It can. But try and think of something nobody else here will know, because in a minute, everyone is going to guess who’s written each fact.’

Gareth didn’t know what to write. He was a simple guy. Nothing particularly inspiring or dramatic jumped to the forefront of his mind. The ace up his sleeve, however, was the fact he generally did not share much of his private life in the workplace; he worked to make money, not friends, so he felt there was little point in mixing the two. This made it much easier to come up with something nobody would know about him. In the end, he kept it straightforward, with something he suspected would be under the radar and unmemorable.

I have six pets. Three dogs, a rabbit and two chickens.

It didn’t take too long for the rest of the group to add their contributions to Bryn’s bag, and for Ceri to hurriedly move on with the exercise. From her urgency, Gareth sensed she was the type of person who loved hearing the juicy secrets people come up with. But he had no doubt she loathed anyone who failed to entertain her, whether it be through playing it safe, or mocking the game with jokes and nonsense.

She unravelled the first card with enthusiasm, as though it was the first chocolate from a Christmas selection box, eager to sink her teeth into the treat inside. She frowned in unmistakable disappointment as she read it to the group, in dismal monotone, as though she had just bitten into a miniature Twix, or coconut éclair. It was Gareth's.

He felt the tingling sensation of his cheeks glowing, and as soon as his eyes met Jodie's, she seemed quite proud to reveal how she had 'figured out' who the culprit was.

'Yep,' he said, acknowledging her accusation.

There was a brief raucous cackle, led by Jodie and Tara's jubilant celebration. They must have missed the point of the icebreaker, and instead decided it was some kind of competition.

'What are your chickens called? I bet one's called *Scramble*,' asked Billy with a cackle.

'Or *Nugget*?' suggested Matthew.

'Yes! Scramble and Nugget,' said Tara. 'Amazing!'

'Not quite,' replied Gareth. 'Eggatha Christie and Beatrix Clucker – book puns.'

'I don't get it,' said Billy with a frown.

'I never read,' conceded Matthew.

Attention quickly dispersed from Gareth and his chickens, as Ceri cleared her throat and asserted herself with a firm 'okay'.

It was good, Gareth thought, to have his moment under the spotlight done, and out of the way – he was glad he didn't even have to share the names or breeds of his dogs with the others, as Ceri rushed to pick out the next card, clearly desperate for something a little less vanilla.

The next card appeared to do the trick.

'Ooh, this is a good one', she squealed. 'It says, *"I recently had a threesome, with my best friend from work and her married next-door neighbour"*.'

Holy shit.

CHAPTER FIVE

Jodie

The group's reaction made her squirm.

'Tara, for fuck's sake!' Jodie gasped, shaking her head at her friend, who stood beaming with a look of oblivious pride, and mouthing 'what?' – revelling in the ovation of Billy and Matthew, whose whooping and calls of 'Oi, Oi' rang unbearably in Jodie's ears.

She looked around in panic. All she could see were smirks on faces and eyes fixed on her. Even Benjamin looked amused, his mouth twitching as Francesca whispered into his ear, whilst glancing sideways at Jodie. Of course, it must be hilarious to her; Little Miss Perfect who shall never put a foot out of place.

This was all wrong. So very, very wrong. She tried to speak, to try and douse the flames of Tara's revelation, but nothing came out of her mouth.

It was bad enough her supposed 'best friend' – a proclamation which may have touched Jodie, in other circumstances – had revealed such a sordid secret, particularly in a work environment, but without context it cast her in an even worse light. She had been incredibly drunk, and her 'married next-door neighbour' was in fact separated from his wife – hence him living in a studio apartment next to hers. She had regretted it deeply the second she returned home, let alone the morning after.

But none of that would matter. Not now Benjamin knew what she had done, not if it disgusted him, in the way she had been disgusted with herself.

'Okay, everybody,' called Ceri. 'Let's do the next one, shall we?'

'Yes,' agreed Benjamin. 'Quieten down and listen please, guys.'

Despite some continued sniggering, as some of the group struggled to recompose themselves, focus returned to the game as they awaited Ceri's next selection.

'All right,' continued Ceri, pulling the next card from the bag. 'This one is *"I have gone from working a Saturday job in a local department store at eighteen, to having my own global department store with almost fifty permanent employees"*. I doubt this one will be too difficult to guess.'

Jodie noticed Ceri rolling her eyes as she made that remark. What was her problem? Probably jealousy – after all, Benjamin must have been twenty years younger than her, and his business overshadowed hers. A multi-million-pound ecommerce versus a woodland retreat which would certainly have benefitted from refurbishment? It was no contest.

As Billy began singing 'There's only one Ben Pearson' in the tune of *Winter Wonderland*, Benjamin raised a hand in acknowledgment, beaming from ear to ear. He looked at Jodie, and winked at her in a way that said, *'Don't worry – all eyes are on me now'*.

It was a look she had seen before, many times. A look which drew her to him from the moment she first met him. On her first day at HomeHub in 2018, she had been so nervous. Despite that, she was excited to be part of the journey. She had done her homework and had read about Benjamin and his incredible success – the youthful, privately educated upstart who was making quite a name for himself amongst his competitors, and in the world of business beyond them.

Then, she saw him in the flesh.

Boyishly handsome, with a smug-yet-endearing smile on his face, as he exchanged pleasantries with his workers. He was going straight to the top, and he bloody well knew it.

'Ah, Benjamin – this is Jodie. She's starting with the Accounts team today,' Claire had said, gesturing in Jodie's direction, as though presenting Benjamin with another valuable possession for his collection.

'Oh, hello Jodie,' he said, still smiling, before offering his hand to her. His eye contact was intense; it was as though he had the power of hypnosis.

'Nice to meet you,' she rasped shyly, praying that her own hand wasn't noticeably layered with sweat as she shook his.

As brief as their first encounter was, she had been instantly smitten with him. He didn't know it, but she did, there and then – one day he would be hers.

Four years later, and she was still waiting for that day.

But she hoped this weekend was where things would change.

CHAPTER SIX

Steffan

Benjamin was a confident guy, Steffan could see that. He would've had to be blind not to. But it was hardly surprising; why wouldn't Benjamin be that way? He wasn't much older than Steffan and was a rich businessman, successful and in control. He had it all. It was difficult not to be impressed by him. Plus, he'd shifted the spotlight onto himself when one of his employees were floundering in a pit of embarrassment, after most of the group had found Jodie's humiliation amusing. If Steffan was completely honest with himself, Benjamin using his presence in this way was commendable, regardless of his agenda.

Looking around the group after Ceri had read Tara's icebreaker card, Steffan had been in the minority. He hadn't laughed. He wasn't one to judge people's life choices – he had made some terrible ones of his own, and he wasn't a hypocrite. Besides, was a threesome *really* such a big deal, nowadays?

The only other person who had apparently not been amused was Gareth. The guy whose card had been drawn first – the one with all the animals. A revelation which told Steffan very little, other than perhaps a willingness to care for other living things. He'd not said much at all since they had been there, so his refrain meant he was either too miserable to have a sense of humour, or he was just trying to be a decent bloke. Time would tell.

Out of everyone, the icebreaker was most beneficial for Steffan. He knew none of these people. He was the outsider, and these titbits of information – and the way the group interacted after each card – gave him a little insight into the members of the group, even if Benjamin being full of himself and Gareth being fairly reserved threw up no big surprises.

Tara was out there, certainly. Although probably a little bit dim, judging by the way she had exposed something Jodie was so uncomfortable with. Unless she was a two-faced bitch. But she was young, and pretty in a way which suggested innocence rather than malice.

'Okay… so we've had Benjamin, Tara and Gary,' said Ceri.

'Gareth,' mumbled Gareth.

'Sorry?' asked Ceri.

'It's Gareth, not Gary,' said Tara with a smile.

'My mistake,' replied Ceri unapologetically. 'Let's see who's next.'

Bryn shook the bag gently, as if to shuffle the remaining cards inside. As he held it open for her, Ceri removed another card and began to read. 'So, this person played football for their country, representing Wales Under 16s.'

'Oh wow, that's amazing,' said Francesca. 'Well, it can't be you, Billy.'

'Why not?' he snapped, eyes widening briefly before narrowing into a glare. 'I'll have you know I had trials for Gillingham when I was a kid!'

'Yeah, when you were about eight,' said Matthew.

'Oh, sorry *Gareth Bale* – how's your career going?' said Billy.

'I only meant because you aren't Welsh,' insisted Francesca.

'Thank God,' said Billy.

Prick, thought Steffan. 'I'm guessing it's Matthew, then?'

'Yeah,' said Matthew.

'Nice one,' said Steffan with a nod in his direction. 'That's awesome.'

'Cheers.'

'And now he's under my wing, learning from the best salesman around,' boomed Billy, wrapping his arm around Matthew who shrugged him off playfully.

'Let's not forget who started the company, Billy,' said Benjamin, smiling as he spoke, but he stared unblinkingly at Billy.

'Of course – *current* salesman, I should say,' replied Billy, laughing nervously.

'Let's move on,' said Ceri, brushing past the tension still hanging in the air.

'Next one, Bryn?'

The ranger nodded with a grunt of agreement, holding the bag out for Ceri once again. She reached for another card and read it aloud, glancing up at the group.

'This person once got a job they hated because they had a huge crush on someone who worked there.'

There was a collective pause, but Steffan saw Jodie's face flush as she began to chew at a fingernail. It was quite obvious who's fact it was, but he wasn't going to say anything – it would've been quite a fun piece of trivia at the time of writing, he was sure, but there was no doubt she regretted sharing it now.

Billy grinned. 'I think we've all been there, right? Getting a job or going somewhere just for the eye candy.'

'Oh, yeah?' teased Tara. 'Who've you got your eye on, then?'

'Nobody,' he replied. 'I mean, I joined the gym once because the girl on the reception was fit.'

‘How did that go for you?’ asked Matthew, smirking knowingly.

Billy sighed. ‘She had a girlfriend.’

Even Steffan managed a chuckle at that.

‘Come on, who was it?’ asked Francesca.

‘It wasn’t anything stalkerish,’ said Jodie, in attempt to brush it off. ‘I was in college so wanted a job… my first job, really. I knew a guy who worked in McDonalds; he was the older brother of one of my school friends.’

‘Ooh, a school crush,’ joked Tara. ‘What was his name?’

Jodie shrugged her shoulders, as if trying to stay nonchalant. ‘Tom, but it doesn’t really matter – I needed a job, he put in a good word and got me in there.’

Francesca leaned forward with a raised eyebrow, clearly interested in the details. ‘But you got the job just to get closer to him? What happened? Was it worth it?’

Steffan watched Jodie pause awkwardly, taking a deep breath as her cheeks maintained their rosy glow, before she looked up again.

‘I fancied him a bit, he was always the “cool big brother” who would show off when we were at my friend’s house, teasing her and things. But nothing came of it – I guess he just saw me as his kid sister’s mate. In the end I got sick of smelling of fries and being covered in grease. I didn’t work there for long.’

‘Didn’t you tell him how you felt?’ asked Tara.

‘No, I was too shy.’

‘Not too shy for Tara and your neighbour though,’ muttered Francesca.

‘Well, however you got there, you made your first step into the working world,’ said Benjamin. ‘Even if it was flipping burgers.’

Steffan felt he had started to gather a clear enough picture of the group. Matthew’s fact meant he was clearly active and competitive – a good person to have on side for any team games during the weekend, but it was people's reactions to each other which was the most telling. There was a definite fragility amongst them all – the sniping and willingness to make jokes at each other's expense just seemed childish to him. Sure, there was banter amongst the troops when he was in the army, but one man tended to give as much back as the next.

Francesca's story about being a model for 'only a shampoo advert' was telling – she tried to play it down initially, but Steffan picked up on a sense of her feeling she was meant for greater things than working in marketing for HomeHub.

'It's good that you decided to work in the real world, in the end,' said Benjamin.

'Would you ever go back into it?' asked Matthew, seemingly interested in Francesca's experience.

'I don't know,' she said with a smile. 'I guess if the opportunity arose – I had barely left school when I did the campaign. An agent spotted me outside Selfridges, when I was shopping with my mother. It was good fun, but ages ago now.'

'You're stunning though, you could definitely be a model full-time, if you wanted to,' said Tara. As there were murmurs of agreement from others in the group, Steffan noticed Jodie scowling, arms folded as though she was withdrawing from the group slightly. A hint of jealousy, perhaps?

'Thanks,' said Francesca, clearly overselling the compliment – her knowing smile told Steffan she was fully aware how attractive she was.

Ceri drew another card. 'Last couple now, guys. This person left a successful career at another company to come and work for HomeHub, believing in the company's vision and the leadership of Benjamin.'

There were a couple of groans, but Billy was undeterred in owning his statement. He began grinning, as though he'd been waiting for this moment.

'Easy,' he said. 'For those of you who don't know, I used to work for one of HomeHub's old stationery suppliers back in Maidstone. I was the manager there, on decent dollar, but after getting to know Ben I just knew I had to jump ship. I could see what he was building, so who wouldn't want to be part of that?'

He paused, as though he had made some kind of grand statement, but Francesca made a loud retching sound, breaking the silence in the most appropriate way.

'I appreciate your words, Billy,' said Benjamin. 'This, ladies and gentlemen, is a fine example of workplace loyalty. Some of you could learn something from that.'

Steffan couldn't be certain, but he thought Benjamin had switched his focus directly towards Gareth as he finished saying his piece. One thing was for sure though, if anyone loved Benjamin more than Benjamin did, it was Billy.

CHAPTER SEVEN

Gareth

What was his fucking problem? *Workplace loyalty*, was he taking the piss? And why was Benjamin looking at him as he said it? Gareth had worked at HomeHub for five years, and whilst it wasn't out of undying loyalty for the cause it was a decent stint. He put the effort in too, but it seemed not to matter because he didn't buy into Benjamin's bullshit. Plenty didn't, but Gareth was as adept at hiding his feelings as he was at poker. Absolutely terrible.

'One more to go,' declared Ceri. She seemed relieved.

God knew Gareth was.

'And the bonus ball says…' announced Bryn, as Ceri pulled the final card – Steffan's card, out of the bag.

'This person can speak a grand total of five different languages,' read Ceri. 'Aren't we a clever bunch?'

'As if,' was the response from Billy. Whilst it was one of the more surprising – and interesting – facts of the icebreaker, Gareth wasn't the least bit surprised at Billy's disbelief. There had been occasions where he had questioned the salesman's ability to use coherent English, let alone master another four languages.

'Can you really?' asked Tara.

'Yeah,' said Steffan. 'English and Welsh, obviously, but then I learned some Dari in Afghanistan and Swahili in Kenya. Bit of Arabic, but not much.'

'Yeah, so you can't speak proper, full-on in five languages then, can you?' said Billy. Steffan didn't reply as he furrowed his eyebrows.

'More than you, though, isn't it?' said Matthew, nudging Billy with his elbow.

'I'm good with English. If everyone else just spoke our language, it would be easier, innit?'

The irony of Billy's not so 'good' English wasn't lost on Gareth.

What an absolute moron.

'I agree with Billy, to an extent,' declared Benjamin. 'If we are honest, the world was a far better place when Britannia ruled the waves.'

'Exactly,' said Billy, as though he had been justified.

Gareth didn't partake in the idle chat that followed the debate Steffan's fact had sparked. He was fed up already. He wondered if there was an excuse he could give that would allow him to leave early.

His eyes drifted around the room. HomeHub really was a circus. Individually, most of these people weren't *too* unbearable to be around, but as a group, they made him want to shrivel up and die.

It was quite refreshing to have met Steffan. His fact – speaking five languages? Gareth wasn't someone who tended to envy others, but he couldn't help being impressed. What a gift, to drop into a new land and pick up the lingo so effortlessly – Gareth had barely scraped his way through GCSE French.

Steffan was quiet too, a little detached even. But he didn't seem too bothered about that – if anything, there was an understated confidence to him. It was unusual to see someone working at HomeHub and not desperately seeking Benjamin's approval, or unapologetically begging for attention by making jokes, or just being the loudest voice in the room. It made Gareth wonder what a bloke like Steffan was doing there in the first place.

In some ways, it only made him question his own place within HomeHub. Why was *he* still there? For all their flaws, the people around him all seemed to belong at the company. Gareth knew he didn't. But then, he wasn't sure where he belonged anymore. If anywhere.

CHAPTER EIGHT

Steffan

After the icebreaker activity, Ceri had called for an early lunch, ahead of the afternoon's itinerary. Steffan sat alone. The canteen may not have been elegantly furnished, but it was spacious, particularly for a smaller group – everyone could have taken a table in pairs, had they wanted to. He was happy to sit in the company of empty chairs, watching the others from a distance. The icebreaker had helped, but further observation would give him an even clearer picture of the characters within the group – to work out who would be best to team up with for further activities, and who he was better off avoiding.

Billy had already made a bad impression on him, with his smart-arse comments and general demeanour, so he was number one on the keep-away-from list. Benjamin would likely be a 'Commander in Chief' within any group; he was the boss, after all. This may not translate to a useful team member during physical activities – especially if he was somebody who preferred to simply delegate as opposed to getting stuck in himself, but then he would naturally command the respect of the team. It was a tough call.

There was an interesting dynamic of duos – Billy and Matthew, Benjamin and Francesca, and of course, Jodie and Tara, though the latter appeared to be a turbulent relationship, if the icebreaker was anything to go by.

'All right, mate?' said Gareth, approaching Steffan's table and sliding into the seat opposite.

Steffan wasn't surprised to have been sought out for company. The only person – other than himself – who didn't seem to be naturally paired up with anyone, was Gareth.

'A'right, la.'

'Your "thing about yourself" was pretty cool, wasn't it?' said Gareth, appearing genuine, if a little uncomfortable about conversing with a stranger.

'Not think announcing a seedy threesome with a married bloke to the room is "cool", no?' replied Steffan with a slight smirk.

Gareth winced behind a half-hearted grin, as though he knew he shouldn't laugh. 'What do you think this next activity is going to be, like?' he gestured towards the pile of rucksacks, lying near to the cabin door.

Steffan shrugged. 'Bound to be a scavenger hunt, isn't it? Be sound, I reckon.'

Gareth nodded and said 'good shout'. The small talk was short-lived, and they sat in silence, as Steffan resumed his observation of the others in the room.

He had noticed the presence of Bryn, who had stayed in the canteen whilst Ceri had waltzed off, presumably to a quieter part of the facility. Bryn was eating a sorry looking sandwich, squashed and limp, which he had unwrapped from some crinkled tin foil. He, too, was watching members of the group.

Steffan couldn't work out if he looked annoyed about something; his lips were pressed tightly together, and he barely blinked as his eyes were slightly squinted whilst they trawled over everybody in the room. The expression didn't change when his eyes met Steffan's, but he did gesture a nod towards him, before his gaze returned to other members of the group. Maybe he just wasn't a 'people person'.

Ceri timed her return to the canteen well. Steffan was chewing on the last mouthful of pasta from his lunchbox. Everyone else had just finished eating too, and were on the verge of becoming restless.

'Is everyone suitably fed and watered?' she asked. Everyone muttered in agreement, before she consulted the notes on her clipboard. 'Okay, next up – it's time for a Scavenger Hunt. Two teams. Two different routes, both of equal difficulty and challenges, and finishing back here at camp – you will know you are finished when you've found something *every* camper needs. All right?'

'What does that even mean?' asked Tara.

Ceri ignored the question. 'Everything you may need is in the bags by the door – compass, wind-up torch, things like that. Though the water bottles will need filling up before you set off.'

It all seemed fairly straightforward to Steffan, but he could see a couple of daunted faces around him.

'Are you and Bryn not guiding us round?' asked Matthew.

'Well, no,' replied Ceri. 'The idea is for you to work together to find your way back.'

'What's the teams, then?' asked Billy.

'Good question,' replied Ceri. 'What I want you to do first, is to get into pairs, please.'

The results of the 'coupling up' were predictable, and Steffan quickly realised that he would be left with Gareth. They exchanged a brief nod and a muttered 'all right' to one another before standing to attention, waiting for the next instruction. He didn't mind – Gareth seemed okay. Obviously, he was quiet, but there had been no bullshit from him, unlike some of the others. Someone Steffan could bear to work with, at least.

For the first team, Ceri placed the two finance girls, Jodie and Tara, with Billy and Matthew, and handed them a clipboard. This left Steffan and Gareth's team to be completed by Benjamin and Francesca.

'Look out boys,' said Francesca, to the sales lads. She winked at them and tilted her head in the other girls' direction. Billy and Matthew burst out laughing.

Steffan looked on as Jodie scowled at Francesca, whilst Tara seemed oblivious, chatting away to her friend on the other side of the room.

'Shall we get started, chaps?' said Benjamin, addressing Gareth and Steffan, as he made for the pile of rucksacks. 'Steffan, I think with your military experience, you can lead navigation – it's been some time since I did this with the boy scouts!'

Steffan smiled and nodded. *Sounds good to me.*

'What do you want me to do, Benny?' asked Francesca, in a whiny, babyish voice.

'Erm, if you fill up the water, whilst we look over the list of instructions.'

Francesca tutted and rolled her eyes, but she did as Benjamin requested.

'So, it says here, we're looking for "gold stars",' began Steffan, as he traced the instruction page with his finger.

'Gold stars? Let's have a look,' said Benjamin, immediately usurping his delegation and spinning the clipboard round to face him. He hummed to himself as he read, and Steffan looked over at Gareth, who was glaring at the back of Benjamin's head with an air of impatience.

'What do you reckon?' asked Steffan, as Francesca arrived with their filled water canteens and began distributing them.

'So, yes, the task is to follow the riddles and clues and what-not, to various points in the forest, collecting "stars". We must collect all of them before returning – fastest team back to camp wins. Oh, and there's a map on the back, too.'

‘Sounds easy enough’, said Steffan, looking at his teammates one by one, who all seemed to agree. ‘Let’s make a move, shall we?’

‘Yeah, the others have already left,’ said Gareth.

They each picked up their rucksacks and made their way out of the cabin, to words of encouragement from Ceri, who wished them ‘good luck’, whilst Bryn warned them to ‘watch out for anything creeping in the bushes’, without giving any hints as to what creatures he was referring to. Steffan decided he was probably joking.

‘Says we head right, out of the cabin,’ he instructed, reading from the list. ‘In fifty metres, it’s our first clue. “*I have some riddles, for you to see. You’ll find them hanging, look out for me*”.’

CHAPTER NINE

Jodie

Jodie hadn't spoken to anyone since the ice breaker. She was *so* annoyed and embarrassed. She still couldn't work it out – why did Tara have to do something so stupid, in front of their work colleagues? In front of *Benjamin*?

The girls walked along the bark strewn footpath, through the woodland, just behind Billy and Matthew. Tara was by her side, but in reality, Jodie wanted to be left alone. She gave a twig a half-hearted kick, the toe of her walking boot sending it skittering into the brush to the side of the path.

'You pair are so bloody slow,' said Billy mockingly, looking over his shoulder.

Tara told him to 'piss off', but Jodie didn't so much as acknowledge him. She continued looking down at the floor as she trudged along.

'What's up, Jodie?' asked Matthew. She couldn't tell if he was being sincere or not.

'Oh, she's still in a mood with me, aren't you, Jode?' said Tara.

She held her tongue, still saying nothing.

'It's not that bad,' said Billy. 'It's quite an eye-opener, actually.'

'What do you mean?' snapped Jodie, finally acknowledging somebody.

'Well, it's like... and don't take this the wrong way, but you seem all "goody two-shoes" in the office.'

'Right.' She wasn't quite sure how he had expected her to 'take it'.

'Not you, Tara. It's not exactly a surprise, coming from you.'

'What the hell? You cheeky shit,' said Tara, with a laugh.

'There's nothing wrong with being professional,' argued Jodie. 'And also, it doesn't look great, in front of the company's owner, when intimate details from your private life are revealed in a work setting, does it?'

Tara stopped laughing. Jodie could see she actually looked guilty. She bit her lip anxiously, before whispering 'sorry'.

Bit late for that, now the whole world knows.

'Right, shall we just get a move on then,' said Jodie, beginning to walk with purpose. *The sooner this is over, the sooner I don't have to listen to you lot.*

The group continued along the trail, in search of their first gold star. They were looking for some kind of structure – Jodie had suggested another cabin, possibly, owing to their team's first clue mentioning '*shelter*'.

As the path began to settle into a slight incline, she felt her chest tightening and her calves begin to burn. She cursed her preference for nights snacking in front of the television instead of going to the gym. It would be a struggle to keep up with the others, before too long.

'Seriously though, I wouldn't worry,' said Billy, 'Ben won't be too bothered about what you get up to in your own time. As long as you do the business, for the business!'

He enjoyed his own, dreadful colloquialism far more than he should have.

'Really?' replied Jodie, hopefully.

'I think he's got enough on his plate with *his* bird to be worrying about what the other girls from the office do in their own time.'

Precious fucking Francesca.

'But nah, honestly,' he continued, 'she just loves it, don't she? Always begging for attention. You've seen her Insta; Lulu Lemon outfits by day, vintage wine and pâté in posh-arse restaurants in Cheshire by night.'

'It does all look a bit Tory,' said Matthew, before laughing awkwardly. 'She is fit, though.'

'Do you not think the stuff online is more for show?' asked Jodie.

'Don't know, really,' Billy continued. 'Obviously, she wears the outfits… and she splashes the cash out on the town. Whether it's for the camera or not, who's to say?'

'Champagne lifestyle on lemonade wages, though, isn't it?'

'Doesn't matter if you're shagging a millionaire,' chirped Tara.

If only, thought Jodie.

The group powered on, moving deeper into the woodland. It felt as though the trees were beginning to tighten around them, like a pack of wolves circling on its prey. The air was rich with the scent of earth and moss. Above them, the sky was barely visible through the tangle of leafy branches. Jodie could feel the weight of it all, restricting her progress as her breathing became more laboured. Where was this bloody star they were looking for?

'Right, what was this clue again?' asked Billy. He seemed to be growing impatient – Jodie wondered if perhaps she wasn't the only one struggling with the hike.

Tara, who was carrying her team's clipboard, cleared her throat. 'For the millionth time, "*What once offered shelter now looks bleak, you can still enter if you can take a leak*".'

'Right, so we know it's obviously a building or summink, don't we?'

Obviously, thought Jodie.

'If it looks bleak, it'll probably be abandoned… might even be falling apart,' suggested Matthew.

'Even so,' said Billy, 'surely it should stick out like a sore thumb in the middle of a forest.'

'Maybe not,' said Jodie, as something caught her eye. She stepped off the path, and the others followed her through the uneven brush which carpeted the ground amongst the tree trunks. The closer she got, the more it came into focus – mostly hidden beneath a thick curtain of unruly ivy and brambles stood a stone wall. It was a structure no bigger than a modest garden shed.

'How on God's green earth did you spot that?' asked Billy.

'I don't know,' Jodie murmured, taking a step closer to the wall. She ran her fingers over the ivy-clad stone, tracing the roughness beneath the leaves.

'It's a bit creepy,' said Tara.

'Don't be stupid, it's just an old building,' scoffed Jodie.

They moved to the front of the structure to find a weathered door creaking slightly, caressed by the wind's soft touch.

'Well, go on then Jodie,' said Billy, gently nudging her in the back.

She stiffened at his touch, holding her breath inside her lungs. Reaching for the door handle, she paused, before cautiously opening the door. It groaned at the hinge, as a wind-gathered pile of leaves scattered over and past her feet.

Looking beyond the doorway, she couldn't see anything for the darkness. The others moved in closer, peering over her.

'It stinks in there!' groaned Tara.

'It's mega old, though,' said Matthew as he clicked on the torch from his backpack.

As the bulb flickered into action, there was a sudden shriek as something flew straight towards them. Ducking and screaming, the group covered their faces and shifted out of the way, as wings flapped loudly above them and into the distance.

'What the fuck was that!?' squealed Billy.

'I think it was an owl,' said Matthew.

'Either that or a pigeon,' replied Jodie, looking around at the higher branches of the surrounding trees.

'A pigeon? Behave yourself,' Billy sneered. 'It was definitely an owl, it nearly took my flippin' eyes out.'

'How did that happen when you were diving for cover before any of us?' joked Matthew.

'Come on,' said Jodie. 'Let's find this star and move on.'

Matthew led the way with caution, his torchlight cutting through the darkness. The moment Jodie placed a foot inside, a chill embraced her body. Her stomach twisted, as dread caused her to shiver. The air was damp, and there was a sense of something morbid in there – a presence, almost, unseen as it lingered in the shadows.

'Jesus, this is rank,' said Billy.

Jodie didn't disagree. The stench was nauseating. It resembled a cocktail of mildew, decay and ammonia.

'What's that over there, Matt?' asked Tara, as she gagged at the back of the group.

'Over where?' Matthew said.

'In the corner,' said Jodie, squinting into the gloom. She raised an arm, stretching her pointed finger out in front of the torch's beam.

'Is that a toilet?' suggested Matthew.

'You're joking,' said Billy. 'So that's what the clue meant by *taking a leak*… I thought Bryn might just have had a secret sex dungeon with a dodgy roof.'

‘You’re so weird,’ said Tara with a laugh.

‘That is the most Stone Age toilet I’ve ever seen, though,’ Billy declared.

‘Not quite,’ said Jodie, rolling her eyes. She moved closer, aided only by torchlight. It may not have been as old as Billy suggested, but it certainly bore the echo of an earlier time – essentially a wooden box, with a hole cut out of the top to constitute a seat. ‘Matt, come here.’

He joined her, sweeping the light over the toilet. There were cobwebs clinging to the corners and years of filth resting over the rotting wood.

‘Where’s the star?’ muttered Jodie.

‘Check inside,’ said Billy.

‘Check inside?’ she scoffed. ‘Why don’t *you* check inside?’

‘Nah, you’re doing great.’

Jodie sighed, bracing herself. Her fingers trembled slightly, as she felt for the edge of the wooden lid. The stiff hinges groaned with resistance as she lifted it.

A sudden rustling was followed by a small shadow scurrying between her legs.

‘Shit!’ she yelped, stumbling backwards. The lid slammed shut with a dull thud as Tara shrieked behind her.

‘What is it!?’ bellowed Billy.

‘I don’t know,’ Jodie gasped. ‘Something jumped out from inside – a mouse, or a rat, maybe.’

‘Was the star in there?’ asked Matthew.

‘I *don’t know*.’

‘Oh my god, just get me out of here,’ whined Tara.

Jodie’s heart was still racing, but she couldn’t give up now. God knew the others weren’t going to volunteer to open the toilet, especially after what had just happened.

After regaining her composure, her fingertips found the lid once again, and this time, she lifted it fully. She squinted inside, holding her breath as if braced for another sudden movement. Nothing. She slowly exhaled, relief flickering through her chest.

'Well?' asked Billy.

'Matt, can you come closer,' Jodie instructed. 'I need more light inside.'

Matthew paused for a moment. 'O-kay…'.

'It's there!' she said, her face breaking out into a grin. 'In the actual toilet pan.'

'Gross,' groaned Tara.

'Are you gonna get it out then, or what?' asked Billy.

Here goes nothing, she thought. Quickly, she reached in and grabbed the star, yanking it out of the toilet.

Holding it up in front of her, the torchlight glowing over her, she looked out beyond the others. 'Let's get out of here.'

CHAPTER TEN

Gareth

'Give us a boost, Gaz', said Steffan.

Gareth was looking up at the first gold star, which was attached to a piece of thick twine and dangling from an oak tree branch. It swayed a little in the lazy wind, glinting as dappled light filtered through the leaf canopy above. Something about it hanging there struck Gareth as being in slightly poor taste, given Ceri's earlier tale. He estimated it was around three or four metres up, so presumably Bryn had used a set of ladders to hang it up there. For them, reaching it was going to be easier said than done.

'At the trunk?' asked Gareth.

'Well, it would be difficult to do it from halfway up the damn tree, wouldn't it?' sneered Benjamin.

Gareth exhaled through flared nostrils. 'I wasn't sure if he meant directly underneath the star.'

You pretentious shitgibbon.

'Aye,' said Steffan, gesturing for Gareth to come to him. 'Just so I can try and get to a bit where there's grip, see?'

Gareth nodded. He could see that whilst the lower section of the trunk was rough and textured, there were no little grooves or crevices to place feet or grab onto. He crouched down onto one knee at the base and Steffan stepped onto his braced hands. The weight instantly made his arms tense.

With a loud grunt, Gareth pushed up from his knees to lift Steffan as much as he possibly could. The muscles and joints in his arms and shoulders screamed in protest, his grip straining under the pressure. Steffan wasn't the biggest guy he'd ever met – just over six feet, a bit taller than Gareth, and whilst he was certainly not overweight, eighty-odd kilos was still eighty-odd kilos. His arms trembled as he battled to remain steady.

Steffan wobbled, forcing Gareth to adjust his footing. For a second, he feared he was going to lose the battle to stay upright. He clenched his jaw, determined to not make a show of himself in front of Benjamin. He couldn't afford to look weak.

'Go on, guys,' encouraged Francesca, who was doing nothing other than standing next to Benjamin, watching, offering absolutely no assistance.

'Argh, shit,' groaned Steffan.

'What is it? Are you all right?' wheezed Gareth. He was still holding on to Steffan's trailing feet and was struggling more with each passing second. Craning his neck to see what was happening above him, he saw Steffan's arm, outstretched and reaching for a nearby branch – his fingers painfully close to touching it.

'Can't. Get. This. Fu—' Steffan panted, before a sudden jerk of weight threw Gareth off balance once more.

Gareth heard a sickening crack, and as if in slow motion, the branch snapped under the strain of Steffan's weight, sending him tumbling down. He took Gareth to the ground with him.

Gareth lay flat on his back, dazed and winded from the impact. A sharp pain radiated from his ribcage as he stared at the swirling branches above him. Loose leaves floated lazily around him, like confetti at a wedding. For a second, all he could do was blink and try to regain his focus – and the ability to breathe.

A shadow loomed over him.

Benjamin, with that smirk, his irritating face bathed in self-satisfied smugness, tilted his head to the side as he looked down on Gareth.

'Well, at least you got the star down, guys,' said Benjamin, holding the yellow piece of plastic aloft. 'There's an envelope with it too. Must be another clue, or something.'

At least the pain isn't all for nothing, Gareth thought.

'What does it say?' asked Steffan, who was also still lying on the floor, covered in debris from the disturbed tree.

Benjamin opened the envelope with an almost deliberate slowness, carefully removing and unfolding the piece of paper which had been sealed inside, as though it was some kind of sacred text.

He cleared his throat dramatically.

'*I'm neither buried below, or up in a tree, but you should hurry before I drift out to sea*', he read.

There was a brief silence, as though they were all contemplating what the clue meant.

'Water, then,' Gareth muttered, pushing himself up into a sitting position.

'Yes, but it says *hurry*, so – on your feet chaps. Chop, chop.'

Gareth sighed quietly, struggling back to his feet. *I'd like to 'chop, chop' you, you arsehole*.

He ran through the clue in his head. *Hurry before I drift out to sea*. The sea? They were nowhere near the coast.

Steffan, dusting himself off and blowing a leaf away from his cheek walked to Francesca, who had the map clutched in her hand. 'Can I borrow that for a sec, please?'

She handed it over without hesitation, and he unfolded it before scanning the page.

'Only water I see on here is a stream,' he said. 'Same one that runs under the bridge near the car park.'

'Why does it say about drifting out to sea? It doesn't make sense,' said Gareth.

Francesca tilted her head, thoughtful. 'It's probably just so the clue rhymes.'

'Good call, Francesca.' said Steffan. 'I think you're probably right.'

Gareth nodded. Francesca beamed at them, clearly pleased to have been useful.

'Come on, less dilly-dallying – more clue hunting,' barked Benjamin, cutting in and snatching the map from Steffan without another word. If he had even been listening to Francesca's input, he didn't show it.

Steffan said nothing, but he made sure to catch Gareth's eye – raising an eyebrow in silent response. As Benjamin trotted on ahead, with Francesca shuffling along behind him, appearing a little deflated.

Gareth and Steffan hoisted their rucksacks over their shoulders and followed suit, following the distant sound of running water.

CHAPTER ELEVEN

Jodie

'I'm telling you, it's some kind of animal house,' said Billy.

He was really starting to get on Jodie's nerves. It was bad enough that he was a complete idiot, but to never listen to what anyone else had to say… what made him think he was *always* right?

'Billy, come on mate,' said Matthew. 'The clue says, "sharp or smooth, flat or round, whatever I am lives on the ground" – what kind of animal is *flat*?'

'The kind that gets in my way on the road,' Billy said, before cackling at his own joke.

'What do you – oh, Billy!' said Tara, slapping his arm with a shake of her head.

'It is *not* an animal,' said Jodie. 'It's talking about rocks.'

'But there's loads of rocks,' protested Billy. 'Rocks, stones, flippin' pebbles. How could we be expected to find the *right* rock? It's got to be a rabbit warren or summink.'

'Maybe it's one of those?' said Matthew suddenly.

The others stopped in their tracks. Jodie checked where he was pointing and saw a stack of rocks piled high. The greys of the stone stood out like a beacon, amongst the brown and green of the world surrounding it. The rocks, varied in shape and size, had clearly been placed carefully on top of one another. Towards the bottom of the pile, the rocks were much larger, with edges softened by the growth of moss – they had clearly been there for some time. But could Bryn have put them there?

'Nah, that's just a cairn,' said Billy.

'A what?' asked Tara.

'A cairn. It's like a marker for hikers – I saw it on some Bear Grylls show one time.'

'I don't think they get many hikers around here,' said Matthew.

'Suppose not,' shrugged Billy. 'Apparently, they use 'em for memorials and burials sometimes as well.'

A shiver travelled down Jodie's spine. Memorials and burials? It was certainly quiet enough for someone to get away with murder, or to at least dispose of the body.

'Shall we just check?' she said, hurrying over towards the stones.

'Can do,' said Billy. 'But we'll be wasting our time.'

'Maybe not,' said Tara, looking at their map. 'We're definitely on the right path, and we've not seen anything else similar to what the clue says.'

'Whatever.'

Despite Billy's pig-headedness, Jodie was relieved to see Matthew and Tara follow suit and walk over to investigate the rocks more closely.

'Can you see anything, Jode?' Tara asked.

'No,' replied Jodie. She felt disappointed. On closer inspection, they did just look like a pile of rocks. Weird, sure – especially when considering Billy's description of what these 'cairns' were sometimes used for, but there was no sign of a star peeking out from the pile.

'Looks like we'll have to move them, then,' said Matthew.

As he picked up a rock from the ground, Jodie told him to stop.

'What's up?' he asked. 'Don't you want to find this clue?'

She turned and looked at Billy, who was watching them with a distinct lack of interest. 'What if he's right. Don't want to ruin a marker – or a *memorial*.'

'We can put it back,' said Matthew, smiling at her. 'Come on.'

The three of them began moving rocks, carefully and systematically. If they had to rebuild this thing, they didn't want to create a harder puzzle than it needed to be.

'Are you coming to help?' Tara called over to Billy.

'Nah, you're all right,' he said.

Jodie looked over her shoulder at him and scowled. Standing there, casually swigging water from his canteen.

What a team player.

She continued to crouch down beside Matthew and Tara, brushing the dirt from her fingers as she shifted another stone. The damp smell of the earth filled her nose, as wood louse and other tiny insects scurried away from the sudden disturbance.

'Found anything yet?' Billy called from behind them. 'Digging through rocks like a bunch of muppets. There's nothing there, I'm telling you.'

Jodie clenched her jaw, ignoring him. The urge to lob a stone at him was overwhelming, but she refused to give him the rise he clearly wanted.

'If it's not here, then we'll put everything back and move on,' she said, forcing her voice to stay even. 'That's kind of the point of a scavenger hunt.'

Billy scoffed but didn't reply.

'There's got to be something here,' Matthew grunted, turning a bigger stone onto its side. Beneath it was nothing but more damp soil and the crumbled remains of old leaves. He let out a frustrated sigh. 'We might be wasting our time here.'

Jodie glanced at Tara, who was chewing her lip, eyes darting between the rocks and their surroundings. She looked uneasy.

'What is it?' Jodie asked.

'I dunno,' Tara said. 'I just... I keep thinking about what Billy said. About the cairns being for burials. I mean, what if this actually is one?'

'Just ignore him,' said Matthew. 'He probably just wishes he was on Benjamin's team.'

He's not the only one, thought Jodie.

Billy faked a loud yawn, continuing his relentless wind-up campaign in the background.

'Oh, piss off, Billy,' Tara snapped, throwing a small stone which bounced off the ground and hit his leg.

'Hey!' He jumped back, raising his hands defensively. 'No need for violence, crazy woman.'

'You're not even helping!' Tara shot back.

'Because it's pointless!'

Jodie tuned them out. Her fingers ran along the edge of a stone that felt... different. It was too smooth, too perfectly round to be part of the natural pile. Her pulse quickened as she carefully lifted it.

A glint of yellowy gold.

She held her breath. It had to be it.

'Guys,' she said, voice urgent. 'Look!'

Matthew and Tara turned immediately.

Nestled in a shallow dip in the earth was the star, slightly dirtied but unmistakable. Jodie let out a triumphant laugh, pulling it free and holding it up.

'See?' she said, looking straight at Billy. 'Not pointless.'

Billy rolled his eyes. 'Took you long enough.'

'You didn't even—' Tara started, but Jodie cut her off.

'It doesn't matter,' she said. 'Let's see what the next clue says.'

'Hadn't we best put this all back together?' asked Matthew.

Jodie looked at the stones they had disturbed. An unease prickled at her. She wasn't really sure why. Maybe it was just Billy's stupid comments getting under her skin. Or maybe it was the way the breeze seemed to have suddenly picked up, feeling colder on her damp, muddy hands.

Whatever it was, she had no interest in staying here any longer.

'Come on,' she said. 'Let's get a move on then. Billy, give us a hand.'

He tutted and groaned, but Billy relented. 'Fine.'

Jodie turned the star over in her hands and removed the paper which contained the next clue.

'*You may find I scrape and scratch, but with me you will meet your match.*'

'What does that mean?' asked Tara. 'They'll scrape and scratch, but be your match?'

'Sounds like Matt's type of woman,' said Billy.

'Shut up,' replied Matthew. 'It's got to be something with thorns, right?'

'There's only one way to find out,' said Jodie.

As they made their way along the path in search of their next star, Jodie felt an odd shift in the atmosphere. Looming clouds had covered the warmth and light of the sunshine, and the thickening density of the trees cast a deeper shadow over their trail.

But there was something else.

As they walked along, their footsteps the only sound against the hushed stillness, Jodie couldn't shake the feeling that they weren't alone – it felt as though they were being watched.

She forced herself to focus, and put her concerns down to being tired and dehydrated, but she determined that the sooner they could get back to camp, the better.

CHAPTER TWELVE

Steffan

'I'm not bloody going in. Not a chance,' said Benjamin.

'Oh, go on, Benny,' said Francesca, 'it's your turn.'

'I haven't seen *you* do anything useful,' he mumbled.

Steffan couldn't take another second of the childish sniping. He tossed his bag onto the grass in dismay.

'It's all good, I'll get it.'

He looked down at the rocky stream bed. It wasn't too deep – probably only knee height at most – but the bank was largely submerged, and even to the untrained eye, anyone could see just how quickly the current was flowing. The trickling sounds of the water burbling along grew louder, as he carefully lowered himself in. It was a calming kind of white noise, which was far better than listening to the bickering between Benjamin and Francesca.

The star was on the other side of the stream. It was tied to a low-hanging branch which sat above the water, and trapped, probably deliberately, within a pooled area that was enclosed by larger rocks.

Steffan trudged through the water, crouching as he went, in a bid to maintain his balance. The strength of the current was crashing against him with relentless, significant force. He took each step slowly, primarily to further reduce the chances of becoming completely drenched, but also because the algae-covered rocks on the stream bed were extremely slippery.

'Nearly there,' called Gareth.

He had reached half-way and had become relaxed. He had found a rhythm and was moving steadily.

'Keep going,' encouraged Francesca.

He tried to. Then, his right boot skated across the smooth surface, and he almost lost his footing.

'Shit!'

'Oh no,' groaned Francesca, 'be careful!'

The calls from the others weren't particularly helpful, but Steffan was determined. In the zone. He reached for the branch, and whilst he remained wary of putting it under the strain of his weight after the last tree's inadequacy, he used it to pull himself the last few steps of the way.

'Got it,' he called out, raising the star triumphantly.

Francesca squealed and clapped rapidly in childlike excitement, as Benjamin looked on. Steffan carefully turned around, and held the star between his teeth, before making his way back across the stream.

As he reached the bank, he dropped the star onto the grass, as Gareth approached him, offering a hand to pull him up and out of the water.

'Good work,' he said, and he heaved Steffan, who pushed himself up with his other arm. He sat down on the grass, to catch his breath.

'Tougher than it looks, that was,' he said.

'Can't be harder than avoiding turban-wearing gunmen in the desert though, surely?' asked Benjamin. Steffan couldn't believe he had come out with such a statement.

'Guess not,' he replied.

'That being said,' continued Benjamin. 'I've seen videos of them on YouTube – they have zero braincells. Just pull the trigger and hope, without any training. Stupid camel-herding idiots.'

Steffan didn't know what to say. He looked at Gareth, who had turned away, but he saw him shaking his head.

He was finally beginning to understand why some of the other lads in the warehouse didn't like Benjamin; he was coming across as an ignorant, stuck-up posh boy.

Finally offering some assistance beyond standing on the side lines, Francesca picked up the star, and opened the clear plastic bag which accompanied it, removing the next clue. She unfolded the piece of paper quickly, but before she could read it to the group, she lost her grip as a gust took hold of the clue. They could do little more than watch helplessly, as it dropped down onto the stream.

Steffan jumped up, as he and Benjamin rushed to the edge of the bank, but it was too late.

'What did you do that for!?' shouted Benjamin.

Francesca gasped in horror. 'It was an accident!'

'You've fucking ruined the entire thing now.'

'I'm sorry,' murmured Francesca.

'What kind of *retard* would drop a piece of paper into a stream? Absolutely useless, honestly.'

Francesca apologised again. Repeatedly. Steffan could see she was upset – but he couldn't help but feel that it was all a bit of an overreaction from Benjamin. Plus, the way he had just spoken to her was disgusting – he knew that if he had spoken to any woman like that, his mam would give him the hiding of a lifetime.

'It might be all right,' said Steffan. 'What does the map say – does anything stand out which could be the next location?'

'Oh, erm, not sure,' muttered Benjamin, fumbling for the paper they picked up at the start of the hunt, and analysing it. 'Not really – it follows along the trail, obviously, but doesn't say where exactly we're to look for the stars.'

'We just need to keep walking then, don't we?' suggested Gareth.

‘Yeah, exactly,’ agreed Steffan. ‘We’ll follow the trail, but just be more vigilant.’

‘So, you overreacted and were mean to me for no reason,’ said Francesca.

‘Well, no,’ scoffed Benjamin, ‘it was still a completely *retarded* thing to do.’

‘Benny, can you stop using that word, please? And just admit you were in the wrong.’

‘Oh, shut up and behave, you silly little girl. You’re just embarrassing yourself.’

What the hell?

Steffan had heard enough.

‘Come on, now. Let’s get moving – I don’t think getting on each other’s backs is going to help us to finish. There’s no need for it.’

He looked to Gareth for some support, but he just watched on in silence.

Benjamin clenched his teeth together behind his closed lips, which didn’t succeed in hiding his grimace, as he glared at Steffan, as though he wanted to smack him. He must have thought better of it, as he hissed a disgruntled ‘yes’, before charging ahead of the pack, and was closely followed by Francesca, who ignited a conversation-cum-argument out of earshot of Steffan and Gareth, who remained some way behind.

‘Could have chipped in with something there, la,’ said Steffan.

‘What do you mean?’ asked Gareth.

‘The way he was speaking to her, man. Fucking bad, like.’

‘Yeah, that’s how he is. She must be used to it, by now.’

‘Even so. I’ve seen it on the barracks. Blokes like that, normally PTSD, in their case – coming back with a right temper on them. They’re willing to speak to their missus like dirt in public, they've likely no issue giving them a slap behind closed doors.'

'I get what you mean,' said Gareth, though Steffan doubted a civvy really could. 'I don't think he's like that though; he's just a horrible prick with a short temper; speaks to everyone like shit if things aren't going his way.'

'Everyone, yeah? He won't want to be a prick with me, or he'll be going headfirst into the stream.'

Gareth started laughing, and Steffan did too. But he was only partly joking. He'd battered people for less.

'Come on,' he continued. 'Let's catch them up and get this thing over and done with.'

CHAPTER THIRTEEN

Jodie

The path was growing narrower, its space becoming impeded by the brambles on either side. The air had grown heavier, as though the forest itself was pressing down on them. It was strange, for Jodie to be in the vast openness of the supposed 'great outdoors', but feel this claustrophobic sensation around her. She was sure the others must have felt it too, but nobody had said anything aloud.

Billy huffed behind her. 'Are we sure this is the right way? Or are we just pissing about and getting lost for the fun of it?'

'The clue said it was this way,' said Tara.

'And the map,' added Matthew.

They sounded tired and frustrated. Even Billy's wisecracks had started to carry an edge. Jodie wasn't surprised. A scavenger hunt was supposed to be something fun, and it had started to become vaguely enjoyable after she had begun participating with the group, following her earlier low mood. But now, it was beginning to drag. It didn't help that her feelings of unease were lingering.

'If it's something that'll scrape and scratch, it's got to be round here,' she said, gesturing to the overgrown prickled foliage that surrounded them.

At least I hope it is.

‘If it’s in these brambles, how are we supposed to know *where* to look? We’ll be here all flippin’ day,’ said Billy, kicking at the dirt in front of him.

‘I don’t know, Billy. Do you have any suggestions, or are you just going to complain all weekend?’

‘Look,’ said Matthew – interjecting before Billy could come out with another wisecrack. ‘We’ll just have to focus, and keep our eyes out for something, if there are any disturbed plants or whatever.’

Jodie tried to do just that. Focus. The problem was, her focus was on the feeling that something was not quite right. It wasn’t just the darker surroundings beneath the tree’s coverage. The silence was the thing screaming the loudest. It was *too* quiet. As though the woods were listening to them – watching and waiting to see what they did next.

Something prickled at the base of her neck, and she immediately turned to look over her shoulder. Nothing. She looked around her. Just Billy, Matthew and Tara.

‘Jode?’ said Tara, looking at Jodie with furrowed brows. ‘You good?’

She forced a nod. ‘Yeah. It was just… never mind. I’m all good.’

They continued to walk as a group, taking a steady, vigilant approach in their search.

It was Tara who spotted it first. ‘Look over there!’

They turned to where she was pointing. Deep within the tangle of brambles, sat another star – its brightness peeking through as it stood out to them.

Jodie stepped forward, carefully feeding her arm through the mass of twisted stems. Before she could get to the star, the army of thorns had latched onto her like the claws of a beast. She groaned as she yanked her arm back out of the bush.

‘Careful,’ said Billy.

'It's well and truly in there,' said Matthew, 'we're going to have to clear an opening so someone can get in to grab it.'

Billy laughed. 'There's not a chance I'm doing it – I'm not getting scratched to shit for some stupid game, it's just daft.'

'I don't think anyone thought you would,' said Jodie, rolling her eyes. 'I'll bloody do it – Matt and Tara, you guys need to pull the branches apart.'

As they carefully took hold of the outer stems of the brambles, Jodie pulled her sleeves down over her palms and put her hood up over her head. It wouldn't offer much protection, but it would have to do. And besides, she wanted it over and done with. She shielded her face with one arm as she lowered herself and ducked into the growth with crab-like movements. Her free arm was stretched out, reaching for its target. She could feel the pressure of the brambles as they prodded at her back, pricking at her jacket. Finally, her fingers brushed the cold, smooth surface of the star.

'Got it!'

She wrapped her fingers around the star and stumbled back out of the thorns. In her hand, she noticed there was something fixed to the back of their latest find, secured with an elastic band. She turned it around.

'What is that – a matchbox?' said Billy.

'Looks like it,' said Jodie.

'What's inside?' asked Tara, as they all approached for a closer look.

Jodie freed the matchbox and opened it, discovering another folded piece of paper inside.

If you haven't mastered rubbing sticks, spark some life into this quick fix.

'What does that mean – are we done?' asked Tara.

'I bloody hope so,' said Billy. 'I wish that old bastard Bryn was here to tell us what we're meant to do now.'

A sudden crunch took Jodie and the others by surprise. It sounded like the breaking of a twig. A figure stepped out and into view. Bryn. Looking at them. Unblinking.

'You found it then,' he said flatly. 'Well done.'

'Bryn,' said Jodie. 'What are you doing here?'

'Yeah, I thought you weren't coming out for the activity?' added Billy.

'Just keeping an eye on things,' he said. 'Looks like you've finished just in time. There's some rain in the air – could well be a storm.'

'So, this was the last thing we had to find?' asked Matthew.

'Aye – didn't you hear what Ceri said? You would know you're done when you found something camper's need.'

'Shouldn't campers know how to start fires the old-fashioned way?' asked Billy.

'I suppose so,' said Bryn. 'Can you start a fire "the old-fashioned way?".'

Jodie smirked as Billy stood there silently.

'So can we go back now?' asked Tara, a sense of hopefulness in her tone.

'You can,' said Bryn with a nod. 'Follow your map, it shouldn't take you long. I'm off to see if the other group have finished yet.'

As they followed the trail back towards the camp, Jodie couldn't help but think about the sense of unease she had been feeling during the scavenger hunt. How long had Bryn been there *keeping an eye on things*? Keeping an eye on *them.*

She thought about the way he had suddenly emerged. The sound of a twig breaking beneath his boot, before he was standing there. Had he been there the whole time, stalking them?

Glancing over her shoulder, she half-expected to see him there, lurking. But he was gone. All that was left was the brambles and the trees, watching them in silence as they left.

CHAPTER FOURTEEN

Gareth

It had been around ten minutes since Francesca had stormed off in a huff, and they still hadn't caught up to her. Gareth couldn't blame her for going. Even a shamelessly spoiled, up-their-own-arse brat can only take so much abuse from the person they've sold their soul to.

That said, getting caught in the crossfire of a lover's quarrel – while stuck in the middle of a forest in Arse End – was hardly his idea of fun.

'She must have gone off the path,' declared Steffan.

'What do you mean?' Benjamin hissed. A search and rescue mission wasn't on Gareth's preferred itinerary, but Benjamin appeared to be seething about it. Ironic, really, given it was all his fault – how could he be surprised?

'Well think about it, like. We've been charging after her on the trail for a while, haven't we? Unless she's blinkin' Mo Farah, and pegging it the whole way, we'd have at least spotted her, wouldn't we?'

'Maybe she has run, for a bit at least. Widened the gap between us?' suggested Gareth.

'She might've, like, yeah. But look across there – you can't see clearly, I know, but you'd catch glimpses in the gaps,' Steffan explained. He was pointing through the trees, roughly in the direction the path would straighten to, after the next bend.

He was right. Gareth could see the gaps he referred to, located intermittently amongst the thicket of trunks and undergrowth. The sunlight filtered through the cracks, breaching the growing darkness within.

'Well, that's just bloody excellent then, isn't it?' cried Benjamin.

'So, what do we do?' asked Gareth, though he already knew the answer.

'Have to turn back from here,' said Steffan. 'Split up, break out into the woods either side. Look for the clearest routes – she won't have gone running through a bunch of nettles. It's pretty dry, but keep an eye out for footprints in the dirt. Or any other clues.'

Benjamin tutted and grumbled, as though it was all such a huge inconvenience to him, and him alone, but he turned back with them to follow Steffan's plan.

He began calling Francesca's name, as he ventured off to the right. Gareth was no hunter, but it didn't take being John of the Priests or Davy Crockett to understand shouting to someone who is trying to evade you, was at the very least, counterintuitive.

Gareth looked at Steffan, who looked back at him as if to say, *'what a total idiot'*, before the former military man also proceeded to the right, likely to ensure the area was suitably covered.

With the other two searching one side, Gareth took the other and headed left amongst the trees. The ground was uneven, as both hidden and exposed roots had disturbed the settled earth to leave ridges and cracks in his wake. Old leaves from previous abscissions crunched and rustled underfoot, though he was treading carefully, to limit the risk of alerting Francesca of his presence.

He could still hear Benjamin, although his calls of 'Francesca, where the hell are you?' grew quieter as the distance between them widened. As he started moving through the depths of the trees, Gareth began to think about what Steffan had said earlier. He wondered if Francesca's actions were merely a reaction to Benjamin's venomous words, or whether she could be subconsciously trying to escape a darker, more vicious situation. 'You're a useless, pathetic liability,' Benjamin had snarled, before adding 'I don't know why I even bother with you.'

Francesca hadn't reacted verbally. She had visibly stiffened, but there was no smile or cheeky response to play Benjamin's vile behaviour down. Instead, her face had gone blank. Without a word, she had turned on her heels and walked away.

Gareth remained doubtful it was anything more than a response to the manner in which she'd been spoken to. He was confident that his own knowledge and experience of Benjamin made hitting a woman unlikely. He was more of an entitled man-child than an overpowering and heavy-handed bully. One who spat and screamed publicly, when things didn't go the way he wanted them to. But it didn't mean he was incapable of inflicting pain in other ways. Gareth knew that first hand. The mind games, underhanded comments, and constant stress placed on him in work were the fundamental source of his spiralling depression.

There was still no sign of Francesca. Benjamin's calls were muffled and unintelligible now, but they suggested she hadn't been discovered on the other side of the path, either.

It had become gloomier, and was much harder to see ahead of him, as the sunlight which offered some visibility through the treetops had faded. The darkened sky promised imminent rain – just what they needed to make the situation even worse.

CHAPTER FIFTEEN

Steffan

Steffan's patience was wearing thin. He hoped Francesca had gone in the opposite direction, and that Gareth would find her – if he hadn't already, because with Benjamin's constant noise, they didn't have a chance of catching her if she was, or had been, nearby.

'Francesca, stop being a silly little girl!' yelled Benjamin. His voice was shrill and grating.

'She's not going to come out, with you saying things like that,' said Steffan, trying to keep his voice down.

'Oh, be quiet,' Benjamin shot back, waving Steffan's comments away. 'She needs to do as she's told.'

Steffan stopped walking. He turned his head towards Benjamin, narrowing his eyes. 'She's not a dog. Plus, she was upset and wanted to get away from something didn't she?'

'What do you mean, "get away from something"?' Benjamin snarled, curling his lip.

Before Steffan could respond, Benjamin stepped in front of him, blocking his path. His shoulders were tense as he squared up, widening his stance. Like a peacock fluffing up its feathers. Steffan glanced down at Benjamin's sides to see clenched fists.

You don't want to do that, pal.

'Look. No offence, right, but the way you spoke to her was minging. Came across to me as bullying, like. Abuse, even. I'm just thinking, maybe you shouting is going to make it impossible to find her – she's not just run off in a tizz, it's like she's hiding from you.'

Benjamin didn't reply at first. Instead, he continued to stand in front of Steffan, with the same stiff posture. Whatever he thought, his display of dominance wasn't working. Then, a smile formed on his face. A cold, calculating smile. It was more of a sneer.

Suddenly, Benjamin leaned in towards him. 'What's your name again? Steve? No, Steffan,' he said, in a quiet, silky drawl. It was as though he was mocking him. 'Steffan, I think you should remember who you are talking to. I am your boss. I can take your job away from you. And don't think I'm not aware of your previous *misdemeanours*. No, I am *well* aware. You need me, don't you? *Yes, you do*.'

He pressed his finger into Steffan's chest and edged even closer. Steffan looked down, and back up at Benjamin's face. His jaw tightened, but he remained silent. Fighting the growing urge inside of him. It was what Benjamin wanted, for him to lash out. But Steffan didn't move. Didn't flinch.

'Oh, do you not like people putting their hands on you?' mocked Benjamin, his voice dripping with amusement. 'What are you going to do? Go on, *I dare you*. See what happens.'

Steffan said nothing. His fingers twitched. His body urged him to react – to knock that smug look off his face and watch him spluttering around in the dirt. He could have done it without breaking sweat. But no. Not here. Not now.

Instead, he smiled. Not in a friendly way. It was a slow, knowing smirk. One daring Benjamin right back, to try something else. He left Benjamin's words hanging in the air.

Benjamin opened his mouth to speak again but flinched as they were interrupted by a voice cutting through the trees.

'Hello, hello,' came the voice again.

Benjamin stepped back, removing his finger from Steffan's chest. He smiled over Steffan's shoulder, with a look of burning embarrassment on his face – like a child being caught stealing from the treat drawer.

Steffan turned around, to see someone trudging towards them through the undergrowth.

Bryn.

The old man's expression was unreadable as he approached. 'Just come to see how you were getting on,' he called out to them. 'The other group has already finished.'

'Really?' asked Benjamin in disbelief.

'Aye. I take it you aren't done, and you seem to be off course. Where's the others?'

'We're looking for Francesca,' replied Benjamin. 'A bit of a… misunderstanding.'

Bryn's gaze lingered on Benjamin for a moment too long. It was as though he knew something wasn't quite right. He turned to face Steffan.

'What about the other lad?'

'Looking over on the other side of the path,' said Steffan. 'Shouldn't be hard to find him. It's Francesca who's the issue.' He pointed with his eyes and the faintest tilt of the head towards Benjamin, indicating he was the *real* issue.

Bryn exhaled through his nose. He clearly wasn't stupid. He understood.

'Right, well, let's go and find your mate. Then we're going to have to find the girl.'

'Yes, that's what we're trying to do,' said Benjamin, in a condescending tone.

'And it's clearly a tidy old job you're making of it.'

Just then, a rumbling of thunder sounded in the distance.

'There it is,' said Bryn. 'We're going to have a storm before long.'

'Oh *wonderful*,' hissed Benjamin.

Steffan started back towards the path.

'Come on, let's go and see where Gareth's got to,' he said over his shoulder. 'We don't want to be out here when the rain and thunder arrives.'

The air was shifting, growing heavier by the minute. A storm *was* coming. But Steffan had a feeling it had already started.

CHAPTER SIXTEEN

Jodie

Jodie's feet throbbed and burned. Her chest stung with a lingering tenderness. Her t-shirt was clinging to her back. It felt like the excessive sweat had glued the cotton fibres to her skin.

I'm never going to do this much exercise again.

As her group arrived back at the canteen, and entered through the cabin doors, it soon became clear that they had reigned victorious in the race to finish first.

Billy was gloating with the realisation, looking at the others with an over-satisfied grin on his face.

'We've won, then?' said Matthew, as though he couldn't quite believe it.

'You have, indeed,' confirmed Ceri, who was pottering around, tidying near the tea urn and collecting dirty mugs and spoons.

Billy burst out laughing. 'Ben's going to be ab-so-lute-ly fuming, in'e?'

'Good work, team!' said Tara, patting Jodie on the back.

Jodie hoped that the win would redeem her, somewhat, in the eyes of her boss. She'd been dreading what he must have thought of her. But she also knew he didn't like to lose. It was why he was so successful. It would all be for nothing if he saw her in her current state. She felt nauseous at the stench of hard work, disseminating from her.

‘I’m going to get a shower, before the others get back,’ she said.

‘Good idea, Jode. You flippin’ stink!’ called Billy, as she began heading to the sleeping cabin, to pick out a change of clothes.

‘That’s rich, coming from you,’ said Matthew.

Jodie had only walked a few paces outside, when she heard another set of footsteps behind her, crunching on the stone pathway.

‘Thought I’d join you,’ said Tara.

‘What, in the shower?’ Jodie replied, aridly.

‘Only if you want me to,’ teased Tara. ‘No, I’m going to get changed, too – Ceri said there’s a bit of free time once everyone’s back, before we have dinner.’

Jodie nodded. She had been looking forward to having some peace, whilst getting washed and changed in a leisurely fashion. It looked as though she would just have to make do with a longer shower.

She slipped out of her towel, draping it over the peg of the first cubicle door, before turning the tap on, at what she hoped would be an acceptable temperature. Why were showers away from home always so difficult to operate?

After a few seconds, she held out her hand to test the water. Lukewarm, on the verge of absolutely freezing. Adjusting the dial all the way to red, she was immediately pelted by what felt like transparent lava. She let out a yelp and winced, jerking her arm back towards her body, before trying to squeeze herself around the violent spray of water to turn it back halfway, and stepping in as it became a less scorching climate.

The water felt incredible on her aching skin. She combed her fingers through her hair. A perfect rain washed away all of the frustration, which had built up like stubborn grime over the last few hours.

Her mind drifted to Benjamin. She imagined how much better it would have been, were it just the two of them there, out in the middle of nowhere. No distractions, beyond the starlight above them, and the calm, melodic sounds of tweeting birds in the trees.

She could hear him calling her name, repeatedly. 'Jodie… Jodie…'. She closed her eyes and reciprocated in her mind.

But Benjamin's voice slowly transformed, becoming higher pitched, and more feminine.

'Jodie!'

She was quickly dragged hurtling back into reality, away from her paradisial fantasy. The shower was still running. But it was Tara calling Jodie's name from outside of her private bubble.

'Jodie, hurry up!'

Is she serious?

Jodie ignored her. Why should she hurry up?

'Jodie, can you hear me?', Tara called. 'You need to hurry!'

Oh my god.

'I'm coming, just wait!'

She exhaled furiously, as she turned the shower off and yanked the towel down, before wrapping it around herself.

With an exaggerated shove on the cubicle door, she glared at Tara, who was standing in the doorway of the shower room. Her eyes were wide and panicked.

'What do you want?' Jodie demanded.

'Francesca's gone missing!'

'What are you talking about, *missing*?' asked Jodie, as she walked past Tara and headed towards their sleeping area.

Tara tagged behind, explaining as she rushed after her.

'Bryn told Ceri over the walkie-talkie thing; Matt just came looking for us and told me. Apparently, she's run off and they can't find her – it's going to rain soon as well, *and* it looks like it'll be a storm.'

'This sounds a lot like a HR issue to me,' said Jodie.

'Claire isn't here, is she,' replied Tara. 'And you helped her to organise these trips, so I guess that means you're kind of in charge of the weekend?'

'So the others aren't back yet?' asked Jodie, ignoring Tara's attempt as issuing her with responsibility.

'No, I don't think so – I guess they're still trying to find Francesca.'

'True. Have they said if they need any help?'

'I don't know, but Matt said he was going to go and search for her. I'll go and see if there's any update,' said Tara, before she left Jodie to get dressed, alone. Finally. Although, it seemed she wouldn't struggle for time alone for a while, with Francesca playing hide and seek. What a child. She just hoped Benjamin and the others gave up and made their way back to camp before too long.

* * *

Jodie took a deep breath to control her anxious dithering. Her concern for the missing group was increasing with every passing moment. Where were they? Were they okay?

Was *he* okay?

It had been around twenty minutes since Bryn had last updated Ceri, as he tried to find and bring them all back. The sky had turned much darker since then. A murky prelude enveloped them, in the grey hue of thick, voluminous clouds, and the increasingly stifling humidity.

She sat pining outside the cabin doors, whilst the others stayed inside. She could hear Billy's grating cackle, running on a headache inducing loop. They obviously couldn't care less. She knew something awful must have happened. It shouldn't take this long to return.

The door opened behind her, and Ceri stepped out onto the decking.

'Still no sign?' she asked, more cheerfully than Jodie would have expected.

'Not yet,' replied Jodie.

'They shan't be long. Bryn knows the place like the back of his hand. I'll find out where he's up to – I've left the bloomin' walkie-talkie in the office.'

Jodie's head was resting in her hands. Heavy with worry. She tilted it to the left, as she watched Ceri strolling over to the office. It looked more like a fancy garden shed, from the outside, with a colourful mix of marigolds and fuchsias sitting in pots either side of the door.

She returned her focus to the pathway. Moments later, a pair of boots came into view. She looked up. It was Benjamin. Thank God! His eyebrows were lowered, and he was charging ahead of the others. His feet were stomping heavily, and he was stiff armed, swinging them back and forth as though he was marching in uniform. He looked furious.

Jodie jumped up and hurried towards him.

'What's happened?' she asked.

He glanced at her, grumbling 'just that drama queen,' and continued past her. Following behind was Gareth, along with Steffan and Bryn, who were either side of Francesca. They were supporting her by either arm, as she limped slowly and squinted her eyes with a look of agony.

'Twisted her ankle,' called Gareth.

Poor little princess.

'How did that happen?' asked Jodie. She fought to suppress a grin.

'I tripped over a great big tree root. Oh, it was terrible.'

'We'll get some ice on it, just now. Limit any swelling,' said Bryn.

They joined the others in the canteen, but Benjamin wasn't in there. Jodie asked where he had gone, but she was met with puzzled looks from Matthew, Billy and Tara.

CHAPTER SEVENTEEN

Gareth

Gareth sat at the end of the table with a fresh cup of tea, joining the rest of the group as they had gathered in the canteen. The energy was uncomfortable. There was a strange tension and discomfort that only someone like Benjamin could cause.

Even Billy didn't seem to be in the mood for making any of his shit jokes. But, given much of the negative focus appeared to be on his corporate hero, it was hardly surprising.

Francesca was sat centrally, with her injured ankle elevated as she rested her leg across the next two seats. Ceri had given her an icepack, which was strapped to her ankle with a bandage. She had her best performance face on – pained, fragile, and milking every bit of attention the situation brought her.

'I hope there's no fracture,' she said, her arm reaching towards her ankle as though she was worried her foot was going to fall off. 'The pain when I fell was unbelievable.'

Fell, thought Gareth. He kept his mouth shut, but he certainly thought something was 'unbelievable'. Thinking back to the moment he found her in the woods, it seemed far too convenient. She claimed she had been there for a while, but he hadn't heard anything to suggest a fall, so he had his doubts. Not that he was going to call her out on it – the more heat Benjamin had on him, the better.

Billy was practically vibrating with irritation. 'This seems all a bit OTT, to be honest. Ben's been out there looking for you, after you run off in a strop and now it seems like he's the bad guy.'

'Yeah, he was a real knight in shining armour, out there in the dangerous woods all by himself,' said Steffan.

'Oh, you know what I mean,' snapped Billy with a frustrated headshake. 'I know you guys were there as well, but you ain't the one's being made out to be a villain, are you?'

'True,' said Steffan. 'But we weren't the ones who made Francesca do a runner in the first place, either.'

Gareth's nose flared as he sighed in annoyance. The last thing he wanted was to sit through another argument. Billy appeared too blind to see reality, his faith in Benjamin almost nauseating, and whilst Gareth agreed with Steffan, there was no point in trying to reason with stupid.

'Guys, let's just be glad everyone is back – safe and sound,' said Tara, cutting in.

'I wouldn't go that far,' said Francesca, gesturing to her ankle – just in case anyone had forgotten about it.

'I'm sure you'll be fine,' said Billy. 'Not like Ben, who's taken himself off somewhere – probably thinks it'd be too uncomfortable sitting in here, listening to this bollocks.'

What was it that the pot called kettle? thought Gareth.

'Anyone want another brew?' asked Matthew, getting up out of his seat.

Gareth sipped at his tea, and glanced around at everyone, as one or two of them handed Matthew their empty mugs. He noticed Jodie had been unusually quiet – surely she wasn't still sulking about that ice breaker? She was chewing on a thumbnail, as if deep in thought, but then stood up casually and mumbled something he didn't catch, before slipping out of the canteen door.

'I just don't understand why he hasn't come to check on me – to see how my ankle is,' sighed Francesca.

'He's probably feeling a bit down about people not appreciating everything he does,' said Billy.

'Wind it in, pal,' said Steffan. 'I know he's the boss and everything, right, but that's no excuse to speak to *anyone* the way he spoke to Francesca, his supposed missus. Calling her "retard" and stuff is just fucking awful.'

'Wait, he actually said that?' asked Billy.

Gareth nodded. 'Yeah.'

'Blimey. He must really have been stressed,' said Billy.

Steffan looked as though he was about to explode. Instead, he shook his head and rolled his eyes, deciding not to bother engaging with Billy on the subject anymore.

Silence stretched between them all for a moment. Gareth's gaze flicked back towards Francesca, who was adjusting her bandage. Matthew returned with a couple of fresh cups of tea, placing them down on the table, before stopping close to her. 'Are you sure you don't want to go and get it checked out properly?'

Francesca waved the suggestion away with a wincing smile. 'No, it's okay. I don't want to be a burden.'

Billy scoffed but didn't say anything. Gareth could feel a headache coming on. The familiar pulsing sensation in the sides of his head was becoming more pronounced. He wished he could call it a day and go home.

'Where's Jodie gone?' asked Tara, somehow only just realising her friend had wandered off.

A couple of the others shrugged their shoulders before Gareth answered. 'She went outside a few minutes ago – not sure where.'

'Is anybody else cold?' asked Francesca. 'I don't know if it's the ankle, but I've got a chill all of a sudden.'

‘Do you want my jacket?’ asked Matthew, putting a hand to the zip of his hoodie.

‘No, it’s okay,’ she replied, shifting in her seat before pushing herself onto her strong foot. ‘I’ll go and get one from my room. Should probably go and see what Benny’s up to, anyway.’

As she hobbled towards the door, Gareth couldn’t help but feel as though there was more drama to come.

CHAPTER EIGHTEEN

Jodie

She found him in the sleeping cabin. The door to his room was closed, but there was a crash from inside. She knocked, timidly, before opening the door and peering inside.

He was sat on the end of one of the beds, breathing heavily. He was bright red with rage. She looked around the room. There were suitcases and bags all over the place. A table lamp was destroyed in the corner, with fragments of the light bulb scattered around it.

'Is everything okay?' she asked, as she began to tidy up the mess.

He didn't answer. He stared straight ahead, seemingly oblivious to her presence.

'Benjamin?'

'She drives me fucking crazy,' he said.

'Who, Francesca?'

'She's a complete and utter nightmare.'

Jodie could see the veins bulging on his forearms, all the way up to his biceps. He wasn't bulky, in terms of his muscle, but he was in great shape. A fit man, who took care of himself. She knew she shouldn't, but she couldn't help but ogle.

She walked closer, and sat beside him.

'What's happened?' she asked, calmly.

'Just an overreaction, that's all. She takes a comment, a harmless comment, and runs with it. Literally. She disappears into the bloody trees, and we can't find her. Next thing, she's twisted her ankle, and it's all about her again.'

Jodie could see through the anger. At that moment, he was vulnerable. She put her hand on his arm. She felt him tense up at first, as though he was taken by surprise, before he relaxed again.

'Don't worry about it,' she said. 'She just likes the attention, that's all'.

He nodded. 'Mm-hmm. Honestly, this whole *trip* is a waste of my time. Claire has some explaining to do, I can tell you.'

Jodie was relieved he had appeared to have forgotten the part she played in the planning of the trip. She didn't bother to correct him.

Gradually, she became more optimistic and daring. He hadn't shaken her hand away yet. She stroked his arm gently. And still, he allowed her touch. A thousand repressed emotions began hammering away, demanding to be released. She knew it was a risk, but she looked down, and slowly manoeuvred her hand to his thigh. He tensed again. Perhaps it was too far. But it was too late, she had done it now. She left it resting there.

'We'd best be getting back to the others,' she said, finally taking her hand away. 'They want us gone before the storm arrives.'

He nodded again. Said nothing. Perhaps he would forget all about it. They could just carry on living their lives, never speaking of this moment again. It was embarrassing, but at least she had finally tried to make a move, despite knowing it was inappropriate, in so many ways.

She began to push off the bed and onto her feet, but as her hand moved away from him, he grabbed her tightly, around the wrist. He looked up at her. He placed a hand around her neck, choking her gently, and pulled her towards him.

What the hell is going on?

She could feel his breath against her face, as he paused, and his eyes pierced hers.

'Benjamin?' she gasped. She was shocked and confused.

He placed his lips on hers forcefully, and thrust his tongue down her throat, with a secure grip still around her neck. Despite her confusion, her instincts kicked in and she kissed him back. Her hand caressed his chest, and she could feel his heart racing behind his t-shirt.

Pushing her down onto the bed, he placed his hands up her top and began massaging her breasts over the laced cotton of her bra. It felt sensational. She stopped kissing him momentarily, as she took a breath and frantically pulled the t-shirt over his head. She felt his skin beneath her fingertips, and rolled over to kneel above him.

This is it. It's finally happening.

The door swung open, and Francesca stood there, holding herself up against the wall. Jodie froze, startled. Benjamin pushed her from on top of him, and she stumbled backwards, losing her balance.

'What the hell, Jodie!?' he shouted.

Jodie sat on the floor, as Francesca and Benjamin glared at her. She was dazed, but she knew it was bad. She tried to speak, but it felt as if her trachea had closed completely. She couldn't breathe.

'What is going on, Benny?' asked Francesca. She spoke coolly. She seemed calm. It unnerved Jodie, somewhat.

'She just… erm… ah… I…' he stuttered, as he moved towards Francesca, staggering.

'She just what? You what? Spit it out!'

'It was her – she forced herself on me!' He continued in her direction, holding his hands out submissively.

'Oh, shut up,' she replied, holding her own hand out before him. 'Don't you dare come near me.'

'But…'

'Don't "but" me, either. You would rather *that*, than me?' she gestured towards Jodie, who was still sitting on the floor. She felt so small.

Benjamin turned and took a passive look at her. She looked back. He began to laugh.

'Absolutely not, Fran. God, do you… wow. Just, no.'

'And you,' said Francesca, turning her attention to Jodie. 'I know you like to share your men, but I'm not Tara.'

She hobbled into the room, and picked up a jacket from a nearby chair.

'I only came to get this. Sorry to have interrupted. Carry on now, you are welcome to each other. I hope you burn.'

Francesca slammed the door, leaving the two of them alone once more. Benjamin rested his head on the door, before repeatedly hammering his fist against the solid wood.

Jodie was struck by a hammer of guilt. She wasn't exactly friends with Francesca, but it was like she had – in betraying her – broken an unwritten rule that exists between all women. But it wasn't just her fault. He was just as much to blame as she was.

'Benjamin, stop doing that. You'll break your hand,' she pleaded, as he continued pounding the door.

'This is all *your* fault!' he screamed, as he spun around, pointing at her. His hand was shaking. Every part of him was shaking.

'My fault?'

'Yes,' he growled. 'If it wasn't for you, throwing yourself at me, like some sex crazed whore… this is your fault! You go and tell her that, now!'

She didn't know what to say. She was mortified. *A whore. Is that how he sees me?*

Benjamin stomped over to her. She cowered. He pulled her up, yanking her by the arm.

'You're hurting me,' she cried, as he dragged her to the door.

'You go. Go now. Tell her that you are a whore. And that this is all your fault. It was all you.'

She sobbed, as she told him again, that he was hurting her. He ignored her. He opened the door, and shoved her out, before yelling 'tell her!' and slamming it shut in her face.

Her wrist throbbed. There were red marks all the way around it, where Benjamin had wrapped his fingers in a vice-like grip. Her heart ached more. She couldn't begin to comprehend what had just happened; how could a moment of passion, a moment she had previously only dreamed about, change into something so terrible, so quickly? The way he had spoken to her. The way he had looked at her, as though she was nothing. She was madly in love with him. And now, he hated her. She would probably lose her job after this, too. She loved her job. It was all such a mess.

One crazy, heart-led decision later, and she may just have destroyed everything in her life.

CHAPTER NINETEEN

Gareth

The darkness had arrived outside. As Gareth looked out of the canteen windows, he gazed at the trees. They had provided a view that was peaceful and green, as the leaves rustled in a gentle breeze earlier in the day. But now, the picture before him had evolved into a far more sinister one – the silhouettes of branches scratched at the air like claws, the shadows beneath them had deepened threateningly. It remained calm and quiet, but what was coming next had begun to appear ominous, as opposed to reassuring.

His attention returned to the room. Francesca had hobbled back into the canteen, returning with the jacket she had gone to fetch. Soon after, she sobbed as she recounted what she had just witnessed in the bedroom.

The rest of the group surrounded her as they lapped up the gory details, like scandal-hungry vultures. Whilst they were no doubt there for the gossip rather than to offer her support, they did just sit and listen – even Billy didn't interrupt.

Gareth zoned in and out, picking up the highlights. A topless Benjamin lying on the bed. Jodie on her knees as she straddled him. It had been Jodie's fault, according to Benjamin. But most importantly of all, it was *all so humiliating* for Francesca.

It was a shocking story, obviously, but it was further evidence that Benjamin was a self-righteous scumbag. Gareth knew Jodie worshipped the company. She was always front-and-centre when volunteers were needed in the office – if there was a charity bake sale, she would be organising it. If customer services needed cover on a weekend, it was guaranteed Jodie would be wearing a headset, answering calls… but to try and sleep with the owner? That was a level of commitment Gareth couldn't quite comprehend.

The canteen door swung open. Bryn stepped inside. All eyes turned to him as he cleared his throat.

'Right then, I've got a bit of bad news,' he said. 'We'll have to knock this evening's wildlife spotting on its head, due to the weather that's coming in. I would also suggest that everyone stays indoors when the storm reaches us – keep out of harm's way.'

'Are you having a laugh?' sneered Billy. 'What are we meant to do instead… sit here twiddling our thumbs all night?'

'I don't control the weather,' said Bryn flatly. 'I know it's not ideal, but it's better to be safe than sorry – and as I have a duty of care to you all, as guests, I must urge you to take heed.'

'This is rubbish,' said Billy. 'I honestly don't see the point in staying here. Where's Ceri, has she gone to tell Ben?'

'And Jodie,' said Tara. She quickly dropped her eyes to the ground when Francesca's head snapped to glare at her.

'Ceri had some work errands to run – bits to pick up, and whatnot. She's left for the evening, so unfortunately you are stuck with me being in charge.'

'Yeah, bollocks to this,' said Billy getting out of his seat. 'I ain't hanging around doing bugger all. I'm offski.'

'Billy, sit down,' said Steffan.

'He's right,' said Tara. 'You can't just leave.'

'Watch me,' sneered Billy. 'Bryn – where's my phone?'

Looking up with a glare, Bryn paused for a second, as though he was weighing up how serious Billy was. 'We were going to hand them back out to everyone in the morning, but I suppose there's no harm you all having them back now there's nothing else going on this evening. Not that there's much point with the service round here.'

'Isn't there wi-fi, though?' asked Tara hopefully.

Bryn sighed. 'Aye, there is. The phones are in that cupboard over there,' he said to Billy, pointing across the canteen.

Billy marched over and threw the cupboard door open, beginning to rifle through the shelves until he came to a plastic tub holding the group's phones. Whilst he did so, Gareth looked up in surprise as Jodie shuffled nervously into the canteen.

She was cradling her arm, and her face was flushed red. Her eyes were bloodshot and glassy. Even if she hadn't emerged with a glowing face due to crying, Gareth was certain she would have soon suffered the same result from the sheer embarrassment of her actions.

Her presence was quickly noticed by the others, with Billy stopping what he was doing to pipe up. 'Where's your boyfriend?'

Jodie looked at him but said nothing, before turning back to the table. 'Tara, can I speak to you?'

All eyes quickly switched towards Tara. She paused, her eyes shifting as though wondering what people were going to think of her. Slowly, she stood up. If she was trying to appear reluctant, she made a good job of convincing Gareth.

She mumbled 'I'll be back in a minute, I guess,' and ambled towards the door, as Jodie turned and walked out ahead of her.

‘And on that note,’ said Billy, holding up two phones. ‘I shall be on my way. Matt, got your phone here, I guess you’re heading home as well.’

‘What? Give it here,’ said Matthew.

Billy laughed and broke into a jog towards the door. Matthew jumped out of his seat to give chase.

As the two salesmen left the canteen, a low rumble of thunder vibrated through the building. The first spots of rain landed on the windows as Gareth looked outside. The storm was right on top of them.

Gareth had decided to go back to the sleeping cabin before the rain started properly. He was in two minds whether to follow Billy and Matthew’s example and leave. But without permission from Benjamin, or even Jodie – who was supposed to be ‘leading’ the weekend’s organisation, he wondered if it was worth highlighting the existing target on his back and risking another telling off come Monday morning.

Instead, he just wanted to ensure his belongings were packed and ready – just in case the decision was made to cancel the weekend once Benjamin came out of hiding.

He pulled at the zip on his bag, as the pattering started above him.

Here comes the rain.

As the sound of thunder boomed outside, he heard voices shouting over the fracas. He opened the door to his room, and they scurried past, laughing and barging into each other down the corridor, carrying their bags out of the main door and into the rain. They looked like drowned rats within seconds. He stood, watching the rain bouncing off the ground, weighing up whether to make a run for it himself, or wait to see if it would ease a little. It was really coming down, now. The leaky gutter dripped like a metronome in front of the doorway, and the building creaked as it was engulfed by a gust of wind – the weather was really putting the structure to the test.

A sudden fork of lightning illuminated the dark sky, taking him by surprise. He had never liked thunderstorms, especially when he was younger. His mum used to tell him it was God moving his furniture, to try and ease his worry. A fair explanation, perhaps, for the rumbling, but what about the huge jolts of flashing electricity flying towards them? Talk about 'all forgiving' – somebody must have really pissed off the man upstairs.

He decided to make a move. The rain hit him like machine gun fire as he sprinted to the car park. Billy and Matthew had obviously both decided it was time to leave. They were starting their engines as he rushed through the downpour in the direction of the canteen and car park. He watched them both throw their cars into reverse, lights on and barrelling out of their parking spaces, with more roaring from the engines as they stamped down on their accelerators after their cars were shifted into gear.

But they didn't get very far.

It all happened so quickly. Another flash of lightning – unnervingly close, was followed by what sounded like a bomb detonating. Gareth flinched, before he then heard the screech of skidding brakes scraping across the rough terrain, and a sickening thud. Finally, he heard screams.

Gareth couldn't believe what he was seeing. He looked over his shoulder to see a picture of horror on Jodie and Tara's faces. They too were just staring in the direction of Billy's car.

It sat trapped beneath a large section of an oak tree, crushed at the front end. Steam rose from the wreckage as the rain continued to pour.

CHAPTER TWENTY

Steffan

Steffan had stayed to wait with Francesca, whilst everyone else had gone off in different directions. He may no longer have been in the armed forces, but he still lived by the mantra of leaving nobody behind – especially if they were injured. He may, however, have been willing to ignore such a rule for somebody like Benjamin.

The explosive bang from outside had taken him hurtling back to the front line – shelling surrounding him in the desert, the ground shaking beneath him as he took cover, praying he came out of yet another onslaught safely and unscathed. With a flinch, he had cowered at the sound of impact, before looking at Francesca and Bryn in sheer confusion. Quickly returning to his senses, he rushed out to see what had happened.

He heard the fear in the screams. He knew whatever was waiting around the corner was going to be unpleasant. He saw Jodie and Tara standing frozen to the spot, and Gareth further ahead of them.

'What's happened?' he shouted, shielding his eyes as he squinted to see through the pouring rain.

'The tree,' shouted Tara. 'It's fallen onto the car!'

Beyond them, he saw the fallen tree. And the car beneath it.

‘Shit,’ he hissed, racing towards it. His boots splashed through the mud as he surged ahead. ‘Gareth, come on!’

Matthew jumped out of his own car as they passed him. Steffan rapped his knuckles on Billy’s window, whilst pulling at the door handle. It was locked. Billy was staring straight ahead, his hands still gripping the steering wheel. A couple more metres, and it would have been him under that old oak tree. Or at least, what would have been left of him.

‘Billy!’ shouted Steffan, as he continued to knock on the window.

Billy squeezed his eyes shut and opened them again with rapid blinks, before looking up at Steffan with a blank stare. The door handle clicked as he unlocked it, allowing Steffan to pull it open from the outside.

‘Are you okay? Are you hurt?’ asked Steffan with sharp urgency. Billy made no reply. ‘Billy! Are you hurt?’

Billy shook his head. Steffan leaned into the car, scanning for any obvious injury and ensuring Billy wasn’t trapped, before unfastening the seatbelt and carefully pulling him out. Billy regained his balance, and Steffan took a deep breath in relief. He was okay.

‘We’d best get away from the car,’ called Bryn, who had arrived on the scene. ‘Don’t know if it’s going to go up.’

Steffan nodded. He didn’t need telling twice, and quickly placed his hand around Billy’s shoulder, before leading him back towards the safety of the cabin.

* * *

Steffan, Billy, Gareth, Jodie and Tara were all back in the canteen, where Francesca had remained throughout the events on the car park. The shock of it all had comfortably overtaken her own drama for the moment. From her reaction, it was clear she couldn’t believe it. None of them could.

‘I think this is the quietest you’ve ever been,’ said Francesca, looking at Billy.

He had barely uttered a word since being hauled out of the car. Steffan appreciated the break it had given his head, but he didn’t want to mention it. It didn’t seem appropriate.

‘Honestly, I thought I was a goner,’ said Billy, shaking his head. ‘I don’t know how it missed me. It was literally, like, centimetres from my head.’

Probably a bit of an exaggeration, but it was frigging close.

‘You’re a lucky boy,’ said Steffan.

‘Oh my god, imagine if you’d died,’ said Tara.

‘It would be a lot quieter in the office,’ quipped Matthew. ‘Without you being a knob all day.’

Billy smiled. ‘Yeah, but you’d be lost without me there to guide you through life, my son.’

‘Yeah,’ said Tara. ‘He might be a knob, but he’s *our* knob.’

Bryn returned inside from the rain, as soaked as the rest of them had been. His expression was even more serious than the stern look he had worn all day. ‘So, bad news,’ he said. ‘Looks like the car wasn’t the only casualty from the tree falling – phone line’s knackered.’

‘That must be why our phones aren’t connecting to the internet,’ said Francesca. ‘None of us have managed to get a signal yet, either.’

‘That’s the problem,’ continued Bryn. ‘The signal is borderline non-existent at the best of times. And because we can’t even use the landline, it looks as though we’ll struggle to call for help. Ceri won’t be back ‘til tomorrow, either.’

There was a collective groan.

‘We’re going to have to go and find help. We can’t stay here, doing nothing,’ said Matthew.

‘What, in that weather?’ asked Gareth.

‘It’s not safe,’ said Bryn. ‘Besides, there’s nothing around here for a few miles. Beyond fields of sheep and cattle. They won’t be much help, however nicely you ask them.’

‘So, what are we going to do?’ asked Tara.

Bryn shrugged. This was clearly beyond his regular duties.

‘I can’t believe she’s just gone, and left the rest of us here stranded,’ said Jodie.

‘We weren’t stranded when she left,’ said Gareth. ‘And besides, it’s not like she’d be able to do anything if she was stuck here with us.’

Steffan saw Francesca eyeballing Jodie, as though she was disgusted that she had dared even open her mouth in her presence.

‘Benjamin might have managed to find a signal on his phone.’ she said. ‘Perhaps *you* can go and ask him, Jodie.’

Jodie looked around, anxiously. Nobody said anything. She slowly got up from her seat, before Steffan also started to make a move. He couldn’t let her go alone, it didn’t seem right. Bryn held out his hand, gesturing for them both to stop.

‘Everyone stay in here, where it’s safe out of the storm – I’ll go and check on him and let him know what’s going on,’ he said.

CHAPTER TWENTY-ONE

Jodie

'Anyone want a coffee?' asked Steffan, starting for the urn on the other side of the room.

'I was just thinking this,' said Matthew. 'I'll get one. You coming, Billy?'

Billy paused for a second, clearly still reeling from his near-death experience, before shifting in his seat. 'Go on then. I could do with a burst of sugar.'

Jodie stood awkwardly, the rest of the group leaving her alone with Francesca. Eyeing the marketing manager as she sat there, wounded both physically and emotionally, Jodie felt as though she was going to throw up. Reluctantly, she sloped down into the seat opposite her. Francesca refused to acknowledge her.

'Francesca, I'm sorry,' she mumbled. There was still no eye contact from across the table.

'Sorry for what?' asked Francesca. Her head position was unmoved.

'For kissing Benjamin. It just happened, and I just… I couldn't help it.'

Francesca finally turned to look at her. It wasn't a glare, nor was it the look of someone who was upset, or hurt, even. It was a look of pity.

'You couldn't *help* it?'

'No, I'm sorry,' she apologised again. 'I… he…'.

‘You’re in love with him, aren’t you?’ asked Francesca. Jodie said nothing, she just looked down at the table to hide her expression of horror. Guilty as charged. ‘It’s so obvious. He knows. He made a joke about it a while ago, about how you will do absolutely anything he asks. Any job needs doing in the office – Jodie will do it. I thought it was unfair, abusing your loyalty like that, exploiting someone in the workplace. But now, I feel like you kind of deserved it.’

Jodie was speechless. *He knew?* She suddenly felt even worse than before. Not for Francesca, although she did feel very guilty now that she was looking directly at her – at the pain she had caused. But, she felt even worse for herself. She was so stupid. She thought that she had concealed her feelings about him well, and that her dedication – her genuine, ambition-led dedication – was shining over everything else. But he had worked her out, had realised her full intentions and was just taking advantage of her, in the interests of himself, and his precious business.

She looked at Francesca, trying to read her, hoping that she was just being cruel, to get her back in some way. But she just saw a look doused in pity, gazing back at her. Hurt, sure. And even a flicker of disgust. But most of all, pity.

‘It was him, instigating things in there, wasn’t it?’

‘No,’ said Jodie. ‘It was…’

‘Don’t. Don’t protect him. I know how he is – I think most people do, if they’re truly honest with themselves. He’s a law unto himself. Maybe you hadn’t seen it in him before today, but now you have.’

Jodie held her tongue for a moment, allowing Francesca’s words to settle around them. ‘But I am sorry.’ She knew apologising repeatedly would make the words seem more and more redundant. But in that moment, she meant it. Despite her mixed emotions.

She hadn’t been sorry for kissing him, or for being pathetically, obsessively, head-over-heels in love with him.

But after sitting there with Francesca, looking at her directly in the eyes, she realised she was genuinely sorry for breaking the rules of the Girl Code. She was surprised Tara, a real *girl's girl*, hadn't been harsher with her on that front.

Now, something within Jodie was sorry she had ever met Benjamin Pearson.

No sooner had the others rejoined them at the table, Bryn barrelled in through the door, the sound of the rain hammering down amplified from outside. He looked flummoxed and was out of breath. Steam was rising from his drenched body. Jodie looked up at him as he sucked in a lungful of air, before making his announcement.

'He isn't in his room.'

CHAPTER TWENTY-TWO

Gareth

Panic hit most of the group rather quickly. It felt like there was just one problem after another. They had all, except for Francesca, rushed out of the canteen to search for Benjamin. Gareth was reluctant, but if Benjamin – and more importantly, his mobile phone – was the only way for them to get help, and for him to hopefully be free of this place, he felt it would be a worthwhile mission.

He had gone with Tara and Jodie, whilst Matthew, Billy and Steffan had formed the other half of the search party. His trio started with Benjamin and Francesca's room, in the sleeping cabin. Just as Bryn had reported, there was nobody inside.

'Where the hell can he have gone?' asked Jodie.

Gareth had no answer. No clue. It was bizarre. All his belongings appeared to still be there, so he couldn't have gone too far. They had turned the room over, checking in bags, underneath the beds and everywhere else he – and his phone – could have been. There was no sign of either.

'This is so weird,' said Tara.

'Do you think he's okay?' pondered Jodie.

Gareth shrugged. 'Don't know. Don't really care. Just want to find him, so we can get that phone and see if it's working.'

'Jesus, Gareth,' said Tara, disapprovingly. 'No need to be a dick.'

'What? I'm not,' he replied. 'He's the dick. He could be dead on the toilet, for all I care. I just want to get this all over with.'

The girls just looked at him with furrowed brows. It was as though he had just kicked a small puppy.

'That's a bit too far,' said Tara. Gareth shrugged again.

'Wait,' said Jodie, suddenly. 'That's a thought – the toilets. Are the others checking there?'

'Seeing as we're over here, and they were starting on the car park, with Bryn, I doubt it,' said Gareth.

Jodie looked at him and nodded, before rushing out of the room. Gareth and Tara followed.

They explored every cubicle of the toilets, to no avail. It was the same result in the showers. Benjamin was nowhere to be found. Their chances of getting help, and maybe even going home that evening were faltering rapidly. He just hoped that the others had been more successful in their search.

After quickly opening each of the other bedroom doors to make sure Benjamin wasn't in any of the other rooms, they made their way outside. The thunder and lightning had passed over them now, and the rumblings had faded away into the distance. The rain continued to fall heavily, and they stood for a moment of reflection. The oppressive mugginess in the air continued lingering around them. They could see further into the woodland after the darkness of the storm had lightened a little, but it would soon be sunset.

'It's hopeless,' cried Jodie. 'We're never going to find him.'

'He's got to be here, somewhere,' said Tara, who seemed more optimistic. 'His car hasn't gone. His stuff is still in his room.'

Gareth nodded in agreement. It was an assessment matching his own. He had resigned himself to the likelihood of being stuck at the camp for a while longer, at least until Benjamin put his toys back in his pram, or asked somebody else to, and came out from wherever he was sulking. Besides, he was famished.

'Shall we go back to the canteen?' he suggested. 'See if the others are there yet.'

'May as well,' said Tara, shrugging her shoulders.

Francesca was no longer waiting alone when they entered the canteen. The other members of the search party hadn't returned yet, but a sodden-haired Benjamin was sat at the next table, leaning back with his feet up. He smiled nonchalantly at them as they walked in. It was as if he was amused at the fact everyone had been looking for him.

'All good, guys?' he asked.

'Where the hell were you?' asked Tara.

'He'd gone to try and find a phone signal,' said Francesca, coolly.

'To get help?' asked Gareth.

Francesca laughed, mockingly. 'Oh, no… business call. Obviously. It's always a business call.'

'Fair enough,' said Gareth. 'Benjamin, I'm guessing Francesca's filled you in…' he continued, and Benjamin nodded. 'Can we use your phone, please?'

'Well, you could – but there appears to be no signal now. Nor that godawful wi-fi this place had on offer. So, it would a bit pointless to borrow it now, don't you think?'

'Have you tried to pick the signal back up?' asked Gareth.

'Obviously, yes. I was literally in the middle of the call – a very important one – when I was cut off. So annoying.'

'Well, this is just brilliant,' said Gareth, throwing his hands up in frustration.

'I would suggest you remember who you're speaking to,' said Benjamin. 'How was I supposed to know a bloody tree had fallen and taken the phone line with it? We're all affected here… I mean, my call was *very* important, and I didn't get to finish it.'

Gareth shook his head in disgust. *This guy is unbelievable.*

'There it is – the headshake. Do you know what, Gareth? I am bloody sick of your abysmal attitude. You are lucky you still have a job. Theo insists you're doing quite well, making us money, and that is the only reason you're still here. Business is business, after all, but you would do well to know your place. You stupid boy.'

There was a stunned silence, surrounding Gareth. He felt a heat rising inside him. He had reached his limit. The trigger had been pulled, and his patience had reached its expiration. He needed to get out, before it was too late. Time and time again, Benjamin had knocked him down, to the point he doubted his capabilities, doubted his worth to the company, and his worth to everything else. He wished he could end that bastard and do them all a favour. Do the world a favour.

He'd imagined taking Benjamin's life before. But Benjamin wasn't the only one he'd thought about sticking the knife into. It would be far simpler to turn the blade onto himself.

Bryn emerged empty-handed, with Steffan, Billy and Matthew traipsing in behind him. They were absolutely soaked. They saw Benjamin sitting there, and the news was relayed to them, amidst the raucous chatter. Gareth could tell some were happier than others to see Benjamin safe. But there was no doubt that everybody was dispirited by the lack of good news on the mobile phone.

'It looks like we're definitely on our own for the night, then,' announced Bryn, finally taking charge. 'I suggest everyone goes and gets cleaned up, 'fore you catch pneumonia. If a couple of you can help in the kitchen, we'll get some supper on the go. Take a brolly with you, there's a couple in one of the cupboards near the door.'

Gareth hadn't said a word since Benjamin's outburst. He had lingered in the background, the words of his boss rattling in his mind, as though his subconscious was provoking him. He was the first to walk out, to get away from everybody. He didn't want to be there anymore. At that moment, he didn't want to be anywhere.

CHAPTER TWENTY-THREE

Steffan

Steffan volunteered to assist Bryn with the food preparation. He had done his fair share of kitchen duty, both on camp in the UK and when deployed elsewhere in the world. He wasn't a great cook, but he knew his way around a chopping board. And a knife.

Matthew hadn't been quite as forthcoming with a willingness to help out, but being the furthest from the exit made it easier for Bryn to recruit him.

'So, what are we making?' asked Steffan.

'Normally Ceri sorts it out, but with her going early it must have slipped her mind. We'll see what we've got, but I'm thinking a quick stew,' said Bryn, as he began to gather a mix of different vegetables. 'If one of you goes into the fridge down there, get some of the beef steak out.'

Steffan loved a beef stew. His mum had made them often when he was growing up. Nothing warmed the soul quite like it. She would defrost the meat and use up whatever vegetables were left over from that week, and leave it simmering all day, creating a simple, but appetising broth.

'I hope we've got bread,' he said. 'Got to have some to dip in.'

Bryn chuckled. 'Don't you worry about that. We've got part-baked rolls, and a couple of loaves leftover from making the sandwiches. The ex-wife used to whinge about it all the time. Said too much bread is unhealthy – blah, blah, blah. Me, I can't get enough of the stuff, I can't.'

'Definitely,' said Matthew. 'Warm with butter. Can't beat it.'

They quickly got to work, with Matthew and Steffan peeling and chopping potatoes and carrots, whilst Bryn methodically sliced the beef into bitesize chunks.

'I can't believe Benjamin's outbursts today. Absolute head case, at times,' said Matthew, who Steffan noticed was far slower with the peeler than he was.

'Aye, he seems to have a bit of a nasty streak in him, the boy,' replied Bryn, without looking up from the chopping board, as he continued to work on the meat.

'I thought he seemed okay, from what I'd seen,' said Steffan. 'But the way he was with Francesca – that seemed a bit iffy to me. Then he got up in my face. He was lucky I didn't pummel him.'

A while ago, Steffan wouldn't have thought twice about hitting Benjamin. The problem was, he wouldn't have thought at all. The time he spent locked up behind bars had changed that. He struggled in there. Not with the other inmates, or even the prison guards, but the day-to-day misery of being isolated from the outside world. The shame he had brought on his family. Once he was released, everything had changed. The attitude of people who knew him had changed – the way they looked at him. Friends ignored him. He was left with a shrunken circle of people who were willing to even give him the time of day.

He had needed help, for a long time. The NHS didn't want to know, despite his military background, and his doctor maintained the variety of prescription drugs to handle his PTSD would do the job. He'd struggled with what he'd lived through overseas. He still did. That was why he started smoking – the weed had helped him to take the edge off. Then that got him booted out. He had left school with nothing worth having – his grades may as well have been printed on cheap loo roll. Away from the army, he was disgraced, and unemployable.

His family had never been flush with cash, but they did their best. His mam had helped to cover the cost of private counselling, and it had helped, for a while. But it didn't heal him. There was no magic cure for what he had seen and experienced. But it had at least helped him to deal with heated situations, to manage his problematic 'short fuse'.

After finishing with the carrots and potatoes, Matthew and Steffan both moved on to the onions, as Bryn quickly browned the meat in a frying pan, before adding it to the huge catering pot.

Matthew groaned, as tears began welling in his eyes. Both Bryn and Steffan laughed at him, before Steffan suffered the same fate. Matthew rubbed his eye, which only made matters worse.

'What have you done that for, lad?' asked Bryn, shaking his head.

They were soon joined by a couple of the others, who were fresh from the showers.

'Bloody hell, who died in here?' joked Billy, unzipping his waterproof jacket as fresh rainwater dripped off it and onto the floor around him.

'Just a cow, and a big sack of onions,' replied Bryn.

'Here, you can take over,' said Matthew, putting the knife down before going to wash his hands in the sink.

Steffan had to agree with his sentiments and headed off to get changed as well. They left Billy, along with Jodie and Tara – who had both already got changed earlier – to assist Bryn. He assumed Bryn would also be intending on showering before too long.

'Wonder where Benjamin's pissed off to now,' mused Steffan.

‘Probably gone into hiding, again,’ said Matthew. ‘You won’t catch him chopping veggies.’

When Steffan got back to the room he was sharing with Gareth, he sat down at the end of his bed and enjoyed a moment of quietness, hearing nothing but the rhythmic tapping of the rain as it continued to fall outside.

He was tired. Hungry. It had been a long day, with tensions running high around him. For what was supposed to be a team building exercise, with a group of people he had little experience of before, he had been submerged into a realm of dysfunctional rivalry and backstabbing. The worst squadron he'd ever been posted in. Led by the most toxic and egotistical commander he could imagine.

CHAPTER TWENTY-FOUR

Gareth

Gareth had burst into tears the moment he stepped into the shower. Quietly sobbing, so nobody could hear him, he asked the faceless audience inside his head why he felt this way. He asked what he was supposed to do, but there was no reply. So, he just stood there, naked, and helpless.

Benjamin had done this to him. He knew that. Slowly, but surely, he had worn down his resistance, his confidence and self-worth. The doubt he had instilled, and the increasingly demanding workloads, a complete lack of respect for him having a life beyond the office. Over time, it had created a fragility, which needed just a simple negative comment to trigger another bout of sadness and frustration.

He hated Benjamin, more than he could imagine hating anyone. Even more than he'd grown to hate himself.

The sound of water running in the other shower cubicles came and went, and he wondered how long he had been in there himself. Too long. His skin felt dry and dehydrated, beneath the layer of shower water. His fingers had wrinkled, the way they used to when he was a child. Often, he'd play in the bath for too long, delaying bedtime on a school night.

It took a while longer, but he pulled himself together, and put his illusory mask back on, before emerging from the shower. He passed Steffan on the way back to his room.

'All right?' he said, forcing a smile.

‘Yeah, just came to get washed up,’ replied Steffan, gesturing towards the towel and pile of fresh clothes he was carrying. ‘Food shouldn’t be that long, hopefully,’

That’s a relief.

His low mood had distracted him from his hunger, but he knew that sustenance would aid in his battle. A release of serotonin. It was strangely contradictory, how he ate to survive, whilst not always feeling as though he wanted his life to go on anyway.

He had dumped his sopping wet clothes from earlier into the bedroom, where they landed heavily on the floor, and left for the canteen before Steffan returned from the showers. After jogging through the rain, he was glad to arrive to the smell of cooked food.

Francesca was sitting back in the same chair, at the same table she had occupied earlier. But he could see from her new outfit that she had also been to get changed at some point. The others were milling around, in and out of the kitchen. Despite them being stranded, and the shock of Billy’s accident, spirits seemed to have improved from earlier, as conversation and laughter echoed through into the next room.

‘How’s the ankle?’ he asked Francesca, walking towards her table, before sitting down in the seat opposite.

She shifted in her seat, wincing as she gasped inwardly, as though she was in a great deal of pain, and placed a hand onto her leg for effect, before saying ‘still hurts, but it’s not too bad.’

‘Well, that’s good,’ he said.

He wasn’t sure what else to say. Despite working just a matter of feet away from her for the last couple of years, he realised he didn’t know that much about her. Not much, at least, beyond what she posted on social media – and he wasn't about to ask her who was playing in the polo that weekend.

Instead, it was she who spoke again. 'Anyway, are you okay? You know, after earlier.'

'Yeah, it was nothing,' he lied.

'For what it's worth, I thought he was completely out of order. He has been all day, to be honest. I don't know what's gotten into him lately.'

Lately? Francesca, love, your fella was born a wanker.

'Where is he, anyway?' he asked.

'Sulking, probably,' she said. 'I moved my stuff out of that room, before. Bryn, bless him, helped me take it into a spare one. We left him on his own in there and I haven't seen him since.'

Gareth figured it made sense, her switching rooms. He was sure she would go running back to Benjamin in no time, just as soon as there was a new pair of Balenciaga trainers she just *had to have*. Despite that, she seemed different all of a sudden. More approachable, and less up herself. It was refreshing. But weird.

All it had taken was a touch of Benjamin-inflicted humiliation, embarrassing her in front of her work colleagues. It appeared even the HomeHub 'elite' were not immune from such gratuities.

Hearing the clattering of pans and chatter behind him, he ventured into the kitchen. It seemed like the right thing to do, showing a willingness – however false – to lend a hand.

'Nice of you to show up and help,' taunted Billy, who – ironically – was leaning against one of the worktops, arms folded.

'Is there anything I can help with?' Gareth asked. He looked around, and there wasn't much being done, by anyone. He'd timed his arrival perfectly.

'You can get the bread out of the oven if you like,' said Tara. 'Everything else should be ready to serve, now.'

He picked up a set of oven mitts and followed the homely aroma of baked goods towards the oven. The bread hadn't turned quite as golden as he would have liked, but it would do.

Fetching a couple of serving dishes, he transferred the bread rolls to them from the baking trays, before carrying them through to the canteen. The appetising fragrances were causing his stomach to rumble angrily, demanding to be fed.

Thankfully, dinner was served.

CHAPTER TWENTY-FIVE

Steffan

He was certain the stew wouldn't have been classified as fine dining, but it wasn't *completely* terrible. Granted, there was far too much salt added, and the vegetables were a little undercooked – or borderline raw, in the carrots' case. The meat was quite tough, too. But Steffan had eaten far worse. Plus, at the stage of hunger he had reached, he didn't really care. Scoff was scoff.

After devouring a couple of bowls of the stew – and polishing off the remnants of gravy with bread and butter – he sat back momentarily and allowed his full stomach a little space. Some of the others in the group were still struggling through their first bowl, as they faced a battle with gristles of fat and overly crunchy veg. Nevertheless, the need to be fed appeared to be universal.

'Enjoy that, bud?' asked Bryn, looking over at him.

'Yeah, it hit the spot. Thanks.'

'Aye. Not too bad on short notice, anyroad.'

Steffan wondered if Bryn was the type of bloke who refused to admit if he had produced something sub-par. There was no benefit to be gained by pointing out the flaws of the meal, but the fact the ranger seemed satisfied with his own efforts struck Steffan as either delusional, or just somebody with low expectations.

Once spoons had been placed down and it was clear that everyone was finished, Steffan began to collect the dishes from around the table.

'Thanks, Steffan,' said Jodie, passing him her empty bowl.

'Good teamwork, everybody!' cheered Tara.

'Yeah, nearly everybody,' said Billy, smirking at Gareth.

There was no reply, but Steffan could see from the way he had curled his lips that Gareth wanted to snap at the bait cast in his direction. Instead, he looked around breezily, as though he hadn't heard anything, before catching Steffan's gaze and getting up to lend a hand with clearing up.

'So then, what's everyone's plans now?' asked Tara. Her eyes darted around, and it was obvious she was up to something. There were mischievous looks from Billy and Matthew, too. They were glancing, in turn, at Bryn, who appeared completely bemused by it all.

'What's are you up to now?' he asked.

'Bryyyyn,' said Tara, fluttering her eyelashes at the older man like a provocative schoolgirl trying to obtain a better grade. 'We might have brought some beers with us…'

'Yes, that's no skin off my nose,' he replied, cutting her off before she could finish.

'Really?' she replied.

'You're all adults, aren't you?' he continued. 'Obviously, don't trash the place, and if you throw up, there'll be a bill from Ceri. But more to the point, I'll make you eat it.'

Tara and Billy laughed. They soon stopped, though, as Bryn's face did not suggest he was joking.

There was a moment of awkwardness, as Steffan collected the last of the dishes.

There was still plenty of food in the pot, so Steffan covered up the leftovers. It was better to save it for later than throw it away.

He looked over his shoulder to check nobody else, namely Bryn, was around, before turning to Gareth. 'What did you think of that stew, then?'

Gareth didn't need to answer. The look on his face said it all.

'That bad?'

'Honestly, I was starving so I ate it. But a day in the office is less painful than chewing that beef. I though it was going to pull out a molar.'

Steffan chuckled. 'I've had a lot worse.'

Gareth hummed a sound of understanding. It seemed as though there was something on his mind – something he wanted to say. Steffan could almost see him shrivelling up within himself earlier, as Benjamin snapped at him.

'You all good, anyway? Y'know, after before.'

'Yeah, fine,' replied Gareth, his eyes lowered. 'I just hate the way he gets all these plaudits, gets richer whilst we, the peasants, are expected to just pick up peanuts and nod our heads to the beat of his drum.'

'Benjamin, you mean?'

'Who else?'

'If you feel that strongly, why don't you bin the place off?' asked Steffan.

'I've tried,' said Gareth, looking at Steffan now. 'Believe me, I've tried. But after so many rejected job applications, you just think "what's the point?" You know?'

Steffan did know. Only too well. For that reason, he didn't know what to say. Couldn't think of a piece of advice to offer. So, he just nodded, and they continued to wash up in silence.

Working together, it didn't take the pair of them long to finish. Despite that, the canteen had been deserted by the time they were done. Steffan guessed the group had gone to gather whatever booze had been brought along.

'I haven't even brought any beers with me,' he said.

‘Nor me,’ replied Gareth. ‘To be honest with you, I don’t really drink anyway.’

Steffan didn’t either. Not anymore. In cleaning up his act, he had tried to live a relatively alcohol-free lifestyle. He wasn’t completely teetotal, but he knew that whenever the first sip of a pint touched his lips, there was a good chance he wouldn’t know when to stop.

But tonight, he fancied a drink. He needed to unwind.

It was understandable, seeing as though he was a relative unknown to them, but he felt a little annoyed to not have been aware of the groups premeditated plans. If he had, he could have brought something along, in case he *did* fancy a beer. Fortunately, there was more than enough to go around.

Soon enough, one of the fridges had been filled up with bottles of various lagers. The girls had even brought a few bottles of wine.

Accepting a kind offer from Matthew, Steffan cracked open a bottle, and even Gareth took one, though he’d insisted it would be ‘just the one’. It would be nice, Steffan thought, to just sit back and relax, and hopefully get to know his colleagues a little better over a few civilised drinks.

The plan soon changed, as Bryn returned, bearing gifts. In one hand, he had an unopened bottle of Penderyn Single Malt, and under his other arm, an old portable CD player and zip wallet filled with discs.

‘Let’s get this party started,’ cried Tara. ‘DJ Bryn in the house!’

Bryn plonked the bottle on the table where Steffan was sitting, as Tara and Jodie rifled through what would undoubtedly be a very outdated selection of music.

‘Only the good stuff, for me, bud,’ said Bryn.

Steffan knew all too well. It was the *only* whiskey his Taid would drink when he was alive. He had always said: ‘Forget the Paddies and forget the Scots, boyo, this is the product of the Lord, in the Lord’s country.’

'Grab me a glass too, would you Bryn?' he called towards the kitchen. He knew he shouldn't, but it would be rude not to.

'I'd be delighted to, young man.'

CHAPTER TWENTY-SIX

Jodie

It had dawned on her that someone would need to go and remind Benjamin to eat. It seemed ridiculous, given the day's events, but as it appeared nobody else had thought to, Jodie had reached the conclusion that it was going to have to be her. She didn't want to go, didn't want to be alone with him again. But nobody else seemed to have even noticed his absence. Whilst the others chatted amongst themselves and began opening more bottles, she decided to leave them to it and slipped away, heading for the sleeping cabin.

Outside, the rain continued to fall. It was relentless, and she wondered if it would ever end. She hunched into her already sodden jacket and shivered as she looked ahead.

With every step closer, she felt her heart beat a little bit quicker. She was worried how he would react to her going back to his room, how he would be with her. After earlier. After the look in his eyes. But she took a deep breath, before swallowing her nerves and ploughing on, her feet squelching along the muddy path.

She let out a quivered breath as she made it to the cabin. Inside, she stepped down the corridor, moving tentatively towards his door. She knocked timidly at the door, but there was no answer. She knocked again, but louder. Still nothing. She heard no sound of footsteps from inside the room – no sound of anyone approaching.

Perhaps he still doesn't want to speak to anyone.

'Benjamin?' she called out, pressing her ear against the door. She knocked again. 'Benjamin, are you in there?'

No reply.

She turned the handle, opening the door slowly.

'Benjamin, there's some food leftover, I was just checking if you wanted…'

Her words were cut short by what lay before her. The room was a bombsite – a far worse state than it had been in earlier. Chairs were upturned, his bed was unmade, with the duvet hanging off, half on the floor. She felt the breeze coming through the wide-open window and gasped. Rainwater dripped from the trees at the back of the building. Inside, the room was quiet, but she could feel an anger within it. Surrounding her menacingly. She shivered as a chill travelled downwards from the back of her neck.

She walked over to the tall, low-set casement window, and pulled it shut. It was only then that she noticed a smear of red on the windowsill. Blood?

Jodie was perturbed as she stared at it, trying to work out exactly what was before her. She followed it down to the wall beneath the window. Spots of more colour on the old beige paintwork, before she saw more trailing across the surface, following a vague pathway towards his bed.

She followed it back to the window. Braced herself, as her stomach tightened. She re-opened the window, and a gust of wind took her breath away as it flooded back into the room. She brushed her hair out of her face and leaned out of the window.

There he was.

CHAPTER TWENTY-SEVEN

Jodie

Jodie stared through the window. Motionless. It couldn't be real. Her stomach was knotted, and she could feel the tingling sensation of the goosebumps that were pushing the hairs up all over her body.

She didn't know what to do as she stood, paralysed, looking at Benjamin with her mouth agape. Her first instinct was to leap through the window, out to the back of the cabin. To check for a pulse. To feel a breath. But something told her it would be a waste of time. Instead, she would have been better going to the nearest toilet, because she knew she was about to throw up. He couldn't be dead. It made no sense.

Almost losing her balance, she ran out of the bedroom to find help, making the terrible error of gulping down the saliva which had pooled inside her mouth, as the contents of her stomach bolted up her throat, and landed on the ground a short distance away from the canteen.

As she retched loudly and uncontrollably, the door opened.

'All right, Jode!?' called Billy, without a shred of concern in his voice.

She looked up at him, as he leaned out of the canteen rather than stepping into the rain. A bead of sweat ran down her forehead, the rain washing it stingingly into her eyes.

She squinted them shut and tried to speak, before the vomiting continued.

'You haven't even finished one beer yet,' he mocked.

She groaned through the searing pain in her oesophagus. Her head was spinning. The sound of footsteps approached, as she saw both Billy and Tara coming closer, treading carefully to avoid what was left of her beef stew.

'Are you okay, Jodie?' asked Tara. She placed a hand on her back and massaged it gently. 'Do you think it was the food?'

'No way, she's obviously just a crap drinker, isn't she,' sneered Billy.

'It's… not that,' said Jodie, trying to catch her breath. 'It's B-Benjamin.'

'Benjamin…' repeated Tara, frowning at her. 'What's Benjamin?'

'He's… I think he's dead.'

She was met with looks of further perplexity from both Tara and Billy.

'Yep. Definitely the drink,' laughed Billy. 'Come on, let's go back in – we'll get you a water, Little Miss Lightweight.'

Why aren't they listening?

'It's not the fucking drink,' she snapped, finding and regaining her composure. 'I just saw him. There's blood. He's not moving. I think he's fucking dead!'

Tara and Billy both stopped. They turned back around to look at her. The bemused expressions on their faces had been replaced by frowns of concern.

'Are you serious?' asked Tara.

'Why would I lie about something like this? Come and see for yourselves!'

They walked towards her, to follow her to the sleeping cabin, but Tara stopped and looked back towards the canteen. She opened her mouth as if to say something, but must have decided not to, instead scurrying to catch up to Billy and Jodie.

'I'll tell you what, Jode,' said Billy. 'I know I said you were boring, but this is a right bloody effort for a practical joke, fair play.'

Jodie just looked at him, with a telling gaze. She didn't need to say a word. It was no joke – she was deadly serious. They would soon see that.

When they arrived at the door to Benjamin's bedroom, Billy and Tara paused momentarily, both giving Jodie an uncertain glance before she ushered them inside.

'See here,' she said, pointing her finger along the floor as it followed the trail of blood which travelled across the room.

'What the hell?' responded Billy.

'It goes to the window, and he's… he's out there.'

'Jodie,' mumbled Tara. 'You aren't joking, are you?'

'Of course she is,' scoffed Billy. 'That's obviously tomato ketchup all over the floor. Fair play guys, this is one hell of a prank. Benjamin, you can come out now!'

'It really isn't a joke,' said Jodie, her voice level.

Tara swallowed heavily as she stared back at her. Billy approached the window, slowly, and stepped over the blood.

'Yeah, this ain't for me,' he said, turning back. 'Tara, you look first. He's gonna jump out or something, in'e?'

'I'm not doing it,' said Tara. 'Just get on with it, and stop being such a wimp.'

He shook his head, clearly unwilling, but still walked over to the window, and leaned out of the window for a moment before recoiling.

'Fucking hell.'

'What?' asked Tara.

Billy turned back and looked at them both. The colour had drained from his face, leaving it a ghostly white. Tara rushed over to the window, pushing past him and peered out, before quickly pulling her head back and putting her hand over her mouth.

'I told you,' said Jodie.

CHAPTER TWENTY-EIGHT

Gareth

Gareth had been nursing his bottle of lager for quite a while, just taking the odd sip. After reluctantly accepting it, he had insisted he would only have that one. He wasn't a big drinker – not for any big, life-altering reason, he just didn't see the point in spending hard-earned money just to feel ill the next day. Hangovers were hellish, and while he often regretted waking up to begin with, suffering the after-effects of a night of beer tended to only make things worse.

As he tipped his drink back, finishing what was left in the bottle, he realised he had become more relaxed. There was an argument that, perhaps, he did need to lighten up a little more. He often envied – through gritted teeth – those who lived life with a more carefree attitude, just working to pay for the weekend. The trouble was, he was a thinker – a deep thinker – and with that he tended to worry about things, big and small. And when he was feeling particularly depressed about life, he worried that booze would somehow motivate him to do something extreme. To do something final.

He sat back in his seat and looked at those around him. Matthew was engrossed in meaningless, but flirty conversation with Francesca, who – against Bryn's advice – had decided to mix alcohol with the painkillers he had given her for her ankle pain. Steffan, meanwhile was chatting with the ranger. They were both knocking back the whiskey Bryn had brought in earlier. Their chat seemed a little more intriguing than the idle gossip of the other two, so Gareth decided to go and join them.

As he rose from his seat, Steffan stopped in mid-sentence and faced him.

'Here you go, Gaz. Have a try of this stuff,' he said, raising his glass towards Gareth.

'Oh, I shouldn't – are you sure?' asked Gareth, looking to Bryn for approval, but secretly hoping not to receive it. He also didn't want to encroach on what appeared to be an expensive purchase.

Bryn gave him a blasé nod of the head. 'Help yourself, bud.'

Steffan handed him the glass, smiling – waiting expectantly for him to drink. Gareth put the whiskey below his nose, smelling it with curiosity, before taking a large gulp. The sweet, earthy flavour engulfed his tastebuds, burning as it trickled down the back of his throat.

'Nice, isn't it?' enthused Steffan.

Gareth wasn't so sure, but he returned the glass with a polite smile and a nod, and headed towards the fridge, to get another beer. With the shot of whiskey in his system, he had passed the point of no return, and figured, why not?

If you can't beat them, join them.

When he arrived back at the table, flicking the cap off his Peroni, Steffan had ventured into the tale of how he ended up in prison.

Gareth listened in disbelief, as Steffan told him and Bryn about how he had been unemployed and skint, struggling to find gainful employment after leaving the army. That was when, one evening at his local pub, a guy he knew from school – Jamie Price, or 'Jam' as he was known, had offered Steffan a solution.

'He wasn't a mate, or anything like that,' said Steffan. 'I knew he was a dodgy little bastard. His whole family are. But I was desperate, see?'

Bryn nodded as he swilled the whiskey around in his glass. 'Understandable, lad. You serve the country, and then you're spat out like gristle off a lamb.'

'Right,' said Steffan. 'But yeah, what I'm trying to say is – I only had myself to blame.'

He explained how he had received the call the very next night. Outside, a battered old white Transit van was waiting for him with the engine running. Jam and another guy called Mowgli – who didn't acknowledge Steffan – were inside.

Jam had explained to Steffan that the house they were going to belonged to an older lady – living alone – who was out of the country.

'So it was a burglary?' asked Gareth. He was shocked; Steffan hadn't given the impression he was the type of person to commit such a crime.

'Aye. The woman had been widowed a couple of years earlier, and just used to buy stuff for the sake of it off the online shopping channels. "Money to burn", Jam had described her as. But anyway, we get there, and it's all going to plan – we get in the house, this bloody massive house, and we're searching for things to take. I'm upstairs searching in her bedroom…'

'Then what happened?'

'I found an envelope with a wad of cash in under her mattress, but that wasn't all.'

'What was it?'

'Her husband's medals from the second World War.'

'Bloody hell,' said Bryn.

'You didn't take them?' asked Gareth.

'Christ no,' said Steffan. 'They just distracted me. Made me ask myself what the hell I was doing there, to this innocent woman – the wife of a hero. I didn't hear the sirens at first, and when I did…'

'They went and left you behind, didn't they?' said Bryn. It sounded rhetorical. As though the ending was predictable.

Steffan nodded. 'I come out of the front door to a cloud of exhaust fumes. Before I know it, there was blue lights everywhere. There was nowhere for me to go, nowhere to run. I just stood there as they cuffed me.'

'That's fucked up,' said Gareth. Steffan looked him with furrowed brows. 'No, I mean… sorry to say it, but you got what you deserved, obviously. But for that *Jam* guy to screw you over like that. Wow.'

Steffan shrugged. He made no reply. Gareth hoped he hadn't annoyed him.

Bryn held his bottle up to them both. 'Having another one, boys?'

CHAPTER TWENTY-NINE

Steffan

It was sometimes hard to go back in time, recollecting the things he had experienced. Steffan didn't mind as much, when talking about his time *after* the army – the stupid decisions he had made, and even the struggles he faced. But his time in combat? That was the tougher subject. Seeing the life fade away from a friend's eyes, after they had taken a bullet or been caught in a grenade's blast radius. The battle between a need to survive and the overwhelming, natural reluctance to kill another person. The human brain was not wired to process such abominable scenarios.

When people did speak to him about the army, or his time in certain parts of the world, he would often try to focus on lighter moments – practical jokes amongst comrades, or explanations for bizarre nicknames. It was better to leave the other stuff locked away, in the darkness, he had thought. It was easier that way.

But some dickhead would always ask the question. *'How many people have you killed, Steff?'*... his answer was perfected, rehearsed and damning enough to move the conversation swiftly on – *The day isn't over, yet.*

'What do you guys think?' asked Francesca, beckoning Steffan, Bryn and Gareth away from their own conversation.

'About what?' responded Steffan, turning to face her.

'Them three,' said Matthew, with a smirk. 'Where have they gone?'

'Matty thinks Tara and Jodie are up to their old tricks,' Francesca said, playfully punching Matthew in the arm.

'No, you're the one who said it!' he squealed.

'Yeah, but you agreed,' she said. 'Anyway, what do you think, Gareth?'

Steffan looked at Gareth, who had puckered his lips and furrowed his brows. He couldn't decide if it was in thought or annoyance.

'Well, they won't want to be outside,' interrupted Bryn. 'Not now it's dark, out.'

'Being eaten by a bear would be a better option for Billy, than a night with those two,' laughed Francesca.

Steffan knew it was a joke – but still – bears in North Wales? There was more chance of Billy being charged by a badger.

Despite the underhanded premise behind their question, Francesca and Matthew did have a fair point. Billy and the girls had been gone for a while – and it was their beer everybody else was drinking, other than Bryn's Penderyn, which Steffan was thoroughly enjoying. He picked up his glass to take another sip, as the door crashed open.

'Benjamin's dead!' yelled Billy.

What does he mean, 'dead'?

'I wish,' muttered Gareth, louder than he probably realised.

'Dead? What are you talking about?' asked Francesca, flippantly.

'Dead. On the floor. Out there.' Billy pointed in the vague direction of the sleeping cabin, as he blurted out fractured pieces of information. He was clearly spooked.

Confusion swept across the group, as voices babbled over one another, rising into a disorderly clamour, which began ringing in Steffan's ears. Billy and Tara were attempting to answer people's questions, barking back, and only making the noise more unbearable.

'Can everyone just shut the hell up, for a minute?' he bellowed, knocking on the table, with only his fist for a gavel.

Silence and order came at once. He looked around at each of them, as they stared back at him expectantly. As though they believed he would have all the answers. In reality, he just wanted to be able to hear his own thoughts.

'So, where exactly is he?'

'Round the back of the cabin – he's gone out through his window somehow,' said Tara.

'And you're sure he's dead, like?'

There was a momentary pause from all three of them, as they looked at each other before shaking their heads timidly.

'We didn't actually check, we were too scared,' said Jodie. 'But there's blood.'

Steffan exhaled slowly, trying to not show outward signs of exasperation. 'So, you haven't actually check— come on…', he marched towards the door, and everyone – even Francesca, began to follow. 'You're going to have to show us where he is.'

Bryn picked up a couple of torches and handed one to Steffan, before the group went out into the darkness awaiting them.

CHAPTER THIRTY

Gareth

There was a sinister feeling lurking within the obscurity of night. With just the glowing beams from Steffan and Bryn's torches offering visibility up ahead, Gareth couldn't shake the sense of being watched through the falling rain. Paranoia was a common symptom of his depression – and whilst his gut instinct was usually right, when he felt somebody was out to get him or was talking behind his back, the drink had only heightened its sensitivity that evening. Ironically, he had taken his beer outside with him, and he raised it for another swig to try and settle his nerves.

Nobody spoke as they walked, their boots and shoes crunching down on the gravel trail towards the sleeping cabin. They were huddled, lagging behind the two leaders, as Francesca hobbled amongst them. Gareth wondered if flocking together was a conscious decision people had made, or just a natural response to the fear coursing through them. He wasn't particularly frightened at the prospect of seeing a dead body, but he could have understood if the others were.

As they arrived at the sleeping cabin, Bryn turned around, shining the light in their direction.

'You lot go in there – look out of the windows if you must, though I'd seriously consider not putting yourselves through it, if those three are right.' The light flickered against the cabin door, as he gestured for them to go inside.

Gareth wondered why anyone would have bothered coming out into the rain if they *weren't* planning to look.

'I'm coming with you,' said Steffan.

'Oh, er, you sure, lad?' asked Bryn. 'Okay, the rest of you – head inside.'

Despite the air of angst within the group, nobody appeared reluctant to try and get a glimpse. It was as though the idea of seeing a real dead body was far more alluring than the reality.

They filed in through the doorway, and followed the corridor to Benjamin's room. On first glance, it looked like there had been a burglary, rather than being the scene of a possible death. Either a burglary, or an infamous Benjamin tantrum – where no inanimate object was safe from being hauled across a room, whether it be a crowded office or his private quarters.

He saw the neck of a bottle, sticking out from under the bed. The unmistakable blue Grey Goose label was still present.

Benjamin had obviously decided to have his own party.

'Oh my word, is that *blood*?' said Francesca.

Only then, did Gareth see the spots of red, spattered on the dark wood of the floor.

'Taking that into account,' he said, 'should we maybe not be in here, putting our hands all over things? In case it's a crime scene, and all that jazz…'

'Okay, nobody touch *anything*,' instructed Francesca, before hopping over towards the window and peering out. 'I can't really see outside – oh, shit.'

'Wait,' said Jodie. 'We've already been in here. I didn't think… I've touched stuff in here.'

'Looks like the police will have you pegged as the killer then,' said Matthew, with a smirk. Nobody saw the funny side.

Jodie looked mortified. 'I didn't kill anybody! He might not even be dead!'

'Are you sure, maneater?' quipped Francesca, who was still stood by the window.

'Yes, I'm sure – what the hell! Why would someone say such a thing?'

Jodie began bawling loudly, in blatant exasperation. Tara started to bicker with Francesca, whilst Matthew and Billy threw aggressive lines of vituperation back and forth. Gareth stood there in disbelief, as he considered just how quickly the group had descended into chaos.

'To be honest,' he said. 'It looks as though he's just been enjoying his own company.' He gestured towards his discovery, but nobody took any notice of him. His words were lost in the crossfire of the unceasing bedlam.

'Guys!' came a stern, hushed call from the other side of the window. Gareth saw Steffan glaring into the room. As rainwater ran down his face, he appeared to be just as appalled at the others as Gareth was. Nobody else had taken any notice of Steffan, as the arguments continued. He repeated himself, loudly, and finally the squabble petered out.

'What is it?' said Francesca.

Steffan looked at her, before casting his gaze at all of them. 'It's not good news. He's not breathing, and we couldn't find a pulse...'

'So, he's... he's really dead?' she stuttered.

Steffan pursed his lips and nodded solemnly.

'But how?' asked Matthew.

The others walked towards the window, to get a better look at Benjamin, or 'his body', which it would be referred to as, from that point on. It was so strange, Gareth had always thought, how once a person dies, what remains is no longer perceived as the person, but merely the body which belonged to them. As though it is only a temporary object used by someone – an outfit, or a shell.

'I'll spare you the gory details, like, but he's taken a hell of a blow to the head. It's hard to see anything else in the dark, but we're not flippin' running autopsies out here, either.'

Gareth took his opportunity to cast his eye over Benjamin. Through the darkness, he could see him lying there, sprawled on the dirt. The rain continued to fall, and it was as though it was washing the blood away – cleansing him as it seeped into the earth. He felt detached for a moment. It was like watching a film in 3D, rather than real life, but a weight in his chest told Gareth that wasn't the case.

He wasn't sure how he felt. It should have been fear, possibly even guilt, but it wasn't. It was a shock, but Benjamin was gone. The question was *how*? Without knowing the answer, Gareth couldn't help but wonder if someone else could be next.

He shuddered, and turned back to face the others, absorbing the reactions from around the room. The girls had all begun to cry hysterically, though it was difficult to decide between Francesca and Jodie who seemed the most upset. Billy and Matthew stood in reflective silence, shaking their heads as they tried to come to terms with the unfathomable confirmation. Gareth was silent, too. He didn't know what to say, in such a situation. Benjamin's death was unfortunate, of course. But it *was* something he had dreamed about.

He had asked the devil for a favour. It appeared the devil had obliged.

CHAPTER THIRTY-ONE

Steffan

Steffan wiped the rain from his brow, listening to the cries of dismay coming from inside the bedroom. Bryn was circling Benjamin's body, aimlessly, as though looking for an answer to explain what had happened. An answer which wasn't there.

Steffan had seen more than his fair share of dead bodies. It never got any easier. If anything, despite the brain's attempts to desensitise the effects of the sights he had witnessed, each time just created a new memory, locked away, waiting patiently to come out to haunt him when he slept. One nightmare after another.

Whether he liked, loathed, was friends with, or had never even met the man before he saw them lying there in front of him, it didn't make much difference. He barely knew Benjamin, and from his brief encounters with him, he certainly wasn't sold – in fact, he was pretty confident he would have developed a great dislike for him. But Steffan had lost just as many comrades who he had no time for, as those he had respected and cared about. Their faces all wore the same, helpless expression, as their souls faded away from them.

The difference on this occasion, was that there were no enemy troops firing bullets in their direction. So, what the hell had happened?

‘Right then,’ said Bryn. ‘We’d best get him moved inside.’

Steffan looked at him, confused. ‘Shouldn’t he be left where he is, for when the police get here?’

‘There’s a problem with that, lad – no phones, remember? They won’t be coming any time soon. We can’t leave him out here, for the foxes to come across. Flipping awful mess that’d be. Besides, poor guy has suffered a dreadful accident – I don’t think the officers will be too worried about him being moved.’

Bryn raised a fair point, despite the obvious risk of incriminating themselves with the forensics team. The prospect of Benjamin becoming a feast for the local wildlife was not a pretty sight to envision. But an ‘accident’? How could Bryn make such an off the cuff statement? Sure, whilst it seemed unthinkable that any of his colleagues were capable of murder, this ‘accident’ was difficult for him to get his head around. There were just too many questions to consider. How did he end up out there? What was he doing on the wrong side of the window, if he hadn’t been put there by somebody else?

‘How do you want to do this then?’ he asked, gesturing towards Benjamin.

‘If you get the top end, I’ll get his feet,’ replied Bryn.

Steffan nodded. He was reluctant to cover the body with his fingerprints and DNA, let alone disturb a possible crime scene, but he followed Bryn’s lead. The mud squelched beneath his feet as he squatted, carefully sliding his hands beneath Benjamin’s shoulders and hooking his fingers to the armpits.

‘On three?’

‘Aye.’

They heaved the body from the ground, as Steffan’s heels sank a little with the extra weight. He tried not to look as Benjamin’s head lolled backwards, drooping and bobbing towards the ground as they carried him towards a more sheltered place of rest.

CHAPTER THIRTY-TWO

Jodie

Nothing made sense. Jodie could not understand how, or why this could have happened to him. As she stood there, eyes glazed and in silence, her head was spinning wildly, as different emotions and questions collided with each other in frantic dissonance.

Nobody else was speaking either. The room was still, in complete silence, as though they were all trying to come to terms with the fact Benjamin was gone. The man she had loved for so long, was dead. He hadn't even reached forty years of age. People just weren't supposed to die so soon. It happened, of course. It would appear in the news from time to time, but not to somebody you knew. It was surreal.

She was convinced it couldn't have been an accident, and he could not have taken his own life – his ego simply would not have allowed it, for one. He was too confident, and self-centred to do such a thing. His arrogance was what she had been so drawn to, in awe of.

What was she thinking? Of course it wasn't suicide. It hadn't truly dawned on her until then, when everyone was together, that someone in the group had to be at fault. Someone she knew. Someone *he* knew.

She could not, however, believe that the others had suggested *she* had played a part in his death. Despite everything that had happened earlier in the day, she was still besotted with him. She couldn't bear the thought of her fantasies never becoming a reality, as they so nearly had, before being cruelly snatched away. But now, she would never know for sure if there could have been a way back for them.

When Steffan and Bryn had lifted his body from the ground, and began to carry him back inside, the others shuffled out in muted tones, and made their way back into the canteen. It was partly to allow space for Steffan and Bryn to manoeuvre Benjamin back into the bedroom, she was sure, but it was obviously to avoid having to come face to face with his lifeless body, without the filter that the night sky had afforded them from a distance. She almost followed them, particularly for the latter reason, but she had to see him. *Really* see him. It was the only hope she had of understanding and accepting it was true.

She heard the outer door, and clunky footsteps approaching. Once Bryn and Steffan made it into the room, she soon regretted her decision to stay. She looked at his face. It was still and calm, yet frozen in a state of fear – something that she had never seen from Benjamin. Nothing had ever seemed to faze him. His eyes stared at the ceiling above him, pupils dilated and unfocused. His scruffy hair was stained red, on a large patch to the left of his crown.

'Are you okay?' asked Steffan.

She looked at him and saw empathy in his eyes. But why? She wasn't the one who was lying there.

'Perhaps you should go with the others, love,' said Bryn.

'I'm fine,' she whispered, lying to him *and* herself. Her hand trembled slightly as she raised a pointed finger, aimed at Benjamin's head. 'Is that how he died?'

'Aye, looks that way,' replied Bryn. 'It's not pleasant – are you sure you don't want to go and catch your breath?'

She lowered herself, kneeling at Benjamin's side and gently caressing his bloodied head. Why did this have to happen? It wasn't fair.

'He stinks of alcohol,' she said, looking up at Steffan and Bryn in turn. It was true. The harsh fumes of spirits took her by surprise.

'Aye,' said Bryn once more. 'Must've been bladdered and had a fall – tripped through the window. That's my best guess anyway.'

She took her hand away from his wound. 'There's not much blood, really,' she said, looking at her dry palm.

'Doesn't have to be. The impact alone can kill you, head injury like that.'

'But what about the blood inside the room? It doesn't make sense if he's fallen outside, does it?'

Bryn sighed. 'I don't know, love. Look at the state of it in here, maybe he hurt himself in the room – bumped his bonce, then in the confusion he's stepped out through the window and collapsed. I'm not a detective.'

Jodie wasn't a detective either, but what Bryn had suggested sounded ridiculous. She shook her head, and that's when she spotted it. Her eyes were fixed on Steffan. She saw his hands. Then his sleeves. Everything was red. He was covered in Benjamin's blood.

He caught the direction of her stare, before looking down at himself.

'Shit.'

He crouched down next to Jodie, and reassessed things, making use of the lighting. He carefully placed his hands beneath the body. Jodie looked on, silently. His eyes widened, and he took a deep breath, before carefully turning the body onto its side.

'What are you doing, lad?' asked Bryn.

'Still think it was an accident?' Steffan asked.

The back of Benjamin's shirt was the same shade of red as Steffan's sleeves. The material was slashed in the centre of the bloodstain.

So, he really has been murdered?

The colour drained from Bryn's face, as he looked down at the evidence Steffan had presented.

'I think we should get back to the rest of the group.'

CHAPTER THIRTY-THREE

Gareth

It was eerily quiet in the canteen. Gareth reclaimed the same seat he had taken before. He had finally started to relax earlier, drinking a beer with the rest of the group. But now, the mood had changed significantly – even after meeting his end, Benjamin still seemed capable of having that effect on things.

Whilst it was understandable that the others had fallen into a sombre state, he felt no misery for what had happened to Benjamin. But it did raise questions that were just as relevant to him as they would have been for the others.

Who would run the company, now? Would they still have jobs to go back to? What happens next?

Of course, nobody had dared ask such things, but he was certain they would all share the same concerns. On the flip side, if Benjamin's death led to the company suffering its own demise, it may yet have served as the steppingstone Gareth had needed, to get out of that pit of misery and find a new, less damaging workplace.

We need to get out of this place, first.

'Does anyone want a coffee?' he asked, looking around at the forlorn faces surrounding him.

Tara looked at him, sullenly and bleary eyed. 'No, thanks.'

Her reply was followed by mutters from everyone else, all declining Gareth's offer, as Francesca reached across the table to pick up a half-finished bottle of wine. Neglecting to fill a glass, she pressed the open top to her lips and swigged heavily.

'Yeah,' said Gareth with a nod. 'That probably makes more sense.'

'Good idea,' said Billy, and he made his way towards the kitchen. 'I need a drink. Beers all round, lads?'

Nobody responded, but Billy soon emerged with as many bottles as he could carry – the necks wedged and gripped tightly between his fingers. He dished them out to everyone, and raised his own bottle, as Jodie, Steffan and Bryn piled in through the door.

'To Benjamin,' he bellowed. 'He played by his own rules.'

'He usually won, as well,' said Matthew, raising his own bottle.

Not this time, though, thought Gareth. He slightly tipped his bottle, but refrained from raising it in unison with the others.

'Erm, guys,' called Steffan. Everyone turned to face him, as he looked back with an expression of deep concern. 'We have a situation on our hands.'

'Yeah, Benjamin is dead – we're all aware,' scolded Billy, his bottle still raised. 'Hence the toast.'

'It's a bit more serious than that,' came a call from behind Steffan. Bryn turned to face the room, after closing the door behind them and turning the latch.

The expression of concern, which had protruded from Steffan's face like a diseased boil, had now spread amongst the room as they waited for Bryn to elaborate.

'What do you mean?' asked Francesca, a slight quiver in her voice.

‘It looks like Benjamin has been…’ rasped Jodie. She closed her eyes and inhaled deeply. ‘He’s been murdered.’

‘Murdered!’ said Billy. ‘What the hell do you mean, *“murdered”*?’

‘There’s what looks to be a stab wound to his back,’ explained Steffan.

‘Well, how did that, like, get there?’ asked Francesca.

‘I presume somebody put it there, with a knife or something,’ said Gareth.

What a stupid fucking question.

She looked at him with a scowl. ‘Obviously, I know *that*,’ she hissed. ‘What I mean is, who? Why would someone do such a thing?’

I could give you a reason, or twenty.

‘Let’s all try and stay calm, folks,’ called Bryn, which Gareth thought was a ridiculous suggestion to make.

He looked around as the chaotic chatter of panic consumed the rest of the group. Gareth, too, was incredibly concerned at the prospect of a killer in the ranks. But who?

Whilst casting his shifting gaze around at the group, he simply couldn’t determine that any of them could have been capable of such an act, despite some having undeniable motive. There was Francesca, the betrayed lover. Jodie, who was complicit in said betrayal, before being cruelly brushed aside and made a scapegoat by Benjamin. Steffan, the latest employee to receive a provocative tongue-lashing, that very day. Christ, even Gareth himself had motive. He detested Benjamin, more than anybody he had ever detested before, but much like he had determined of the others, even he wouldn’t have been able to kill him – no matter how salivating it was in a daydream.

‘So, what do we do?’ he asked, looking at Bryn to take control.

‘I’m just trying to think,’ the ranger said, closing his eyes as if he was trying to drown out the noise. Gareth looked on at him, glancing around at the table – people were still caught up in the moment.

'Guys, can you all just. Shut. The. Fuck. Up?' barked Steffan. He seemed genuinely aghast, his expression resembling that of a secondary school teacher at the end of half term – the stage when they have just about had enough of the bullshit.

It worked. Everyone, including Gareth, stared at him as he urged Bryn to continue.

'Right, so whilst I'll be the first to admit I had this down to a horrible accident – a drunken fall, most likely. But as Steffan here has just told you, it appears Benjamin has suffered a stab wound in addition to his head injury.'

'A drunken fall?' asked Billy.

'He stinks of alcohol,' explained Jodie.

I did try and point out the bottle on the floor, thought Gareth.

'In the circumstances,' continued Bryn. 'We have to assume that one of *you* were involved.'

More raised voices ensued. The group broke out into a raucous exchange, which was reminiscent of the House of Commons during Prime Minister's Questions. Gareth half-expected calls of '*order, order*' to come from Steffan's direction. Instead, Bryn continued, projecting over the others.

'I need everyone to remove everything from their pockets. Now!'

Silence. Again.

'You can't really believe one of us had anything to do with it?' said Francesca.

'There's nobody else here,' said Bryn, his expression still.

'I ain't emptying my pockets for you,' sneered Billy, before taking a swig of his beer.

'Why, got something to hide?' asked Steffan. He took a step towards the table. 'We just want to get to the bottom of it – so if everyone can slowly reach into their pockets and put everything on the table in front of them, that would be great.'

Everyone except Billy stood up from their seats. Even Francesca, although she used the table for support, leaning on it with one hand and rummaging in her pockets with the other.

'What are you even looking for?' asked Tara.

'A knife, obviously,' replied Matthew.

'It's bloody ridiculous,' muttered Billy, continuing to sit. He was shaking his head and his arms were folded.

Gareth looked down at the table. There wasn't really anything of interest – sweet wrappers, phones, soggy tissues and a couple of car keys. As everyone's empty pockets hung outside of their clothes, all eyes moved to Billy.

He looked around at them and scoffed. 'Oh, whatever. If it'll stop this nonsense.'

Gareth watched as Billy's eyes shifted from one person to the next. One by one, he placed a hand into each pocket, dropping the contents onto the table. Small change, a chewing gum packet bounced off the surface. He came to the last pocket and paused.

'Billy?' said Steffan.

His hand emerged from inside his jacket, revealing a retractable utility knife. He placed it down on the table. 'There. And before any of you say anything – no, I did not use it to stab Benjamin.'

'How are we supposed to believe you?' asked Francesca.

Billy shrugged. 'Honestly, I don't give a shit if you believe me or not. It was in my pocket after the scavenger hunt, that's all.'

Bryn walked over to the table and picked up the knife, exposing the blade. He brought it to his nose and sniffed it, before running a finger along the smooth steel and inspecting it - presumably for any residue.

‘Unless he’s done a decent job of cleaning up, it looks clean to me.’ He chuckled, before adding. ‘And unless he’s stronger than he looks – *much* stronger, he’d have done well to do enough damage to kill someone in the way Benjamin was. Especially with *that* thing.’

‘I am strong,’ said Billy – clearly irked by Bryn’s comment. ‘But I never done it.’

‘Who did then?’ asked Tara.

Bryn looked at her, before casting his gaze around the entire group. ‘That’s what we need to find out.’

CHAPTER THIRTY-FOUR

Jodie

Jodie felt so lost. Helpless even. She stared absently into space, waiting for Bryn's next move. He had just asked everyone to congregate around one table.

Conversation began to pick up around her. Mutterings between one another buzzed in her ear, whilst bottles and glasses clinked down on the tables, as people sipped their beverages. It seemed such a strange thing for everyone to be doing, at such a shocking and devastating time. Benjamin, their boss, had just died and they were drinking as though it was nothing. As though it were something to celebrate.

How can they be so relaxed?

She thought back to the first time she had seen Benjamin. The day she had started at the company. The self-assured tone in which he had introduced himself had made an instant and lasting impression on her – he was incredibly alluring, and quickly became the emperor of her thoughts.

But now, he was gone. Forever. When she closed her eyes, she could see his face, hear his voice and smell his unique musky scent. But as real as it felt, she knew that it wasn't, and never would be again.

Her eyes began to swell. Teardrops flooded and pooled, and as she fought desperately to contain them, the pressure became too much and soon her face was streaming uncontrollably.

'Here you go, Jodie,' said Francesca, placing a wine bottle in front of her. She looked at Francesca smiling wryly at her, and back at the bottle. She erupted. Her hand swatted the bottle, sending it hurtling across the room. It smashed, leaving stains of red across the white painted wall.

'What the fuck?!' gasped Billy, as everybody else stared at Jodie in confusion.

She breathed heavily through gritted teeth, as a tsunami of emotions came crashing out from within her.

'If you didn't want any wine, you could've just said so. *God*,' scoffed Francesca.

'Just shut the fuck up, all of you!' Jodie screamed. She was practically foaming at the mouth.

'Jode, calm down,' said Tara, moving towards her friend with cautious steps.

'Calm down? Benjamin has just been killed. And you're all here, drinking like nothing has happened!'

'We're drinking *for* him. Look, it's shit – I'm gutted, and to tell the truth, I don't think it's sinking in properly,' said Billy. 'But, it's not like one of us have killed him.'

'Isn't it?' snapped Jodie.

'What do you mean?' asked Billy, screwing his face up in confusion.

'What do you think I mean?' she said. 'Nobody else is here. Like Bryn said earlier, there's nothing – nobody – around here for miles. Who else can it have been?'

'She's right,' said Matthew.

'But none of us would do that!' exclaimed Francesca. 'Why would anyone?'

'I don't know,' said Jodie. 'Maybe it was you? I mean, who could blame you, after what you saw earlier?'

Francesca gasped in ever-dramatic horror at such an accusation. 'That's crazy. I can't believe you've said that!'

'Seems a bit far-fetched, considering Francesca's twisted her ankle,' chirped Gareth, to which Francesca nodded and gestured her hands towards her injury – her leg still rested across the unoccupied seats beside her.

'That's true,' muttered Jodie. 'What about you then, Gareth? They say it's always the quiet ones, don't they?'

'Oh, fuck off,' said Gareth dismissively, with a shake of the head.

'I don't think this is helping anyone,' said Bryn, who Jodie noticed was staring directly at her, with a look which she took as both empathy and an instruction to pack it in. She lowered her head. She felt exhausted.

'What's the plan, then?' asked Billy.

'We need to put together a timeline of people's movements,' said Bryn. 'We can't be sure exactly when the… accident happened, but we know it's some time between the last time everyone saw Benjamin – before we started making grub, and Jodie finding him.'

Francesca snorted. 'Yeah. Convenient that.'

'What's convenient?' snapped Jodie.

'Oh, you know…' replied Francesca with a smirk, leaving her insinuation up in the air. Jodie could have punched her.

'Ladies, please,' said Bryn. As he glared at Jodie, she swallowed heavily. Why did he keep looking at *her* like that? She wasn't the guilty one. 'Obviously, everyone here has been in and out of the canteen during that period. What we need to work out is who saw who, and if anyone was unaccounted for at any point. Make sense?'

'Not really,' said Steffan. 'I mean, it's not like we were showering together, like.'

'We didn't all go for a shower then, either,' chirped Tara. 'Some of us had one after we got back from the scavenger hunt. Me and Jodie did, anyway.'

'Okay,' huffed Bryn. 'But did anyone go back to the sleeping cabin alone?'

‘Gareth did,’ said Jodie, breaking her silence. Everyone looked at her, before moving their focus onto Gareth, who began to blush.

‘Yeah, I did,’ he said. ‘I went for a shower – then Steffan saw me coming out of there, on our way back to the room.’

‘What about *before* your shower?’ suggested Billy. ‘Surely you weren’t in there that long?’

‘I didn’t time myself, but it’s not like I’ve thought “oh, I know, I’ll just pop into Benjamin’s room on the way and kill him”, is it? For fuck’s sake.’

He seemed annoyed. Had something struck a nerve?

‘What about the rest of you?’ asked Bryn.

‘I went at the same time as Matt,’ said Billy. ‘Went over there at the same time, came back here at the same time.’

‘And I went around then, too,’ said Francesca.

It was useless. Everyone, it seemed, had an alibi. Perhaps there was more than one person involved. A team effort. But who? That was the question. Without the answer, Jodie didn’t know who she could trust.

CHAPTER THIRTY-FIVE

Steffan

The room had fallen silent again, as though nobody knew what to do next. Steffan stared blankly into space, thinking back to times of combat – or rather, the times between combat, where they would wait for the next order or piece of intel to reach their base. There was tension, and no matter how experienced he or his fellow soldiers were, they were human, and worry would creep into their thoughts. It was natural.

He knew what needed to be done. He was certain everyone else did, too. They needed to work out who the killer was and detain them – tie them to a chair if they had to. But based on Bryn's failed attempts at identifying suspects so far, he wasn't sure how successful they would be in exposing the culprit.

'We're going to have to assume there is a killer amongst us,' Bryn had said. 'That means you don't go anywhere alone, at any point.'

'But what if you go somewhere with the killer?' Matthew had asked.

'Then you're buggered.' Bryn replied. He laughed to himself. It was easy for him to be relaxed, given he had pulled out a shotgun from a locked storage cabinet and was keeping it close by.

Unlike most of the others, Steffan hadn't continued drinking. He wanted to remain as alert as possible, as the night wore on. Jodie's outburst had forced that decision upon him. She was clearly in an unpredictable frame of mind. And besides, if there truly was a killer in their ranks – and it seemed worryingly plausible that there was, he needed to be focused on his own survival – at least until they could alert the authorities, when Ceri returned the next morning.

As he mulled things over in his mind, he glanced up at the windows. That's when he saw them. They were faceless in the dark but were undoubtedly staring back at him from outside. Steffan could feel it.

The killer. It had to be. No sooner had he spotted them, did they slip away into the darkness, but he was already on his feet, moving towards the door.

'There's someone out there!' he shouted as he threw the door open. He stopped a few steps later and looked around. Nothing.

Bryn had followed behind and stood in the doorway. Steffan turned to see a look of bewilderment on the old ranger's face.

'What is it, lad?' he asked.

'I saw someone, just there,' replied Steffan, pointing towards the window.

Bryn scoffed. 'It was probably just a shadow from a tree blowing in the wind, or something. Your mind's playing tricks on you.'

'It was a person, I'm sure of it,' said Steffan. He had no doubt whatsoever of what he had seen.

'Okay, if you insist,' said Bryn, heading back inside. 'Hang on.'

'Who's there?' called Steffan, his words swallowed by the impenetrable darkness of the woodland. He squinted his eyes into focus, but even though the rain had halted, it offered little improvement to the limited visibility surrounding him.

He looked at Bryn, who stood beside him with the shotgun in hand. It was an old 12-gauge, pump action Winchester, which Steffan hoped the old guy held the relevant certification for. Nevertheless, it was a weapon which would serve a little better as both a deterrent and protective tool, than the rubber-headed mallet Steffan had picked up and was gripping tightly in his right hand.

'Any ideas?' he whispered, gazing back out into the blackened trees.

'Like I said, I think it's your mind playing tricks on you, lad,' said Bryn.

'I know what I saw. What do you think is best to do, you know the place better than anyone else.'

Bryn paused for a moment, before exhaling slowly, as though his patience was wearing thin. 'Head back inside with the rest of the group, I reckon.'

'What if they – whoever it is – comes back?'

'If there *is* someone out here, and they're daft enough to even think about coming back, we've got the shooter right here, so they'll not be much of a threat with their brains painted all over the place. Let's go back in, come on.'

Steffan looked at Bryn again. On the face of it, he didn't see someone who had it in him to point the barrel in the direction of another man, let alone squeeze the trigger – just an aging, somewhat grumpy fella who had obviously long had a gripe with life. But he nodded and turned on his heel, to make his way back to camp.

'I can't get my head around what's happened here, tonight,' said Steffan.

'Aye,' replied Bryn. 'I should expect you've seen plenty of fallen comrades in your time, though, God-bless-yer…'

'Well, my fair share, yeah – but that's not really the same. Plus, we knew who the bastards were, whilst they were firing at us.'

Bryn nodded. He didn't get it, Steffan knew that. But he didn't mean any harm – he was just an old boy, who respected the veterans, even tried to resonate with them through patriotism, despite never actually serving himself.

They were just a few yards away from the canteen, when Steffan caught a glimpse of a dark figure moving quickly out the corner of his eye.

'Oi!' he shouted, as the figure vanished round the side of the buildings. His feet pattered loudly in the puddles as he began to make chase.

'Wait, lad!' called Bryn. 'Where are you going?'

'Didn't you see them!?' asked Steffan, slowing as he turned around. 'We need to catch them!'

Bryn paused, momentarily. 'Take it slow, try and catch them out. I'll go around the other way. And be careful.'

Steffan nodded, squeezing his fingers to tighten their grip on the mallet's handle as he made his way in the direction of the assailant.

As he edged closer towards the dark corner, between the wooden shack and entrance to the car park, Steffan became increasingly aware of the sound of his own breathing. He slowed it down as much as possible. He wasn't scared, he just didn't want to give them – whoever they were – any advantage, should they decide to go on the offensive and ambush him.

There was no sign of anybody. It was baffling. Despite the lack of visibility, it was obvious to him there wasn't anywhere else they could have gone, other than around the building – where Bryn would be waiting for them.

He continued. Slowly. Methodically. Listening.

Suddenly, the ground ahead crunched underfoot.

Where are you?

Steffan felt a heavy blow to the side of his head. And then nothing.

CHAPTER THIRTY-SIX

Jodie

Jodie had begun to feel awkward about her behaviour earlier. The outburst, throwing objects and accusations around the room. But she was certain *someone* in the room was to blame. How could they not be? They were in complete isolation, with nothing but nature surrounding them. Regardless of what Steffan *thought* he had seen. The outside world was miles away from them. Even though his body lay no more than fifty metres away from her, she realised Benjamin, too, was a long way from them now. She shuddered at the thought.

As she stifled a yawn, she longed for the warmth and safety of her own bed back home. She wished they had never arranged this stupid weekend. Wished they had never gone there. There would be no sleep that night – for any of the group.

She had blended into the background, ultimately being ignored by everyone else as a result of her own actions. It had been pretty quiet since Bryn and Steffan rushed outside, anyway. People continued to exchange fleeting small talk, as they waited for them to return. She really wanted to raise the question again – *which one of you did it?* – but they hadn't got anywhere so far, and she doubted that would change any time soon.

It had been a few minutes since Bryn and Steffan had gone outside, chasing the mysterious figure who may or may not have been outside the window. She had her doubts – it was ridiculous to think someone else was out here in the wilderness, especially in that weather, creeping around the retreat. *Unless...*

'Where have them two got to?' asked Billy, interrupting Jodie's thoughts as he seemingly aimed the question to nobody in particular. He walked towards the windows at the front of the cabin, peering out into the darkness.

'Maybe they've found a werewolf?' suggested Matthew.

'Or the Abumible Snowman,' said Tara.

'How the fuck do you bum a snowman?' asked Billy.

'It's *abominable*,' said Gareth, rolling his eyes.

You're telling me, thought Jodie.

'Do you not think we should go and see if they're okay?' she asked.

Francesca gestured towards the door theatrically. 'Don't let us stop you.'

'Come on, guys. We need to do something,' said Tara, getting out of her seat. 'We can't just sit around, doing nothing.'

'Bryn said nobody was to go anywhere alone,' added Gareth.

'It'll be safer if we all go together,' said Matthew, who shrugged as he followed suit.

Jodie nodded to each person in turn, as they stood, assembling, and waited to head outside together. The only person who remained seated was Francesca, which was understandable due to her injury, but Jodie doubted she would have bothered regardless.

'You can't all leave me here!' she said, ever the distressed damsel.

Matthew sat back down very quickly, to accompany her – as though he was her knight in corporate uniform. Jodie could tell he fancied her – which meant she could guarantee Francesca would have worked it out too. She'd be *absolutely* loving the attention. She probably didn't even care about what had happened to Benjamin.

'Okay… shall we?' said Jodie, gesturing towards the door and leading the way.

There was no immediate sign of Steffan or Bryn outside. Or any activity at all. Not a sound could be heard beyond the whispering of the steady breeze, as it drifted amongst the leaves and branches of the forest. Now that the rain had stopped, Jodie thought it could have been quite a peaceful evening – if she ignored the fact the love of her life lay dead in a nearby building, and now two other people had vanished without a trace.

'Well, this is hopeless, isn't it?' groaned Billy, kicking at the gravel beneath his boot.

Jodie hated the fact she agreed with him. Bryn and Steffan could have gone anywhere. She had assumed they would be patrolling close by, but, if there really was somebody outside, they could have given chase far into the woodland.

'This might not be the best idea,' began Gareth. 'But thinking logically, would splitting up not give us a better chance of finding them?'

'Could we not just go and wait inside?' said Tara, her teeth chattering through what Jodie guessed was a combination of both fear and the chill which was now in the air.

Although it *was* the most logical way of speeding up their search, Jodie wondered if Gareth's suggestion was a little too convenient. Splitting the group up would be exactly what a killer would have wanted. She hoped Bryn and Steffan were actually close by, in case he had a sinister motive.

'We can't wander too far,' she said. 'We don't want to get lost.'

'No, that makes sense,' agreed Gareth.

'Fine,' huffed Billy. 'Me and Gaz, you and Tara. Two pairs, meet back here in a couple of minutes.'

Tara began to protest, before Gareth interrupted. 'Don't be a dick, Billy.'

'What are you trying to say? That girls can't stand up for themselves? They need brave, strapping blokes to keep them safe?'

'Well, we'd be screwed if that was the case – I can't see any strapping blokes here,' said Jodie. Billy scowled at her. *Sexist wanker*, she thought. 'Gareth, you go towards the car park with Tara, just have a look around. Then *Sir Billy of Mansplaining* can protect me whilst we go in the other direction.'

Whilst Billy tutted, Gareth and Tara seemed happy with the arrangement.

As they agreed to regroup in five minutes' time, she and Billy parted ways with Gareth and Tara. It was strange, but she felt as empowered as she ever had. In some ways, she no longer felt any fear at what – or who – they may find. With Benjamin gone, she didn't care what happened to her in that moment.

And besides, if they did come across a crazed knifeman during their search and she found herself in need of a human shield, Billy would finally serve a purpose.

Determined, she charged ahead as Billy dawdled behind her.

'Steffan?' she called out, but only the whistle of the heightening breeze responded. 'Bryn?'

'Quieten down, will you? I don't wanna get killed,' hissed Billy from behind her.

'Billy Big Balls isn't *scared*, is he?' she said, refusing to look back at him. 'Steffan?' she called, louder.

‘For fuck’s sake, Jode. You got a death wish or something?’

She stopped, suddenly. Turning round to him, with a sadistic grin on her face. Her eyes looked straight through Billy’s as she replied. ‘Why, do you want to kill me?’

‘What?’

‘I said, do you want to kill me? Are you jealous? I mean, you’ve always had your nose buried right up Benjamin’s arse, haven’t you? Do you wish it was you and him in that bedroom?’

‘What are you talking about? You’re flippin’ mental, Jode.’

I’ll show you mental, she thought. Stepping towards him, Jodie clenched her fist tightly and swung it towards his jaw. The cracking sound of the impact was followed by Billy stumbling backwards, barely maintaining his footing on the muddy track.

‘Ow,’ Billy groaned, putting a hand to his chin before looking back at her in bewilderment. ‘What was that for, you crazy bitch?’

Jodie didn’t respond. Instead, she charged past him, ignoring his calls to ‘wait’. She’d had enough. She needed to get away. From Billy. From everyone. But where? Bryn had said it was not safe for them to be alone, but she didn’t care. Not anymore.

She made it to the sleeping cabin and headed straight for her and Tara’s bedroom. She entered, and slammed the door, before leaning against it and lowering herself to the ground. It was too much. What was she going to do?

‘I loved him,’ she sobbed.

CHAPTER THIRTY-SEVEN

Gareth

'Do you think something bad has happened to them?' asked Tara.

'No, I doubt it,' Gareth said, hoping to reassure her. 'Everyone's just on edge – Steffan has obviously convinced himself he's seen something, so has got the bit between his teeth and isn't giving in until he finds this imaginary person.'

Tara didn't seem to have been persuaded. 'But something must've happened – or someone must be out here. They've clearly gone somewhere, and how else do you explain, y'know, *the murder*?'

It was a fair point. Gareth had tried to work it out, but he felt as though every scenario he built inside his head was unfathomable. Ridiculous. But then, wasn't his boss being murdered, on a team-building retreat *also* ridiculous and unfathomable?

He looked at Tara. He could see how worried and fragile she appeared. He didn't know her very well, but she had always seemed nice enough. A normal girl, who – like the others – found herself in abnormal circumstances. It convinced him to double-mark her off his hypothetical suspect list. It was progress.

'Do you not think it's possible one of the others – who we *know* are here – could have killed Benjamin?'

Tara's eyes widened. 'What do you mean?'

'I don't know, it's just… as everyone keeps saying, we're in the middle of nowhere, so the chances that someone else just happened to be here and decide "yeah, I'll kill that random guy, for no reason whatsoever" seems unlikely.'

'And one of our mates doesn't?'

Mates is a strong word.

'I suppose. But as I say, they're the only ones we know are actually here.'

Tara had no response. They continued in silence, eyes peeled whilst strolling side by side, before stopping in the middle of the car park. Looking around them, nothing seemed untoward.

'Well, they're not anywhere around here,' declared Tara, with a sigh and disheartened shrug of her shoulders.

Gareth looked at her and shrugged too, before turning to go back in the direction they had just come from. *What a waste of time.* Tara followed, scurrying in shorter footsteps than those of Gareth's, to catch up to him.

'Wait,' he whispered, freezing on the spot. He held out a hand in front of Tara, to gesture for her to stop moving. 'Can you hear that?'

As he continued to listen, he could hear a sound from behind the first cabin. It was growing closer. Footsteps. Heavy footsteps. Gareth could also hear his heartbeat pounding in his chest, and Tara's increasingly quivered breaths, as panic began to take hold of them both.

'Do we run? I'm gonna run,' Tara murmured.

Gareth placed a reassuring hand on her shoulder, with the added intention of preventing her from suddenly charging away and leaving him alone to be slaughtered.

'Behind the car,' he whispered, pointing to Matthew's black BMW and ushering her with a gentle push. It was the nearest thing to offer them cover.

Who are you? he wondered, as he watched from behind the car – braced to run and escape at a split second's notice. Moments later, none other than Bryn wandered cautiously into the open. Gareth and Tara sighed in unison, relieved to discover a friendly face.

He did a double take as they emerged from behind the car. 'What are you two doing out here?' he asked, clearly confused. He looked to be on edge.

'Looking for you and Steffan,' replied Gareth.

'I see… have you found him?'

A surge of dread coursed through Gareth's chest. 'No – we thought you were together?'

'Aye, we were,' said Bryn. 'We split up. Stupid thing to do, I know. Lord knows where he's got to, running off like a macho man.'

Tara groaned. Gareth looked at her, before his attention returned to Bryn. This was bad. Really bad.

'We need to get back inside,' said Gareth.

Tara needed no further encouragement to dash back towards the safety of the canteen. Bryn nodded, and followed suit, with Gareth alongside him.

'What the hell are we going to do now?' Gareth asked.

'Not much we can do, lad,' grunted Bryn. 'Go back inside, and hope that he comes back safe and sound.'

Gareth wasn't so sure it was the best thing to do. What if Steffan was hurt, or worse? He cursed the warehouseman's stupidity, rushing out into the unknown. Now, nobody knew where he was, nor did they know where to look.

CHAPTER THIRTY-EIGHT

Steffan

He could hear something. There was a ringing in his ears. It was constant and high pitched. But there was something else. It sounded like voices. Incoherent and muffled, but it was definitely people's voices. Everything was painted black as he desperately tried to see beyond the darkness and blur of his lost focus.

The voices continued. They weren't loud, but they were not whispers, either. One voice grew louder, as though it came closer, but he could not tell which direction they approached from. Though he could not understand the voices, they did not sound happy. They sounded concerned, frightened even. Who were they? He did not know.

He felt dizzy. What had happened? Where was he?

He was tired. A sleep would help.

CHAPTER THIRTY-NINE

Gareth

Billy had just wandered back into the canteen unaccompanied. Not only had the search for Bryn and Steffan led to only one of them being accounted for, but Jodie had now not returned to the group. This trip was beginning to look like the Ten in the Bed nursery rhyme.

'So, you just left her to it?' asked Gareth, to which Billy nodded – somewhat sheepishly.

'Well, somebody needs to go and see if she is okay,' said Tara.

Don't look at me, thought Gareth.

'Gareth, will you come with me?' she continued.

For fuck's sake.

'I'm not so sure it's the best idea,' said Bryn, as he poured himself a fresh tumbler full of Welsh whiskey. 'With what happened to your man earlier, and now Steffan being missing. Perhaps best we wait here for him to return, so we're all together, like.'

'But we're not *all together*, are we?' said Tara. 'Yes, Steffan's disappeared, and I hope he's okay, but Jodie is on her own. We need to get her back, too.'

'Yeah, well. That all seems a bit fishy to me with Steffan,' said Billy, who was making the most of his injury as he held a chilled bottle of lager against his cheek. 'Big strapping lad from the army – who none of us really know, by the way –

goes and disappears? A betting man would be putting money on it being him who killed Ben…'

'You don't think he did… do you?' asked Francesca.

'If it wasn't him, it's got to be one of the rest of us,' said Matthew.

'Exactly,' said Billy, appearing satisfied the results of his Poirot-like analysis were conclusive.

Though it would have pained him to concede out loud, it seemed a plausible suggestion even to Gareth. Sure, Steffan came across as a decent lad in their interactions, but he *had* only met him that weekend. They all had. Also, in that time he had already witnessed Steffan squaring up to Benjamin in the woods – and he had even made comments about causing him harm. His criminal record didn't help, either. Perhaps Billy was right? If so, they needed to be careful, just in case Steffan was still close and decided to come back out of hiding to silence the rest of the party, which would mean they all remained in grave danger. Jodie – who was still alone – included. They'd have to go and bring her back.

'Okay, let's go and get this over with,' he said to Tara.

'As I said, lad…' began Bryn.

'If you're so worried, will you let us take the gun?' suggested Gareth.

Bryn scoffed at that, shaking his head. 'Don't be daft. It isn't a toy.'

'Right, okay then. We'll just have to take our chances, won't we. Tara, shall we?'

'Be careful, you two,' called Francesca, as Gareth and Tara made their way towards the door.

'So, Steffan…' said Tara. 'Do you think he's actually killed Benjamin and done a runner?'

Gareth shrugged. 'I really don't know. Maybe.'

He looked around at their surroundings. It didn't seem quite as claustrophobic as it had before. The dark aura which had been shrouding the camp appeared to have lifted a little since Steffan had disappeared. But he was not quite ready to commit to a guilty verdict just yet.

'God, I guess you never really know somebody – well, I didn't know him anyway, but you know what I mean.'

Gareth had nothing to say. As they entered the cabin, his eyes were drawn towards Benjamin's bedroom door. He felt a tingling sensation on the back of his neck as he stared at the simple wooden frame, knowing behind it lay the body of a man who had left Gareth damaged and holding onto his *own* secrets – his own darkness.

Even though Benjamin was dead, Gareth knew that his demons had not instantly vacated his mind. In fact, it left him questioning whether or not this was the ending he really wanted – or, more importantly, needed.

Tara knocked gently on the door to the bedroom she was sharing with Jodie, before turning the handle and discovering it would not open.

'I didn't think there were locks on the doors?' asked Gareth, puzzled.

'No, I don't think there are,' replied Tara, before putting her ear against the door. 'Jodie, are you in there? It's me. I've come to see if you're okay.'

'Leave me alone,' came the muffled reply from inside the room.

Tara glanced at Gareth, and he rolled his eyes in response.

What a bloody child.

She obviously didn't want to see or speak to anyone. Gareth wasn't sure why they had bothered to go and check on her. He pressed his ear to the door and could hear her sobbing gently. It made him feel uncomfortable. This wasn't his thing – reassuring and consoling people. After all, how was somebody with so much internal baggage of their own supposed to find room to empathise with to others? What was he supposed to say?

‘We aren’t going to leave until we know you’re okay, babe,’ called Tara, her voice gentle but firm.

Silence.

Gareth sighed. ‘Jodie, can you open the door? It’s not safe to be alone.’

Still nothing. She was being stubborn, and if he was honest, it was understandable – he could relate to her wanting to shut herself off, especially after what had happened. But it was for that reason they needed to get her out of the bedroom. They needed to stick together, whether they liked it or not.

‘Come on, Jode,’ Tara pleaded.

There was another prolonged pause, but finally, the door opened. Just a crack, enough to see Jodie peering out at them. She opened it further and stood before them, looking at them with red, swollen eyes. She didn’t say a word.

Tara wasted no time in throwing her arms around her friend, wrapping her in a tight hug. She whispered something Gareth couldn’t hear, whilst he shifted uncomfortably, glancing around the room instead of directly at Jodie. He wasn’t here to play therapist.

‘Why won’t you just leave me be?’ she asked with a sneer.

Gareth exhaled sharply through his nose. He knew this was a mistake.

‘We’ve come to take you back to the canteen, so everyone’s together,’ explained Tara. She stroked Jodie’s shoulder with her thumb and smiled gently.

‘Why now? I’m fine in here on my own.’

‘Basically, Steffan’s disappeared,’ said Gareth. ‘So you need to come back and join the rest of us.’

Jodie’s eyebrows knitted together. She looked at him, puzzled. ‘What do you mean, *disappeared*? Has he been attacked too, or something?’

'No,' Tara said quickly. 'Well, we don't think so. Bryn came back, but there's no sign of Steffan. People are saying he might have run away.'

'Why would he…' began Jodie, but then she stopped herself. The colour drained from her face as though realisation struck. 'It was *him*?'

Gareth wasn't sure what to say. Nor did Tara, it seemed.

'We don't know for sure,' Gareth said eventually. 'But obviously it's better to stick together, you know, safety in numbers. Shall we go then?'

He was starting to grow very impatient. It mustn't have been well hidden, as Jodie eyed him suspiciously.

'What's wrong, Gareth? You'll be all right, won't you? He's your mate.'

Gareth bristled. 'I mean…'

'Maybe you were both in on it – you don't exactly seem sorry about Benjamin.'

'This again?' groaned Gareth with a sigh.

'Gareth, maybe you should head back – I'll be fine here,' said Tara.

'Yeah, fine. So long as you're sure – I'm sick of these bullshit accusations, anyway.'

Jodie clicked her tongue against her teeth, shaking her head at him.

'Of course,' replied Tara. 'We'll be back in a minute.'

Gareth nodded to her, before turning on his heel and stormed off down the corridor. Behind him, he could hear Tara continuing to try and reason with Jodie, her voice containing a mix of frustration and concern.

He was just about to exit the building when Jodie screeched from inside the bedroom. 'For the last time, I am not going back to that fucking canteen. Just leave me alone. Okay!?'

Christ, just leave her, if that's what she wants.

Gareth paused in the doorway as Tara stomped back out of the bedroom.

'Fine, suit yourself. If you want to get butchered by some maniac, be my guest.'

She charged out of the room, slamming the door behind her before leaning against it and looking up at the ceiling in dismay.

'Here's hoping,' Jodie called after her.

Gareth continued making his way back to the canteen. Tara could catch him up if she wanted. He wasn't in the mood to wait. The way Jodie had just spoken to them had left him seething – and the more he thought about her persistent accusations, the more it wound him up. Yes, he didn't like – rather, he despised – Benjamin, and he couldn't care less that he was dead, but that didn't mean he had killed him, and the fact she seemed so hellbent on convincing herself of it, it just made him wish he had. Just so he could rub her stupid, bunny-boiling nose in it.

'Blimey, you've got a weed on you, Gaz. Anyone would think you actually liked Ben,' said Billy.

'What's that supposed to mean?' Gareth asked.

'I think he's saying you quite clearly didn't get on with Benjamin,' said Matthew.

'Oh,' said Gareth. *Was it that obvious to everyone?*

'What is it? Can't handle the booze?' mocked Billy.

'No, it's not that – I've barely had any,' said Gareth. 'Just Jodie, banging on about how I'm some kind of murderer's accomplice. Mad bitch.'

'When… before?' asked Francesca. 'Just ignore her.'

'Yeah, and just now.'

'Oh, so that's why you left the two girls all alone and in danger,' said Billy. 'Maybe you and Steffan have been working together after all – you set the victim up, and he finishes them off.'

'Are you serious!?'

Billy just laughed scornfully. There were sniggers from Francesca and Matthew.

Gareth felt his cheeks burning, as his embarrassment refused to disguise itself. He looked down, to avoid making eye contact with anybody. The laughter rang loudly in his ears, echoing in his head. The same old feeling of being targeted. It was what came with working with these people, he knew that. It was like they would gang up, prodding him with steel rods, pushing and goading him towards breaking point.

It was never going to change. Even without Benjamin there, making his life a cascade of misery, the toxicity of that place would enable him to live on, mocking Gareth. Encouraging him to take that one, small step off the edge of the cliff. Perhaps, he wondered, he should just allow himself to fall into the darkness.

'Fuck the lot of you,' he murmured, as he swivelled out of the chair and made for the door.

He ignored Bryn's call to stay. Blocking it out as he stared straight ahead, refusing to look back. He crossed paths with Tara on the way out. He glanced momentarily in her direction but did not acknowledge her. She looked furious about something – Gareth presumed it must have been more resistance and arguing from Jodie, given she had not accompanied her back to the canteen. The lovelorn cow must really have had a death wish.

With the way he felt at that moment, Gareth contemplated a reality where she was not the only person who had one.

CHAPTER FORTY

Steffan

When Steffan opened his eyes again, he found that he was still enveloped in isolating darkness, confused and lost. He blinked in attempt to regain focus, but even with the complete absence of light he could feel his vision would have been clouded in the brightest room.

What happened? Where am I?

The ringing in his ears had subsided and had been replaced by a deafening silence. Nothing. He could hear absolutely nothing.

Was he dead? Was that what this was? This place. Where the dead went after it all ended. But, if after death there *was* nothing, why did he feel this sense of consciousness?

His head still pounded. The pain pulsated around his skull as though it was pushing and struggling against an overtightened bonnet. It made him want to vomit. The acid in his stomach was trying it's hardest to break free as it burned against his insides. Did people throw up in the afterlife? Surely not. It was supposed to be peaceful.

He groaned before sighing heavily and closed his eyes again.

CHAPTER FORTY-ONE

Jodie

Jodie heard the lumbering footsteps of someone in the corridor. As they grew louder, two scenarios crossed her mind. First, perhaps Steffan, or whoever the murderer was, had come to claim their next victim, which she was ready for – she would fight, but without placing any importance on the outcome. If it wasn't a killer approaching, it must have been someone coming back to pester her. *Again.* She really could not be bothered with that – she would much rather have a knife placed inside her.

No sooner had the unidentified person's movement grown louder as they approached her door, that they passed without stopping. It was perhaps due to her newly found lack of concern for her own safety, but she braved opening the door to peek at who it was.

It was just Gareth. *What's he doing back here again?*

She hadn't been discreet, so he must have heard her opening the door, but he did not turn around. She guessed it would be obvious to him that it was just her behind him. Looking at him, he appeared rather mopey. His head was tilted downwards, and his shoulders were slumped, as he ambled along aimlessly before wandering into his bedroom.

She didn't care that he seemed upset, but it did leave her curious as to what had happened. But still, she wasn't about to go and ask him, so she shed him from her mind and left him to it, instead slipping back inside her own room and closing the door behind her.

Although she was alone, sat in her own pit of misery, she felt strangely comforted in the knowledge that Benjamin – or at least his body – was close by. Despite that, she could not bear to go and be in the same room as him. The sight of him lying there, lifeless, had already been scorched hauntingly into her mind. It was an image she would never be able to forget. She wasn't religious, far from it, but if her own death was the only possible way to reconnect their souls, to be with him again, she would gladly embrace it.

As she settled down once more, with her spine pressing against the door, she closed her eyes and folded her arms around herself. Exhaling slowly, she tried to remember earlier images of him, rather than the heartbreaking last.

Her mind took her back a few years, a few months into her time at HomeHub. Benjamin was sat in their office at a spare desk – he often did this, seat hopped from department to department. She thought it was so inspiring how hands-on he was with the running of the business. How did he find the time?

From two desks away, she could smell his aftershave. The way he absently chewed his lip as he read something, engrossed by what was on the laptop screen in front of him. She just watched. He hadn't seen her, of course. But then, he never did. She could remember the exact shape of his pointed jaw, imagined caressing the light stubble across its surface. The sunlight from the window bathed him in a warm glow, making it appear as though he was an angel from Heaven. Not an angel – a god.

If he had taken his eyes away from the screen for just a second, he would have noticed her, noticing him. Perhaps he would have smiled. Perhaps he would have said her name.

Another memory rose from the depths of her longing. The 2019 Christmas 'work's do' in Chester. A night they had walked side by side down the cobbled streets of the city centre – well, not together exactly, but on the same path, close enough to hear his footsteps in sync with hers. He had been talking to someone else, laughing and joking, unaware that she was absorbing every word, every sound, storing it inside her. She skipped forward a couple of steps, just to get closer, to allow the warmth of his presence settle over her like a blanket.

It had all felt so real then. It still did now.

He may have never been hers, but that didn't matter. She had carved a version of him who did. Who always would. A Benjamin who was always there, and had been waiting for her all along.

And now, as he rested, he waited for her still. On the other side of the wall.

CHAPTER FORTY-TWO

Gareth

He pulled his right leg back and let out a growl of fury as it swung forwards, his foot connecting with his bag as he kicked out. It flew halfway across the room, leaving its contents sprawled all over the place. His breathing was heavy, and his nostrils flared as he seethed with gritted teeth. This place, this situation, was pushing him to the brink of despair, and he didn't know how to cope with it. His fingers twitched uncontrollably, and his chest tightened against his ribcage. They were symptoms he often experienced when he was faced with conflict.

He may have taken himself away from the canteen, but another set of four walls were not helping him. He needed to breathe. He needed to get away, now. His anxiety was consuming him.

It had always been this way, or at least for as long as he could remember. Even when he was younger, back in school, a teenager trying to navigate his way through puberty and exams. He recalled the sense of overwhelming emptiness after Carly had dumped him via a solitary text message.

She had been his first 'proper' girlfriend, getting together during the Summer holidays before Year 11. The relationship had lasted until the beginning of the final term, as GCSEs loomed. A long time, or so it had felt back then, and all he received was a single line, which read *'wer ova soz x'*.

Even without an explanation, it made sense why she did it. He had kept refusing to go and hang out with her whilst he was knee-deep in revision. The future – whilst he had no idea what it entailed – was important. And besides, he wouldn't have been allowed to go out had he wanted to. It was all right for her; her mum wasn't bothered what she did, and Carly was only interested in the 'now'.

He wasn't sure how he was supposed to react, and though he knew he felt a kind of sadness to have lost Carly, he didn't cry. Boys weren't supposed to do that. So instead, he shut himself off from the world. Stayed in his bedroom, wishing he didn't exist anymore – it would have been better if he hadn't been born. He knew he was a disappointment, why else would his parents treat him with such contempt?

As he had lay on his bed, staring at the ceiling and imagining an alternate reality, on where he wasn't such a burden, his mum had opened the door. The first thing she remarked on was how untidy his bedroom was.

'I'll sort it,' he mumbled.

'You best had. And you can stop lozzocking around, as well. I'll bet you've not done your maths revision, have you?'

'I'm not "lozzocking". I've had a shit day.'

'Language!' she gasped, as though she'd never heard such foulness leave someone's mouth before.

'Sorry.'

And then, the old adage was uttered. One he had heard many times, from so many adults at the time. *Plenty of people have it worse than you.* He knew that. He wasn't a fucking narcissist. But, being told you weren't at the top of life's shit list had never helped anyone – having your problems downplayed like that never did.

If his younger self had been able to tell just what the future had held, maybe he would have done more than lie there *thinking* about removing himself from the equation. At least then, he wouldn't have lived to experience the latest situation he found himself in – trapped in hell as it masqueraded as a secluded forest.

He paced the cabin bedroom as though a lightbulb moment was coming any second, but unfortunately it did not. So instead, he left again and made his way back out into the night. He wasn't sure what his plan was as he paced along the pathway towards the car park. He didn't have one. But he knew he needed to get out of there. In fact, if he never had to see a single person from this place, ever again, then that would have been perfectly fine with him. They were complete arseholes, the lot of them.

He looked at his old Focus. How he would love to have been able to simply jump in, turn the key and cruise away, without as much as a brief glance in the rear-view mirror. But that wasn't happening, not whilst the exit was blocked by the fallen tree. And what was left of Billy's car.

As he approached the wreckage, he shook his head and cursed his own misfortune. It was bad enough being *told* he had to attend this stupid weekend trip, never mind the fact he had then physically been forced to stay, unable to leave. Stranded with nothing but his demons for company.

Looking at his options, he wondered just how long it would take to find someone who could help him. He knew what Bryn had said, but surely there had to be something he hadn't mentioned within a reasonable walking distance? An old, isolated couple, living in the same cottage they had raised their long-moved-on kids in, maybe. Or a charming little country pub. Anything. *Anyone*.

Gareth hadn't seen anything on the way there that day, but maybe he had been distracted. He could try and climb over the tree, and hope the bridge was stable enough, before going to explore.

It was that, or the alternative. He would have to stay where he was and wait. The thought took the last of his motivation away from him, and he slowly slid down to the ground, his back leaning against the side of Billy's car, as the first spots of fresh rain began to land on him.

Kill me.

CHAPTER FORTY-THREE

Jodie

Jodie wasn't keeping an eye on the time, but her internal clock told her it must have been at least ten or fifteen minutes since she had spotted Gareth going into his bedroom. She had heard the brief thrashing around of various objects, before the door slammed once again, and the sound of his footsteps – which seemed to have far more urgency in them than when he had come in – passed her room, and faded back out of the cabin.

She wasn't sure what the commotion was about, but the sounds coming from Gareth's bedroom had distracted her from her daydreams. There was one thing she now knew, though – he clearly had quite the temper when nobody was around.

Perhaps it *could* have been him, after all. Maybe *quiet, shy Gareth* was a persona he used to mask his more aggressive and dangerous, true personality. The kind of person who lashes out in a rage. He may not have even *meant* to kill Benjamin. It could have been an accident, or a fight which had gone too far, and now his conscience was poisoning him with guilt, making him even angrier in the process.

She flinched suddenly, as a knock on the door interrupted her train of thought. Could it have been Gareth, coming to finish off his next victim?

'Jodie are you still blocking the door?' came a voice.

Tara! What is she doing back, again?

'I thought I made myself clear. Go away,' called Jodie.

'No… I know… just, can we come in please?'

We?

'Please let us in, Jodie. We need to all stay together – for safety reasons, like,' said Bryn. His deep voice echoed through the hollow door far more than Tara's.

With a sigh, Jodie stood up and opened the door, keeping her palm rested on it – just in case they didn't get the message, and she needed to slam it shut on them.

'Like I told Tara earlier, I'm absolutely fine.'

She could tell from the look in Bryn's eyes that he was not happy to be told 'no', despite his efforts to hide it, speaking in a softer tone. 'Look, I understand everyone's had a bit of a shock, and this weather leaving us stranded is a bit of a sticky situation, but come on now.'

'A shock?' hissed Jodie. 'Our boss has been killed!'

'Aye, well. I'm sorry about that, love.'

'Are you? It's not like you knew him. Why would you care?'

Bryn did not reply. He just stared at her, pursing his lips, as though he had grown tired of trying to persuade her.

'Please Jodie, I'm begging you,' said Tara. 'You're in here, Gareth's bailed and gone to bed now, too. Steffan's done a runner. It's all too much. I need you.'

Jodie looked at her friend. The fear and concern in Tara's face made her realise that she wasn't the only one struggling with the events that had happened.

'Fine,' she said. 'But you won't find Gareth in his bedroom.'

'What do you mean?' frowned Bryn.

'He went in there. Sounded like he trashed the place for some reason. But then I heard footsteps going back out again.'

'Right, okay,' said Bryn. 'And you're sure it was him leaving?'

'Who else would it have been?' asked Jodie with a scowl.

Bryn nodded but proceeded to go and check Gareth's bedroom anyway. As he emerged from there, a moment later, he shook his head at them.

'What the hell is going on?' groaned Tara.

'He can't have gone far, can he?' said Jodie, starting towards the exit.

'We'd best flippin' well find out,' grunted Bryn as he rushed to catch up to them.

As she emerged outside, Jodie was forced to do a double take, as she saw who was approaching.

Matthew and Francesca, laughing as they made their way away from the canteen. Running. Francesca was *running*.

The look on their faces, upon realising they had been spotted, was quite the picture. Jodie smiled at them.

I've been waiting for this, bitch.

'Where are you two going? Back to the canteen, for Christ's sakes,' boomed Bryn. 'And how the heck are you running, girl?'

'I think we know the answer to that one, Bryn,' said Jodie.

They gathered around the canteen table Francesca and Matthew had occupied. Gareth had been forgotten about for the time being, and Jodie knew she was going to enjoy what happened next.

'So, explain yourself then', she hissed, posing like a pissed-off teapot with a hand on her hip.

Jodie raised her eyebrow, as Francesca looked around sheepishly at the others, noticeably longest at Matthew, who was beside her. She said nothing. It was, Jodie thought, possibly the first time she had ever seen the HomeHub 'It Girl' lost for words.

‘Honestly, right, it’s not what it looks like,’ said Matthew, breaking the silence.

‘Really?’ replied Jodie. ‘Because it looked like you were both running somewhere. What happened to the twisted ankle?’

‘It healed,’ said Francesca, in a more hopeful tone than a convincing one.

‘Or you were never hurt,’ said Tara, from behind Jodie, who nodded in agreement. Francesca just looked down at the table in front of her.

‘So, I’ll say it again,’ Jodie continued. ‘Explain.’

There was another, awkward silence, as the group – or what was left of them – awaited a response from Francesca.

‘Oh, you lot are back,’ called Billy, emerging from the toilet with his hands wrestling the fly of his jeans. He looked around, a confused expression on his face. ‘What have I missed?’

‘Not much,’ said Jodie, not taking her eyes from a dishevelled Francesca. ‘Fran was just going to tell us about her miraculous recovery – and, why she and Matt were running off somewhere.’

‘Running off? They were in here before I went to the loo. Wait, what recovery?’ Billy looked more confused than ever.

‘Okay,’ groaned Francesca. ‘I can explain.’

‘Go on then,’ said Jodie, crossing her arms in wait.

‘I faked the twisted ankle,’ she began. ‘I mean, Jodie, you know as well as anyone what Benny was like – and he was being so horrid, I just…’

‘You just what? Did it for attention?’ scolded Jodie.

‘No… I mean, yes, maybe. Oh, I don’t know… I guess I just thought it might make him stop being so mean, if he’d realised I was hurt. He might be *nice* for a change.’

‘And just now,’ said Jodie, looking at both Francesca and Matthew, ‘where were you going?’

'It's not what you think,' started Matthew again, before Francesca rested her hand on his arm.

'Stop, don't worry,' she whispered to him, before looking back at Jodie and the others. 'Me and Matty, we… it all started after the Christmas party. Benjamin had stormed off in a mood about something and left me on my own outside. Matty found me, got me home safely, but of course we'd had a lot to drink. And…'

'And you cheated on Benjamin?' said Jodie, a level of judgement in her tone that even she realised was bordering on unreasonable.

'You know what he is like!' pleaded Francesca.

'What he *was* like,' muttered Jodie. Another stark reminder of the fact that he was gone. And, despite how disgusting Francesca and Matthew's foiled plans were, they were technically no longer cheating on the boss.

But maybe that was part of the plan.

'So, which one of you did it?' she asked.

'What do you mean?' asked Francesca.

'*I mean*, his body isn't even cold and you're running around like schoolkids without a care in the world! Which one of you killed him? Or was it both of you?'

'We didn't! We wouldn't have done that!' pleaded Matthew.

'No, you're a decent guy, Matt. Or at least, I thought you were. But I don't believe you did it. Was it just you then, Francesca?'

'No! How could you suggest such a thing?' screeched Francesca, taking a step towards Jodie, who remained unmoved. 'Despite what you may think, I love him, or at least I *loved* him at first – despite the fact he never loved me. He never loved anything, or *anyone* as much as he loved his precious business.'

Loved him? Don't make me laugh.

'Where were you earlier, when he was killed?'

Tara leaned in towards her, quietly reasoning. 'Jodie, we don't even know when it happened – and we all went back to our rooms earlier, remember?'

'Exactly,' said Francesca. 'And besides, I've been nursing my ankle injury all evening.'

'*Fake* ankle injury,' snapped Jodie.

'Yes, my fake injury,' said Francesca, rolling her eyes. 'Regardless, I have been sat in here, beyond going and getting myself changed – like everyone else has. Think about it Jodie – the opportunity just wasn't there, whatever you may think of me.'

Jodie held her head in her hands. It was useless. How was she going to get to the bottom of this? How was she going to expose Benjamin's killer?

Bryn cleared his throat, making Jodie jump. 'Sorry to interrupt. But in case everyone's forgotten, we're still missing a man.'

'Two men,' corrected Tara, quietly.

'Yes, well. If the rest of you can behave yourselves for five minutes, I'm going to scout the area, see if I can't find at least one of them.'

'On your own?' asked Tara.

Bryn smiled and held his shotgun in front of him. It was an unnerving smile, Jodie thought. 'I think I'll be okay, love. Shan't be long.'

CHAPTER FORTY-FOUR

Steffan

It was 2013 again. September. It wasn't as hot in Kabul as the last couple of months had been, but the air was still dry. Steffan had been counting down the days until he was on the plane home. He couldn't wait to see his family again. This was his second stint in Afghanistan, and he was hopeful it would be his last.

The things he had seen. The people who had been lost. It had all started to take its toll on him. He glugged down another mouthful of contraband vodka and enjoyed the sensation, as it left a warmth in its path whilst seeping down into his gut. Going home and booze – they were the only two things holding him together, keeping him going.

What he didn't need was Private Maya Clarke catching him. She walked into the tent he was hiding in, and it felt as though his heart stopped. That was until she looked at him with an expression that wounded him. *Disgust*.

'Steffan, I thought we'd talked about this?' she said, in a tone which exuded both annoyance and despair.

Steffan looked back at her, and he felt a throb of guilt inside him. They'd grown closer, towards the end of their last tour, and whilst they agreed it would have been inappropriate to allow things to evolve into anything more, the feelings they obviously had for each other were still there. He didn't want to let her down, truly. But drinking was the only thing that allowed him to block it all out.

'Please, Maya', he slurred. 'Just hear me out, yeah?'

'What is it you want to say, Steffan? You know you're drinking too much, but it helps you to forget the bad stuff you've seen out here? Yeah, I've heard it all before.'

'But you don't understand!'

'I do understand.' She glared at him. Through the blurriness affecting his vision, he could see it. 'We all understand. We've all seen some horrible things, and it's not right. It's shit, I know it is. But we're not all drinking ourselves into oblivion, every chance we get. Are we?'

'I'm sorry,' he sobbed.

'You need help, Steffan.'

He continued to sniff, and he watched her leave him once more, before wiping the tears away from his bleary eyes.

It could have been the excessive self-pity and loathing he was feeling for himself, or the excessive volume of dodgy vodka he'd consumed, or both, but suddenly he felt extremely dizzy as the contents of his stomach began to evacuate.

The pain in Steffan's gut, and the burning in his throat, felt very real as he continued to retch. He opened his eyes and saw only darkness around him. Where was he?

The confusion began to subside a little, as he came around slowly. Things started flooding back. He remembered he had been looking for someone in the woodland. At a nature reserve. A killer, perhaps. His boss had been murdered. What was his name again? Benjamin. He had seen someone and chased them. But that was when his memory ended. As though he had simply fallen into a blissful asleep. The side of his head was sore, and a throb pulsated. He'd been hit in the head. By the person he was chasing. The killer? It must have been.

The smell of vomit and damp wood was stomach churning. His mouth had become dry, through dehydration. But he did not know where he was. He listened carefully, but could hear nothing beyond the beating rhythm behind his ear, and his heavy, laboured breathing.

Slowly, he tried to climb up off the ground. It was then that he realised that both his hands and feet were restrained. They were tied together somehow. He couldn't manoeuvre very well at all.

Was he a captive? But who would have done such a thing? If it were the killer, why would they not have just finished him off, rather than tying him up? They would have, if they had been any good at their job.

One thing was for certain, he decided – whatever it took, he needed to get out of this place, wherever *this place* was, before they did come back.

CHAPTER FORTY-FIVE

Gareth

Gareth sat in the driver's seat of his car, wallowing in helplessness. He could not move it anywhere, but somehow, it felt like the safest place he could be at that moment. Away from the chaos around him, leaving him to an anonymous existence in the unpopulated lands surrounding him.

He wondered if anyone had noticed his disappearance yet. Obviously, he had walked out on the group earlier, but they would have just assumed he had gone to bed. But he would not have been alone, there. Not as alone as here. Not with Benjamin rotting away in the same cabin. Jodie was probably still there too, pining after her lost love.

They likely wouldn't have been concerned enough to check on him in the first place, let alone worry that he was missing. He didn't mind. Not really. He felt no affinity towards them, and in that moment, no real love for himself either. If death came now, perhaps it would be a blessing.

He had occasionally debated with his conscience about the best ways to end his own life, but he was left just short on a conclusive answer every time, because he would not have the bottle to go through with it anyway. He couldn't *kill himself*; he was too weak.

Yes, suicide was just another addition to the substantial list of what Gareth Parker would undoubtedly be useless at.

He wondered if he was jealous of Benjamin, in that moment. Of course, he had received a helping hand, but the smug bastard had yet again successfully achieved something Gareth would be incapable of. It really was not fair.

But then, life wasn't fair. That was another thing he had often been told – by teachers, relatives… it was the stock response of people who had been conditioned into bottling up their problems. It wasn't the only repeated phrase he could recall. There was the old favourite – 'man up', or the more vulgar 'grow a pair'. Although, Gareth thought the suggestion that adding such delicate parts to the body's anatomy would somehow make a person anything other than *more* fragile, was quite ironic.

He shrugged off his self-pity and sighed, as he stared out through his raindrop-covered windscreen at the fallen tree. The barrier to his freedom. But not, he realised, an invincible barrier.

They were in the woods. Bryn worked in the woods. Surely, he would have the tools to resolve the issue. Wouldn't he?

Only one way to find out.

He opened the door to his car and stepped out. He looked around at the cabins nearest the car park, towards where he had seen Bryn, earlier that day. There was a garage-sized extension to the rear of the 'office' cabin, which he decided would be the most logical place to start looking for something he could use – a chainsaw would be ideal, but Gareth would have taken a chisel if that was the only thing on offer.

As he searched through strained eyes, it was difficult to see anything, with only the gentle glow of moonlight creeping in through the open door. It was not the tidiest of spaces, that much was obvious to him, as he stumbled over a couple of old tins of paint and odd screws, wincing as they went clattering across the concrete floor. He reached what appeared to be an old, repurposed sideboard, and found what he was looking for. An old chainsaw, which bore the rough texture of rust in places. It could have done with a little bit of TLC, but would no doubt get the job done. *If* he could get it started.

Despite the darkness, he lifted the chainsaw off the work surface and placed it on the ground to start it. It would make a fair bit of noise, he realised, and wondered if it was a good idea to potentially alert the murderous psychopath who may or may not have been lurking around the place. But he decided they would have had to have had a death wish of their own to try and attack someone wielding such a destructive potential weapon. If they wanted to lose a limb, he would let them come, and shake their severed hand to acknowledge their bravery afterwards. Not to mention thanking them for ridding the world of Benjamin.

He had used a chainsaw once or twice before, and wasn't a complete novice with tools and machinery. After a few hopeful attempts at pulling the starter cord, it became clear that there was no life in the thing. It needed fuel.

His search of the shed continued, but there was no sign of any tanks or containers holding what he required. There were a couple of empty cans, but it appeared Bryn had neglected to replenish his stock. It made sense, given he hadn't suggested getting rid of the tree earlier. That was unless he was just a lonely old man, and the storm had simply created the opportunity for an evening of company.

There didn't seem to be any other cans of fuel anywhere, and Gareth had started to admit defeat. He found a stool and perched on it, resting his elbow on the worktop next to him. He gazed into space absently, wondering what to do next. In the dim light, he spotted a photograph of a smiling man pinned to the wall where he was sat. He looked to be a similar age to Gareth and there was something familiar about him. But the man bore a striking resemblance to Bryn.

So much that Gareth could have believed it was a picture of the ranger in his younger days, had he not been pictured holding a smartphone. Even modern-day Bryn didn't appear to possess one of those.

The sound of emerging footsteps from outside the shed almost caused Gareth to fall off the stool. Quickly, he darted away from where he had sat and crouched behind a couple of stacked boxes, hoping he was concealed enough to avoid being seen by whoever was out there.

He held his breath and gulped anxiously, as he waited for them to reveal themselves. Was it Steffan? Was he the murderer? A shadow filled the doorway, blocking most of the light from reaching inside the shed. The door opened a little more, revealing that it was Bryn, armed with his shotgun in one hand and a torch in the other, which clicked on as he pointed it into the darkness.

The beam creeped closer to Gareth, and his heartrate began to quicken with every millimetre.

'Anybody in here?' he called. There was a slight quiver in his voice, but largely he sounded calm and determined. 'Gareth, is it you?'

Bryn stepped further inside the shed, and Gareth realised he would soon be discovered. It was far better to come out voluntarily, than be found hiding – it would be far less suspicious. But what explanation would he give for being there? Should he just tell the truth?

'Yeah, it's me,' said Gareth, raising his hands almost instinctively, a reaction which made him appear like was a wanted criminal, finally caught by law enforcement.

'What are you doing in here? How did you get in?' said Bryn, his tone more quizzical.

'I was looking for a chainsaw, to cut the tree,' said Gareth. 'The door wasn't locked, but I couldn't get it started though – I think it needs petrol.'

Bryn looked back at him, as though he was pondering Gareth's explanation.

'Put your hands down, what're you playing at…' he said, taking another step into the shed before stopping. 'I've not had chance to get more fuel. Farmer a few miles up the road does me a good deal on a two-stroke mix but he's away at some show. I did ask Ceri to get some instead on her way home…'

Gareth caught Bryn's eye wandering in the direction of the photograph. His attention was, just for a moment, firmly set upon the wall of mystery. He tightened his grip on the gun. Gareth gulped.

'Oh,' Gareth said with an awkward chuckle. 'Looks like I'm stuck here, then.'

'Aye,' grunted Bryn, his eyes snapping back onto Gareth. 'Looks like we all are. Come on, you'd best get back to the others. I'll lock up here, save anybody else wandering in without permission. Don't want someone else getting hurt.'

Gareth nodded and walked past Bryn, back outside. 'Is that your son?' he asked, gesturing towards the photograph on the wall.

'Nephew,' grunted Bryn. 'He *was* my nephew. Dafydd. Died five years ago.'

'I'm sorry.' Gareth didn't know what else to say.

Bryn looked at him with a cold, unblinking stare. 'Let's just get back, come on now.'

He nodded and made a conscious effort to avoid any more eye contact. He didn't want to piss off the guy with the gun any more than he already had.

CHAPTER FORTY-SIX

Jodie

'I just can't believe what I'm hearing,' groaned Billy. 'Explain again – you and *you*, were…'

Jodie cringed at Billy's visual aid, consisting of a pointed finger being placed through a 'hole' he had created with the other hand, as he continued to try and come to terms with Francesca and Matthew's revelation.

'It's nothing against you, mate,' said Matthew. 'We didn't tell anyone. Nobody could find out, obviously.'

'I don't understand why you'd do it though,' said Billy. 'And Fran… what were you playing at? You had the life of dreams with Benjamin – he's minted.'

Was minted, thought Jodie. Another reminder.

'It's not all about money,' said Francesca.

Jodie had to suppress a snort at the claim – who was *Her Ladyship* trying to kid?

'No, I mean, I get that,' said Billy. 'But it's just about loyalty, innit?'

Jodie could understand where Billy was coming from, even if he had articulated like a child. He was one of Benjamin's most loyal employees, himself. He had worked for him for years and had also been a sales rep for one of HomeHub's UK-based suppliers before that. It was well known that he was renowned for sucking up to Benjamin, idolising him. It would have seemed quite pathetic to her, had Jodie not been just as in awe of Benjamin herself.

Also, she considered, Matthew was also one of Billy's teammates in the sales department, and they had developed a bond which was akin to her own, with Tara – so it was a bit of a double-whammy for him to find out about the secret this way.

'Billy,' said Matthew. 'I'm sorry, yeah?'

'Whatever, Matt. I'm just trying to get my head around it all. This day has been completely flipping mental.'

That's an understatement.

Before Jodie could continue painting a mental picture of Jodie and Matthew's sordid betrayal, she was interrupted by the canteen door opening, and Gareth appearing before them.

'You're still alive then,' she said, with what she realised was an inappropriate level of sarcastic disappointment in her tone.

Gareth smiled wryly in response. His face was pale, as though he had just encountered the ghost of Benjamin. She studied him curiously as he walked in and took a seat, without uttering a single word. Jodie could tell something was on his mind, but then, there must have been a lot on *everyone's* mind.

A moment or two later, Bryn returned, following Gareth. He, too, was displaying the expression of a wildly deteriorated mood.

What happened out there?

'Okay then, ladies and gents,' said Bryn. 'After another scout of the area has only returned Gareth, here, who I found snooping around in my shed, I think it's for the best if you all go and get some sleep.'

'Are you joking?' asked Billy. 'It's only nine.'

'I'm sorry, boyo,' replied Bryn. 'I must apologise if you thought I was pulling your leg – I meant nothing humorous in what I just said.'

He stared at Billy, with a cold, unmoving glare. There was a definite change in his mood since his return.

'What I think Billy means,' began Tara, 'is that there's a murderer on the loose. If we go to sleep, he'll just come and kill the rest of us!'

'What makes you so adamant that this "murderer" of yours is a "he"?' asked Bryn.

Jodie looked at Tara as she frowned back at Bryn. She opened her mouth as if to respond but held her tongue. She caught Jodie watching her and held eye contact for a moment longer than was normal. Bryn was quite right; the general consensus did seem to be focused on a male culprit – Steffan, in particular, the recipient of much suspicion, but she held doubts about Francesca after her exposed lies.

It genuinely could have been any of them.

'He, she, they, them… who gives a shit what they are, other than the fact they're a flipping murderer!?' protested Billy.

'It's a fair point,' said Gareth, breaking his silence for the first time since his return. Of course, he *would* be open to the idea of blaming a female, if it was him.

God, Jodie thought. *Mrs Marple can have her fucking job back.*

'Look, I can assure you, there's nobody unaccounted for around here now,' said Bryn. 'And besides, I'll keep watch – I don't sleep much, any road.'

'I don't think any of us are going to,' said Matthew.

There were disgruntled mutterings around the room. Nobody made a move to do as they had been instructed. Jodie couldn't blame them.

'Okay, I've got an idea,' she called out. 'Everyone's in pairs in the rooms anyway… why not take it in turns to sleep. If anything happens, the person who's awake can just scream as loudly as they can and warn everyone else?'

'I'm not in a pair,' said Francesca.

Of course she wasn't. But then, with Steffan missing, neither was Gareth.

'You can come in with us,' said Matthew, placing a reassuring hand on her arm.

'I'm not sharing with you two,' sneered Billy.

Francesca looked delighted at that.

'Look,' growled Bryn, raising a hand to silence the group. 'I don't give a monkey's who bunks up with who, right… you just need to sort yourselves out and get to bed. Pronto.'

'You can just take Steffan's bed, Billy,' said Gareth. 'It's not like he'll be needing it.'

Jodie nodded in agreement, but Billy appeared ready to protest once more – probably at the prospect of lying in the bed of the most likely murderer, but Bryn clapped his hands together like the slam of a vault's door, silencing the group before anyone could say anything else.

'That's decided then,' he said. 'Get some sleep, everybody. This nightmare will all be over by the morning.'

CHAPTER FORTY-SEVEN

Gareth

Whilst it may well have been true that Gareth – along with everybody else – would be able to go home the next morning, putting at least some of this horrendous experience behind them, it seemed a hell of a long time to wait.

He had been sat upright at the head of his bed for a few minutes, with Billy taking the same position on the other bed in the room – the one Steffan was supposed to be in, had he not vanished into the night.

'There's not a chance I'm going to be able to sleep,' groaned Billy. 'Especially in the bed of a murderer – I mean, what if he comes back here?'

'Mm-hmm,' responded Gareth. He wasn't really listening to Billy's complaints anymore. He had been droning on about how unfair the whole situation was since getting back to the room, and Gareth's mind was elsewhere.

'I'm surprised you didn't get any sort of indication, sharing a room with the guy,' said Billy, turning to face Gareth.

'What, for the matter of seconds we were in here together at any one time?' said Gareth. 'Besides, whilst it may be the most likely explanation, how can we be sure Steffan actually killed Benjamin?'

'Well, who else would it have been?'

‘Literally anybody,’ said Gareth. ‘I know you think he was great, but surely you must be able to accept that he could be a real dick?’

‘I don’t think he was a dick, as such. He’d just expect effort and hard work. You know?’

‘So having HR on people’s backs all the time is a healthy environment, is it?’

Billy shrugged. ‘If it gets results.’

Gareth thought back to the time when he had been hauled into Claire’s office for a ‘return to work meeting’. He had been at home for the last couple of weeks, isolating after testing positive for coronavirus. HomeHub had not implemented the same ‘working from home’ plan that many other businesses had, as Benjamin had decided it was perfectly acceptable for an ecommerce business – selling products such as flat-packed garden sheds and board games, and not PPE or medication – to be self-classified as essential.

Annoyingly, Benjamin had been proven right, in the sense that sales quickly sky-rocketed, as customers sought to improve their homes, occupy the kids and ultimately make life without freedom a little more bearable.

Whilst in isolation, Gareth *had* continued to work from home. The influx in custom demanded it, so whilst it wasn’t ideal, at least he was able to keep on top of things.

‘How are you feeling?’ Claire asked, opening the meeting. From the way she had pulled her paper closer to her, and increasing the distance away from him on the other side of the conference table, she certainly hadn’t wanted to catch anything if he was still contagious.

Gareth wondered drily if that was what it was like to have been a leper.

‘Not too bad, thanks,’ he replied. ‘Still got a bit of a cough, but not as bad as I was.’

Claire cleared her throat and nodded sullenly. 'Good. So, I just need to go through this questionnaire as you have had a period of time away from the office due to illness.'

'No problem.'

'It's all fairly standard. The first question is just why you were absent, which is obviously Covid. Second question is if you are now feeling well enough to be back in work, so I'll just write what you've told me.'

Gareth nodded. It may have been a formality, but it just seemed a bit excessive – he had still been 'in work', albeit not 'at work'. It wasn't as though he had been stuck in a hospital bed like so many had been and still were.

'Okay, moving on. Would you say that you remained contactable in the event of emergencies – work related emergencies, of course – whilst you were absent?'

Was this a real question? Claire looked at him expectantly.

'Yes, I would say so,' he said. 'I was working whilst at home.'

'Okay,' she said, appearing unconvinced by his response. 'It is just that it has been raised you were slow to reply on occasion. Do you agree with that?'

Oh, for fuck's sake.

'No, not really. I was chased up a couple of times by Benjamin and Theo, but I was already in the middle of replying, both times.'

Claire looked at him, her face expressionless as always. 'Right. It's just that when you are out of the office for any reason, there will still be times that the company needs to be able to keep in touch.'

'I get that,' he said. He was becoming agitated. 'But I was contactable, and did keep in touch. I was working, the same as everybody else.'

Without responding, she began to make further notes on the form in front of her. Gareth couldn't believe how ridiculous these insinuations were, but he began to feel a sense of guilt building up, as though he had actually done something wrong. That was what this place had done to him.

In the end, he had been issued with a formal warning as a result of the company's 'findings'. It was bullshit. He knew that, and Claire must have known it, too. But there was no point in arguing, it would have only made things worse in the long run.

'I'll tell you who *is* a dick though,' said Billy. 'Bryn.'

'Do you think?' asked Gareth.

'Sending us to bed like fucking children. He's having a laugh ain't he?'

'I suppose,' said Gareth, pondering. 'I don't know if it explains why he's kind of miserable, but I found out before that he had a nephew that died.'

'What?' said Billy. 'How do you know that?'

'Saw a picture of him on the wall, when I went into Bryn's shed.'

'Christ, that's a bit weird, innit?' scoffed Billy. 'What were you even doing in his shed, by the way?'

'Looking for something to get us out of here – to shift that tree. I found a chainsaw, but it didn't work.'

'Well, *obviously*. Don't you think Bryn would have had the brains to cut the thing himself, if he could? How did this nephew of his die, anyway – young was he?'

'I don't know,' replied Gareth. 'He shut me down quite quickly when I asked. Dafydd, I think he said his name was.'

'*Dafydd*, boyo,' Billy said, in an awful attempt at a generic, regionless Welsh accent. 'The only gay in the village, ey?'

'What?'

'Little Britain,' said Billy. 'Don't you remember it?'

Gareth nodded. 'Yeah.'

'Good times. They don't make stuff like that anymore – all the *woke snowflakes* would have a meltdown.'

'Right.'

'There was a Dafydd who worked at HomeHub, once upon a time. He was bent as well, rumour has it.'

'What happened to him?' asked Gareth.

'I think he was sacked. Benjamin has mentioned him a couple of times, joking about him. But I don't really know.'

Gareth shivered. 'You don't think it's the same one, do you?'

'I don't know, do I?' said Billy, before he yawned loudly. 'Anyway, if you're just going to sit there, I might as well try and get some kip.' He leaned out of the bed, reaching to switch the lamp off. 'Make sure you wake me up if Steffan comes back to do us in.'

CHAPTER FORTY-EIGHT

Steffan

The more he struggled, the more the binding seemed to be growing tighter. Freeing himself was beginning to feel like an impossible task. He grunted and wheezed as he tried once more, squeezing his arms outwards and tugging from the wrists, desperately trying to loosen the grip on the rope around them.

'Come on, man', he growled, as he pushed with every last drop of his energy.

The rope just would not budge. The knot held strong in its defiance.

He exhaled, his body relaxing like a deflated balloon. He may have come around now, reclaiming his senses and awareness, but physically he was exhausted. He felt helpless. His cheek rested on the coarse surface beneath him. He could smell the earthy notes of the timber flooring, amongst the staleness of the mould which was rotting its host quietly beneath the surface.

What was he going to do? He couldn't afford to just lie there, accepting his fate. Whatever that may be – though he knew it couldn't be good.

But he was so tired. So restricted.

So, he *would* lie there, just for a while. Just until he could muster the energy to try again. Hopefully then, he would break free.

CHAPTER FORTY-NINE

Jodie

She would have given just about anything to be able to fall asleep. It wasn't for the want of trying. She'd lay there, forced her eyes shut and tried to picture a world where this day had not happened. She even tried counting sheep. With a sigh, she turned onto her back and listened to the rain as it pattered steadily on the roof.

'Can't you sleep?' asked Tara.

'No,' she grumbled.

'I don't think I'll be able to either. I'm too scared.'

Tara had offered to take the first watch in their room. Out of everyone, she was the only person Jodie had ruled out of being Benjamin's killer. Except maybe for Billy. If it had been anybody else left in the room with her, she wouldn't have been quite so willing to sleep – or at least try to.

'Try not to worry,' she said. 'If you *can* sleep, I don't mind staying up – not that my brain is giving me much choice.'

'Why, what are you thinking about?' asked Tara.

'What do you think?' She realised she had snapped at her friend and immediately apologised.

'It's okay,' said Tara. 'I'm sorry that I didn't realise you fancied him *that* much. I thought you just thought he was hot, or you have a power kink. I don't know.'

Jodie looked at her. If only she knew.

'Don't you think, in a way, him being such a massive arsehole with you is the closure you need to focus on. You know, to forget about him?'

'I don't think it's just that,' she said. 'He's dead – lying there, literally in the next room. We don't know who it was, why it happened. It's a mess.'

'It *has* to have been Steffan. He's the outsider of the group, right?'

'I suppose so. Look, why don't you try and get some sleep. There's no point in us both staying up.'

Tara agreed and switched out her light before shuffling further under her duvet. She seemed convinced of Steffan's guilt, but Jodie wasn't so sure. She just could not settle on him without proof. Whilst he had run away, it didn't mean he was running from his own crime. Tara had said it herself; he was an outsider – he had no reason to help them, but perhaps he had gone into the depths of the forest out of desperation to find assistance. He had seemed convinced by seeing someone through the window; maybe he had followed the shadow and lost his way. Or maybe he had just left in search of a way home.

Beyond Steffan, theories continued to fly around in her head, suspicions involving just about everyone, colliding and battling to cancel each other out.

Gareth had a problem with Benjamin, and he hadn't even tried to disguise it – with all the comments he had made. He even seemed pleased Benjamin was dead. His mopey quietness was shifty – he didn't let people in. Jodie barely knew anything about him. It could have been because he had something to hide. The temper he'd displayed –

when he thought nobody was around to notice – replayed over in her mind.

Francesca had been cheating on Benjamin. Her illicit affair apparently going on for months. Despite that, she had been humiliated by him earlier that day, and whilst

Benjamin had blamed Jodie for coming onto *him* in the bedroom, Francesca seemed unconvinced. What had she said to Jodie? *Don't protect him. I know how he is.* A scorned lover seemed too obvious, but then she had faked her twisted ankle – a cover, perhaps?

Then, there was Matthew. He could have been protecting Francesca's honour. But then, wouldn't the very public falling out have opened the door for things with them to go public – if not immediately, at some point? That was if Francesca and Benjamin broke up, of course. Perhaps he had seen an opportunity to remove the competition. It was unlikely, but anything was possible and *someone* was guilty.

'Jodie?' said Tara, interrupting her thoughts.

'What's up?'

'I'm sorry for being harsh about Benjamin – about how you need to move on. I know it's not that easy, but I just hope you will be okay.'

Me too, she thought.

Jodie smiled at Tara, forcing herself to put on a brave face of reassurance. 'Don't worry about it. I'll be okay.'

CHAPTER FIFTY

Gareth

Something was bothering him about Bryn's nephew, Dafydd. How had he died? It was a morbid thing to think about, but after what Billy had said – about another Dafydd working for HomeHub, a person Benjamin would make jokes about, Gareth couldn't help but wonder if it was the same person. He just didn't know why it was bugging him so much. Maybe it was the way Bryn had shut the conversation down in the shed, but whatever it was, something didn't sit right with him.

He climbed up off his bed and tip-toed past Billy, so as not to wake him. He was flat out, snoring with his face pressed into the pillow. His mouth was open as a result, making him look arguably more moronic than usual. Gareth left him in his pit of drool and opened the door, before closing it as quietly as he could behind him. As he took his hand off the handle, the latch clicked into place more loudly than he had anticipated. Gareth clenched his jaw, wincing as he hoped it hadn't disturbed Billy.

As he crept along the dimly lit corridor, he arrived at the room where Benjamin's body lay. He scowled in the door's direction before continuing. Benjamin would have been the one who could have given him the answers he sought. But not now.

He heard voices from Tara and Jodie's room as he moved past their room. Evidently, neither of them were able to sleep. He reached Matthew and Billy's room – or Matthew and Francesca's, per the reorganisation that evening.

With a gentle knock on the door, he waited for an answer. He couldn't hear anything from inside, but he hoped that they, too, were yet to submit to their exhaustion. He knocked again, with a little more force, before he heard movement from inside.

'Who is it?' came a weary call from the other side of the door.

'It's just Gareth.'

'What do you want?' asked Matthew, opening the door. His eyes squinted as he switched a light on.

Gareth invited himself inside, before Matthew had chance to even contemplate such a request. He was holding onto a hairbrush. Gareth smiled at it, before looking back at Matthew. 'I don't think that'll protect you from anything more dangerous than knots and tangles.'

'First thing I could pick up,' mumbled Matthew, looking down at the hairbrush, before tossing it onto a pile of clothes which sat at the foot of one of the beds.

'I came to speak to Francesca,' explained Gareth, as he perched on the edge of Matthew's empty bed – or at least, Matthew's *side* of the bed, as he noticed that the two singles had been curiously pushed together to form a makeshift double. They had certainly not wasted any time in taking advantage of things becoming common knowledge.

'What do you want to talk about?' asked a yawning Francesca.

'It's about Benjamin,' replied Gareth, at which she rolled her eyes. 'Well, kind of, anyway. Did he ever talk to you about a *Dafydd* who worked for him?'

Francesca paused for thought. Gareth could see the cogs were turning in her mind.

'Who's that?' asked Matthew, as he joined the conversation, taking a seat at the head of his bed. He looked with confusion, first at Gareth, before looking to Francesca for an explanation.

'There was somebody called Dafydd who used to work for HomeHub, back in the early days – before any of us. I remember hearing Benjamin talking about him to Theo, a while back. Some stock had gone missing from the warehouse, and he'd joked that this Dafydd person must have returned.'

'So, he was on the rob?' asked Gareth.

'Apparently so,' she nodded. 'All Benjamin told me, when I asked, was that they could never prove he had stolen anything, but there were a few other incidents which led to him being sacked, and that he hadn't heard anything from Dafydd after he'd left.'

'So, you don't know if he *died*, or anything like that?'

'How would I know that?' asked Francesca. 'No, I haven't got a clue.'

Gareth nodded, pausing for thought. None of this helped him to join the dots.

'Hang on a minute,' said Matthew. 'Where has this name come from? Why are you asking about it now?'

Gareth took a deep breath, as he looked back at both Matthew and Francesca's confused stares. He knew he was only going to confuse them even more – either that, or they would think he was an utter lunatic.

A knock at the door interrupted his thoughts.

'Hello, it's Bryn. Can I come in for a moment, please?'

Shit!

'Er… okay,' called Matthew as he stood up to go and open the door.

'Wait,' Gareth whispered, as quietly as he possibly could, given the situation. 'I need to hide!'

'What on earth are you talking about?' hissed Francesca.

‘Trust me,’ he whispered again. ‘I’ll explain in a minute.’

Bryn knocked on the door again, placing an unmistakable sound of urgency in the vibrations his fist inflicted on the wood. Gareth’s heart raced as he scanned frantically around the room. Then he had it. Quickly, he slid himself beneath the bed, and prayed he could keep his breathing under control.

If Bryn was who he thought he may have been, he could not afford to be heard.

‘Sorry to disturb you,’ said Bryn. ‘I’m just checking in on everyone, making sure they’re all right, like.’

Gareth could see Bryn had stepped into the room. He watched the movements of his boots in fear, hoping that was all he would see of him. If his grizzly old face appeared before Gareth’s own, it would be Game Over.

‘Yeah, we’re okay,’ said Matthew. The nervousness in his tone was not well hidden.

‘Are you sure, lad?’

‘Honestly, we’re absolutely fine,’ said Francesca cheerfully. ‘We’re just trying to sleep, that’s all.’

‘My apologies, I shall leave you to it,’ said Bryn, before he ventured further into the room. Gareth found it more difficult to catch his breath, increasingly so with every creak of the floorboards beneath Bryn’s heavy boots.

Please don’t find me. Please, just leave.

He heard a metallic rattling from somewhere behind him, as Bryn said ‘I’m just going to lock the windows, whilst I’m here. Make sure nobody else can get in.’

And to make sure nobody else gets out, you mean.

Francesca and Matthew murmured in agreement, as Gareth watched Bryn’s footsteps, relief building as they grew closer the door, and further away from him. But then, they stopped.

‘Just one more thing,’ he said. ‘You haven’t heard anyone knocking around have you? It’s just Gareth wasn’t in the room with Billy just now when I checked on them.’

Beneath the bed, Gareth’s pulse became frantic, the panic taking a firm hold of him once more. Would they expose him? Was this all a test… did Bryn know he was in the room all along?

‘No, not at all,’ said Francesca. ‘As I say, we have been trying to sleep.’

Bryn grumbled to himself. Gareth thought he was going to hurl.

‘It’s not the first time he’s wandered off tonight,’ said Matthew, finally chipping in with a useful response, hopefully trying to throw Bryn off the scent.

Everyone was quiet for a moment, before Bryn spoke a final time. ‘True enough, young man. Well, you’d best get some sleep now. Goodnight.’

‘Goodnight,’ said Matthew and Francesca in unison, as the door was closed behind Bryn. They both exhaled sharply, and Gareth could feel the tension in the room evaporate, ever so slightly.

He waited for a few moments, before climbing out from under the bed. Unsurprisingly, he found demanding stares waiting for him. It was time to tell them of his fears.

* * *

He told them everything he knew, and of his concerns about Bryn. Gareth waited for one of them, either of them, to say something. As they absorbed what he had told them, they simply looked at him, at one another, in complete disbelief.

‘I don’t understand how you’ve reached that conclusion,’ rasped Francesca.

‘You’re adding *Dafydd* with *Dafydd* and coming up with *Bryn is the murderer*,’ added Matthew.

He exhaled, slowly. Calmly. They didn't believe it – didn't take him seriously. Of course they didn't.

'Bryn isn't some kind of crazy murderer,' said Francesca. 'He was so lovely, helping me take my things into another room. He's keeping watch, right now – keeping us *safe*.'

'But don't you think it's at least a possibility?' asked Gareth. 'That it could be Bryn – that Dafydd, his nephew, is the same Dafydd who worked for Benjamin?'

'I don't know,' said Francesca. 'In theory, I guess. But why would Bryn kill him if it was? It's not Benjamin's fault that his nephew is dead, how could it be?'

Gareth could not answer. Again, he felt the surge of frustration pulsating, the anxiety within him living and breathing. It was like a parasite, using his body as its host whilst it wreaked havoc on his mind. The look on the faces of Francesca and Matthew, their complete refusal to accept what he had told them, made it clear that he was fighting a losing battle. *Another* losing battle.

He shook his head and walked towards the door.

'Where are you going?' asked Francesca.

'Don't know,' Gareth lied. He knew where he needed to go. What he needed to do. Even if he was right. He needed to find out the truth.

'Go to bed, mate,' said Matthew. 'You're obviously just tired. We all are. It'll be over in the morning.'

He paused, gripping the door handle tightly. The chill of the cold brass surface was warning him of what awaited him. It was a risk, he knew that. Confronting Bryn about his nephew, it could be suicide. Something he had never been brave enough to face before.

This time, he would have to be. He was fed up with being doubted by these people. By everybody. By Benjamin. Just once, he would prove them wrong – prove himself right. Irrefutably right. He would walk out of this door and return with evidence that would have them quivering like the children they were. If he survived to tell the tale.

He stepped out of the room and approached the door leading out of the cabin. The handle was stiff. Unmoving. It, too, was laughing at him.

Try again, Gareth… maybe next time, Gareth… I'm just another door you cannot get through, Gareth.

It was locked.

Why was it locked?

Bryn.

He rapped on the door to Matthew and Francesca's room, bursting through it before anyone could answer. Matthew stood before him and stared with a frown. 'What now?'

'The door won't open,' Gareth said. 'It looks like it's locked.' He was hoping, stupidly, that this would offer some kind of confirmation that he wasn't just overtired. And wasn't insane.

'Yeah, Bryn's probably locked it like he did with the windows,' explained Matthew tiredly. 'Just go back to bed, yeah?'

Gareth stood outside the room and watched as Matthew closed the door again, leaving just the knots of the pine door staring back at him. He was trapped. A feeling he knew only too well.

He wondered, if perhaps he *was* mad. Imagining things, driven crazy by everything that had happened to him and had tortured his mind. Was he more broken than he realised?

Admitting defeat, Gareth decided to take Matthew's advice and go to bed. Despite this, he guessed he would be unlikely to manage any sleep – there was no way that somebody as loud-mouthed as Billy would not snore for the whole night... far be it for him to allow a frivolous act like rest to prevent him making his presence known.

The strange thing was, Billy was *not* snoring when Gareth entered the bedroom. He couldn't have been… he wasn't even there.

Weird.

Battling his mind's urge to spin back into overdrive, Gareth told himself that Billy had probably just gone to the toilet. Nature calls, even in times of crisis. After a couple of minutes, Billy was yet to return, and so he decided to go and check – just to be sure.

'Billy,' he said quietly, wandering into the bathroom. 'Are you in here?'

The lights were not on, and in the darkness, he soon realised neither of the cubicles were occupied.

Where is he?

Gareth ambled back down the corridor, racking his brain for a logical explanation to his whereabouts. No such answer was forthcoming. He could no longer fight against the screams of doubt from his subconscious.

Billy was missing, he was sure of it. And now, he was convinced he knew who was responsible.

Enough is enough.

They were all going to die. Gareth could confront Bryn now. He wasn't going to be the next person on Bryn's hit list. Whatever he had done with Billy, it could not have been good news… after all, Benjamin was *dead.*

Benjamin.

The thought struck him instantly. He charged back down the corridor and placed his hand hopefully onto another door handle. Praying for some luck.

From the moment he placed a foot inside the room, the atmosphere surrounding Gareth changed. An uneasiness swirled around him. The stench of death.

There he was. Benjamin Pearson. Possibly the closest rival to Gareth's own psyche, in the battle to tear him down – mentally, and emotionally. For far too long, this man had chipped away at everything Gareth was. And now he was dead.

For the first time, Gareth truly believed it. It was not that he hadn't before, but there was something about being in the presence of the body which just provided true confirmation.

He just stared for a moment at Benjamin's ghostly complexion. Bloodless. Lifeless. But still, he looked as though he was not at peace. His body was tense, as though he had just been let down by a supplier on a hugely profitable order. After all, nothing could have been worse than losing money, to a man like Benjamin. Not even a lethal blow to the back of the head. Or a knife in the back.

'This is all your fault,' he whispered to the corpse. Part of him expected a snarling, patronising reply. *Watch your mouth, Gareth – remember who you're talking to.*

But there would never be a response.

He stood up, and walked over to the window, and found that his gut instinct was correct – the window was unlocked.

He was going to get out of there.

He didn't have much time. After quickly stuffing his belongings back into his bag, he looked down at the outfit he was wearing. Blue jeans and a light grey hooded sweatshirt, he decided, was not fit for an escape mission. He had seen enough action movies to know that this was the part a costume change would take place. Unfortunately, a full SWAT uniform was not going to materialise out of thin air. He glanced across the room, remembering that Steffan had left everything there before his sudden departure.

As he emptied everything out onto the bed, it didn't take long to piece together a collection of more appropriate attire. It was unsurprising, of course, that Steffan would have packed with far more experience for this type of occasion than he. Black combat-style workpants, a North Face rain jacket and even Steffan's choice of hat – a black beanie, offered far more camouflage than Gareth could have hoped for from his own gear.

He changed into Steffan's clothes, discarding his own. And after switching from trainers back into his own walking boots – which were still a little soggy inside, from the walk through the woods earlier in the day – he made his way back to Benjamin's room, resisting the urge to break into a full sprint.

'See you later,' he said, breezing past Benjamin's body in hope that he would never have to see him again.

After throwing the window open wide, he peered out before climbing into the darkness. He took a moment to breathe in the damp air, and looked in both directions along the back of the cabin. He was one step closer to freedom.

CHAPTER FIFTY-ONE

Jodie

Jodie was listening to the conversation taking place around her, but what she really wanted to do was go to sleep. She was exhausted, and, as Bryn had said, this nightmare was all going to be over tomorrow.

Of course, it wouldn't be over for her, not really. Benjamin would still be dead tomorrow. The man she had loved for the last few years. It may have been unreciprocated, but that did not matter – in the end, she had lost him that night. HomeHub had lost him that night. The two most important things in her life – one gone forever, the other never to be the same as a result.

And now, Billy – of all people – had decided to invade her bedroom and had been rabbiting on at her and Tara for what had felt like ages, about Gareth doing a runner, and his suspicions of *why* he had now gone.

'He's lost the plot, I'm telling you,' he had said. 'Talking all this bollocks about Bryn's nephew. If they even existed. He was trying to deflect from his own guilt, he was. No question.'

'What about Steffan, then?' asked Tara. Jodie cursed her for encouraging the man who needed no encouragement to hear – and force everyone else to – the sound of his own voice.

'Simple. Either they were in on it together, or Steffan's dead an' all. Gaz probably slipped up talking to him and had to do him in on the sly. Keep him quiet.'

Jodie could understand where Billy was coming from. After all, she too had accused Gareth earlier. But he and Steffan, by all accounts, barely knew each other, so it seemed unlikely that they would have surmised some kind of grand plan to murder their boss. Plus, Steffan was ex-army. She couldn't see Gareth being able to overpower him in a fist fight.

But then, Benjamin certainly hadn't lost his life to someone's bare hands.

They were interrupted by a clunking sound from next door.

Benjamin's room.

'Did you hear that?' she asked the other two.

'Yeah, what was that?' replied Tara.

The three of them exchanged concerned glances. Jodie lifted the duvet from over her and climbed out of bed.

'What do you think you're doing?' asked Billy.

'We'd better go and look,' she said, walking towards the door.

'Are you mental?' he exclaimed. 'Actually, don't answer that… you've been properly unhinged tonight, too. But you can't go in there – what if it's… well, it won't be a friendly face greeting you in there, will it?'

'You are such a wimp,' hissed Jodie. 'Tara, let's go.'

Tara hesitated and opened her mouth as though she was going to protest, before seemingly thinking better of it and doing as she was told.

Jodie nodded at Tara, before opening the door. She wasn't afraid. She could tell Tara was, but it didn't matter. They'd been through a lot together. She knew Tara had her back –

she was a good friend, despite her big gob sometimes letting her down.

There was nothing unexpected awaiting them. No surprises. Benjamin was in exactly the same place as before. Resting on his bed, eyes closed. As though he were dreaming. Despite him no longer displaying a face full of colour, full of *life*, she could still see the boyish handsomeness he had charmed her with. The strong, razor sharp jawline and pronounced cheekbones. She could still see Benjamin.

'Weird,' said Tara. 'What do you think the noise was?'

'Dunno,' shrugged Jodie, not taking her eyes away from Benjamin. 'Maybe it was the wind or something.'

'Maybe. Are you coming back to bed?'

'In a minute – I'm enjoying the quiet. Billy's driving me up the wall in there.'

As Tara whispered a gentle 'okay' before leaving her alone, Jodie continued to gaze at Benjamin. She placed a hand on his chest, knowing that she would not feel his heart beating, but whilst hers continued to, she would do everything within her power to find the true culprit and make them pay. Whether it was Gareth, Steffan, both of them, or the entire fucking world. She would make them pay.

'I'm so sorry,' she whispered. A single tear trickled down her cheek, before she began to sob quietly.

Knowing Tara would be wondering what was taking her so long, she looked towards the door, reluctantly accepting she would have to leave him. Alone.

But, she did not want him to be alone. It wasn't right. It wasn't fair. He didn't deserve to be ignored. Someone needed to take care of him. Protect him. Carefully, she lowered herself onto the bed, and lay beside him, taking him into her arms in a delicate embrace.

CHAPTER FIFTY-TWO

Steffan

Steffan was frustrated. Blinded by the darkness. Restricted by the shackles he was bound to. As he sat there, staring out into the shadow of his imprisonment, he still could not understand what was happening. *Why* was he there? *Who* had tied him up, and taken him captive?

He did not even know *where* he was.

The rage he had worked so hard on overcoming, that he had promised he would not relent to, had started to overpower his will to remain calm. The confusion fuelled it. He could feel it burning inside him, about to be ignited once more.

He heard a sound. A quiet, metallic scrape – a rattle, in fact. A key. He closed his eyes, turning away from the sound to his left. In doing so, he realised at that moment, the binding around his wrists had relented in its attempts to constrain him. It was looser – loose enough for him to slip his hands free.

A warm orange light glowed through his closed eyelids, before the sound of panicked footsteps followed, scuttling across the surface, and he prayed whoever had just joined him did not notice his newly unrestrained arms resting behind his back.

Not daring to try and catch a glimpse of his captor, Steffan chose instead to focus on listening to their movements, picking a time to safely reopen an eye. They were frantic, rushing around and moving things around. Their breathing was heavy. Perhaps, he wondered, they would be too preoccupied to notice him.

He placed all his chips on the table, and hoped luck was on his side.

As the beam of their torch illuminated whatever they were looking at, or rather *rummaging through* on a desk in front of them, it offered Steffan very little in identifying *who* they were. They hadn't said a word since joining him in his makeshift prison cell. He continued to watch him, as they tossed everything aside. Whatever they were looking for, it must have been important. But it didn't explain what he was doing there.

The inside of his thigh had begun to itch. He almost reached to scratch it without a thought, before remembering they were supposed to be secured behind him. But the urge was unbearable. He sighed, audibly, and the other person instantly stopped what they were doing. Whilst their eyes were not visible, he could sense them staring at him. Stood, cautious and still.

He closed his eyes again, as he heard a hissed whisper of 'shit!' He couldn't be certain, but it sounded like a woman's voice. Not that gender made a difference at times of warfare. He knew that.

The hectic footsteps had slowed right down, as they were replaced by cautious movements towards him. They were wise to be taking their time – but Steffan was certain they had no idea just *how* wise. He could feel their closeness in the vibrations of the wood flooring, and could smell them as they crouched down before him.

'Are you awake?' the voice whispered. He was correct. It was a woman. She sounded familiar.

He held still, his eyes closed, as he listened to her anxious breaths before him. A chill took him by surprise as a gloved hand touched his face, gently nudging his cheek as though she was making sure he had not regained consciousness.

In an instant, he opened his eyes to be met with Ceri's startled face gaping back at him. Before she could snatch it back, he grabbed hold of her arm by the wrist, and yanked her down onto the floor, smothering her mouth with her own hand as he rolled on top of her.

Her screams were muffled by her leather glove, which would have been halfway down her throat had she not clamped her teeth around her fist.

'Shut the fuck up,' growled Steffan, spit dispersing through his own gritted teeth. 'I don't want to have to hurt you.'

He knew that was a lie. The urge to let go of his self-control was growing by the second. It was colossal.

She continued to wrestle with him, and he could feel her sharp fingernails trying to claw at his face through the glove of her free hand. Steffan gripped the collar of her jacket and threw her head against the floor repeatedly, as her screams became a whimpering sob.

If she didn't relent, he was going to kill her. He would have no choice. He wouldn't be able to prevent it. Despite her efforts, there was no way she could match his strength. He was an ex-squaddie, and she was just a random middle-aged woman, who for some still unknown reason had decided to tie him up and keep him as a prisoner.

He could feel her tiring. The fight was wearing her down. Rolling her over, he stuffed the binding from his wrists into her mouth and pressed her face into the ground with his own weight. As she used her free hand to flail at him in desperation, attempting to remove him from on top of her, he wrestled with the remaining binding, which was secured around his ankles, wriggling a foot out from within it.

It was time to run.

'Keep quiet for me, all right?' he grunted as he pushed himself up and onto his feet.

Ceri reached for his ankle as he turned towards the door, and Steffan planted the laces of his boot into her face, quite literally knocking the stuffing out of her mouth.

‘Come back here,’ she screamed as he made his way to the door, but he did not have time to look back to check if she was following.

Outside, he was met by the sight of Bryn, charging over towards the building he had just exited. He had his shotgun in his hand, and for the first time since meeting him, Steffan thought he looked prepared to use it.

‘Stay right there, son,’ Bryn ordered. Ignoring him, Steffan darted towards the trees. He had no idea where he was going, or where he would end up. But as the sound of shotgun shells echoed in his ears, anywhere else seemed a better option than staying put.

CHAPTER FIFTY-THREE

Gareth

The sound of gunfire rippling through the forest made Gareth leap out of his skin. Although the rain had stopped again, he had been struggling to find his bearings in the unfamiliar woodland since making his escape from the camp.

The shots sounded close, but he could not see or hear anything else untoward – no footsteps rustling in the undergrowth, no voices calling his name. But given Bryn had been cradling his shotgun like a newborn baby for much of the evening, he was certain it was him pulling the trigger.

Wherever the shells were being fired from, it meant the alarm had been raised, and Bryn was aware of his disappearance. It must also mean that Gareth's suspicions were correct, and that there could not be any witnesses of Bryn's crimes unaccounted for. Gareth still hadn't worked out why Bryn had done it.

The one thing he did know, was that he needed to get the hell away from there, and quickly. It was proving to be a far more difficult task than he had anticipated, however, and whilst tree after tree looked to be one and the same in the darkness, he could not help but feel as though he had followed the path back on himself.

As he looked around, trying to decide which direction to take, he heard a rustling nearby in some long grass. He turned on his heels and sprinted off the path to take cover behind the trunk of an old fallen tree, when a four-legged beast – no bigger than a cat or small dog – wandered into the open from the long grass. Gareth allowed himself a sigh of relief, as he realised it was just a fox, no doubt looking to scavenge for a midnight feast rather than attack him.

The fox noticed him then. It stood perfectly still, mirroring his own posture, its eyes fixed on him, as if waiting to see his next move. Gareth looked back, unmoving. He didn't want to frighten the poor thing. A moment later, it bounded out of sight.

Whilst he was pleased to discover he was safe, at least for the time being, he knew that he needed to keep moving. Following the path had not offered him any reward up to that point, so he turned and made his way further into the forest floor, and just hoped that his next encounter would be with someone who could help.

CHAPTER FIFTY-FOUR

Jodie

'What was that?' squeaked Tara, cutting Billy off mid-sentence.

Jodie frowned. It sounded like an explosion going off outside. Before another. And then another.

'Dunno,' said Billy, who looked at both Jodie and Tara in confusion. He jumped up from his perch at the foot of Tara's bed and opened the door slightly, peering through the gap before opening it further and stepping out into the corridor.

Jodie followed, before Tara trailed behind – more out of fear of being left, than anything else, Jodie suspected – and joined Billy at the window which overlooked the front of the retreat's row of cabins.

Another blast sent vibrations through the glass pane, as they watched Bryn aiming his shotgun out into the woodland.

Billy ducked. 'Holy shit!'

'What is he firing at, I wonder,' Jodie said, musing out loud.

'Maybe Gareth tried to jump him,' suggested Billy.

'Or Steffan came back,' said Tara, shuddering as she spoke.

Whatever it was, Bryn was visibly incensed, his feet were shifting from one to the other in restless anger. His ears must have been burning, as he glanced over towards where the three spectators were standing in the window, and Jodie felt his glare land directly on her. A chill went down her spine as he kept his eyes fixed firmly in their direction whilst reloading the gun.

He pulled the trigger one more time, before making his way over towards them.

'Quick, he's coming, hide,' whispered Tara.

'Don't be daft, he ain't gonna shoot us, is he?' sneered Billy. 'He'll just be checking on us again, probably. Reassure us that everything's fine, like we're little kids.'

Jodie wasn't convinced. The expression on Bryn's face, which grew clearer with each step he made, did not look like he had earlier in the evening. There was a darkness to the scowl he wore.

After unlocking the front door, he threw the door open, and Jodie took a step backwards as he charged inside.

'I thought you lot were supposed to be sleeping?' he said, with a hoarseness to his voice, which could have been a result of him screaming at whoever he was trying to blow the brains out of, increased blood pressure, or a combination of both.

'We were,' Jodie lied. 'The noise from that thing woke us up.' She nodded her head in the direction of the shotgun, which was resting in his arm.

'Right,' he grumbled. 'Well, the good news is Steffan has gone now, and I don't think he'll be coming back. So go back to bed.'

'Does that mean Steffan really is the killer?' asked Billy.

'What about Gareth?' asked Tara.

'No sign of Gareth, and Steffan didn't stop to chat or confirm,' Bryn replied with a shrug.

'So, you shot him?' asked Tara.

'I don't think so... well, I don't know. I couldn't see through the trees,' explained Bryn. 'But as I say, he won't be back, so bed. Now.'

'All right, Dad,' said Billy, holding his hands up in mock submission.

'To be honest, Bryn,' began Jodie. 'I don't feel particularly comfortable around here anymore.'

Bryn looked at her, as though he was staring right into her soul. It made her shiver once more. He moved towards her, until his nose was almost touching hers. She could smell the stench of whiskey on his breath.

'There's nowhere else for you to go,' he growled. 'So, I suggest you toddle on back to bed, love. Okay?'

Without another word, he stepped back out of the cabin, not taking his unblinking eyes from Jodie's for even a second.

He locked the door, and they watched him stagger away.

'I guess we're going to bed then,' shrugged Billy.

Bryn had done nothing to make Jodie feel any more at ease. In fact, he had only made her worry more. She followed the other two back into the bedroom, and climbed into her bed.

CHAPTER FIFTY-FIVE

Steffan

Steffan's lungs were burning with every breath. He wheezed and panted as his need for speed was challenged by the dodging of tree roots and shrubbery underfoot. A million emotions were thrashing around in his mind, as the voice ordering him to keep going, to get away, bellowed over them all.

Despite the way Bryn looked with the shotgun in his hands, braced to use the weapon, Steffan was still shocked that he had gone through with it. He had *actually* aimed the thing in his direction and pulled the trigger. He had been prepared to take a life. Steffan's life. And now Steffan had no choice but to retreat and try to find safety.

He stopped running momentarily. He was doubled over and sucking at the cool air around him, trying desperately to get his breath back. The sudden cardio session had done his headache no favours at all. Had he not already emptied the contents of his stomach earlier, whilst tied up and semi-conscious, he would undoubtedly have been hacking his guts up after his dash through the forest. His fitness levels were nowhere near as impressive as they used to be.

Looking around, there seemed to be no obvious direction for him to take – beyond avoiding the one he had just travelled from. Steffan had acted on instinct, battering Ceri before breaking out of captivity, but there was no plan for this stage. With no supplies, not even water to drink – and he was already dry-mouthed – his next step would need to be the right one.

He needed to go back and help his fellow comrades. Deserting them was not who he was. He had been left behind in the past, and that had not ended well for him. The problem was, he just didn't know how to save them, not without assistance of his own.

In his mind, he tried to picture the roads his mother's car had been on, when they approached the Wellderness Adventure retreat. If he could find one, it would be a start. All roads lead somewhere. Somewhere that didn't have a shotgun shell with his name written on.

He decided to go to the right.

CHAPTER FIFTY-SIX

Jodie

Jodie still could not force herself to fall asleep. It wasn't helped by Billy's incessant snoring. With Gareth gone, Billy had been adamant about not spending the night alone, in case he and Steffan were truly the murderous duo and decided to come back. After they'd been sent back to their rooms, following disturbance with the gunshots, he had dragged his mattress through into Jodie and Tara's bedroom. He had made himself comfortable on their floor, before somehow falling asleep in no time at all.

To his credit, he had offered and proceeded to wait outside whilst they changed into their pyjamas. They hadn't bothered putting them on earlier, but Jodie had hoped it may have helped with her insomnia. But now, the rhythmic crescendo of his nasal passage made Jodie wonder if she would have preferred him to be awake and silently perving in the corner.

The main reason Jodie couldn't sleep was Bryn. There was something haunting about the way he had looked at her. The way he had spoken to them. He had seemed like a nice enough bloke earlier on. A little bit grumpy, maybe, but nothing more sinister than that. But the manner in which he had come barrelling in, and the way he had ordered them to go back to bed, as though they were disobedient children… it just seemed as though a different side to him had begun to seep out from behind a mask. A side unleashed by whiskey and fear or frustration. Perhaps there was more to him than they had realised.

After all, he was a stranger to them all. An *intoxicated* stranger at that, who they had entrusted with their safety for the night.

It had reminded her of Phil. He had been her mother's boyfriend a decade ago. Jodie was fifteen at the time, struggling with self-doubt and teenage angst. She was the girl in the friendship group that the boys didn't notice. Not like *that*, anyway.

Phil was nice at first. He made her mum happy, which was something Jodie hadn't seen any man achieve since her dad had left. The men in between were always dickheads, short-lived romances which would never last. Phil had been different. A little bit older than the men her mum usually went for, but that was okay. The way he made her mum laugh, and the way he showed an interest in her kids – he was the best thing to happen for her in a long time.

But then he moved into the family home.

It was at that point when he started drinking, and his true colours emerged. He was horrible then. The names he would call her mum, the things he would say. It was dreadful. Even Jodie wasn't safe from his abhorrent, venomous tongue. He would mock her about her 'puppy fat' and goad her over her lack of male attention – how she never seemed to talk about boyfriends.

And then things had become physical.

Her mum didn't notice. She didn't know what was happening – or at least pretended she didn't. And Jodie couldn't tell her the things he had done. She didn't want to ruin her chance at happiness. And what if she hadn't believed her? What if she had taken his side?

Jodie shuddered. Bryn had unearthed these thoughts, but she quickly compelled herself to reseal the box inside her mind, locking the memories away as she always had. But it didn't change what was happening there and then. What she thought may happen next. Bryn was still there, angry and armed, and that was what worried her.

'Tara?' whispered Jodie. 'Are you awake?'

'Yeah,' replied Tara, also whispering. Billy continued to snore.

'Can't you sleep?'

'Not with that pig in the corner, no.'

Jodie stifled an awkward snigger, before refocusing herself. 'I've got a bad feeling about what's going to happen here.'

'What do you mean?' asked Tara.

'Did you see Bryn before? The way he spoke…'

'I think he was just pissed,' said Tara. 'And pissed off.'

'Suppose. But what if, I dunno, Gareth was telling the truth? Maybe Bryn isn't everything he seems.'

'What. Like an imposter?'

Jodie paused. 'More like a murderer.'

CHAPTER FIFTY-SEVEN

Gareth

It was utterly hopeless. Despite going off-piste, away from the paths and trails and deeper into the forest's maze, Gareth was still no closer to finding refuge. The darkness had well and truly smothered his surroundings now, and his bearings were even worse than before.

He knew that he was alone, but he could not shake the feeling that he was being watched. His paranoia had continued to grow as he shrank further within himself. He was small fry in this environment. A helpless townie out of his depth. It reminded him just how much he had hated going on school trips into more rural areas of north Wales. Being sent home with a letter to his parents, instructing them to send their child with waterproof clothing and suitable footwear, was never a welcome addition to his schoolbag. But at least those trips were safe. He'd had responsible adults to lead the way, to ensure nothing bad would happen to him. And daylight. What he wouldn't have given for some daylight at that moment.

Although, he was well aware that despite its hindering qualities preventing his already appalling navigation skills, the lack of visibility had provided him something of a cloak from others, from Bryn and his bloody shotgun. He had to use that to his advantage.

He continued walking cautiously, regularly casting his eye over his shoulder. Beyond the crunch of leaves and twigs, and the gentle swish of grass as the breeze caressed it, Gareth could not hear anything untoward. The soles of his feet were becoming sore, and his socks – now damp from the boots – had started to rub. He could feel blisters forming on his heels and toes. A tightness in his calves urged him to take a break. He was hungry. The temptation to give up was almost too great, but still he plodded on, cursing Benjamin and his damned business as he went.

CHAPTER FIFTY-EIGHT

Steffan

Steffan's head throbbed as he continued to march, struggling through the pain. His dry throat was scratching as the need for hydration took its toll on him. There had been no sign of roads, or even the slightest indication of an end to the woodland, but he remained hopeful in his pursuit. He had to.

The sound of decaying leaves disintegrating beneath the weight of his boots offered a strange reassurance. It reminded him of his power. He was stronger than this place. He would defeat it. He had overcome far worse.

It was another sound that forced him to pause in his tracks. To listen and assess. His own feet had stopped moving, but debris continued to crack and snap nearby. He wasn't alone.

Bryn.

There was not much urgency to the movement, as he continued to listen. It exhibited a cautiousness, perhaps even more so than his own. The footsteps were slower, and more prolonged. Measured and wary. But they did sound heavy. Maybe he wasn't as unfit as he had first thought. And even if he was, he had age on his side against Bryn, who must have been struggling in his own pursuit.

But he did have the gun. As much as Steffan would have backed himself to outrun a man almost twice his age, he wasn't as confident about his chances of dodging any more hot slugs which flew in his direction. And the footsteps were drawing closer, which meant the gun was too.

He needed cover. There was plenty to choose from, but nothing foolproof. There were no big rocks, conveniently positioned like they would be in the movies. With the options that *were* available, he would likely have been a sitting duck, trapping himself, waiting to be discovered and blown to pieces.

Instead, he decided to take the alternative option. Hunt the hunter. If he kept moving, he would have a much better chance of evading Bryn or – if he needed to – taking him down, ambushing him from behind. He just needed to figure out exactly where Bryn was.

Steffan listened a moment longer, to be certain of the direction the movement was coming from, before positioning himself up against a nearby tree trunk. It was narrower than he would have liked, but it would suffice. Slowly, he rolled himself around the bark until he could peer around it. He watched. He waited.

He crouched slightly in preparation – ready to go with a split second's notice, before reaching down to pick up a broken piece of wood. A snapped off limb from the tree above him, repurposed as a club. The aim was to circle around the back of Bryn, opening up a clear path to escape, but the branch held a decent weight, if Plan B came into play.

The footsteps grew louder. He was close.

It was time to move.

Steffan proceeded with caution, still crouching. His eyes were firmly set in Bryn's direction, waiting for him to come into view. But this was a mistake. While his movements were steady and controlled, holding his focus meant he didn't spot the second fallen branch lying before him. He didn't notice its bowed shape, and the offshoots still adorned with green. Not immediately, at least. Until it was too late.

The toe of his right boot knocked into the branch, sending him off balance. As he tripped, all he could hear was the angry rustling of the leaves at the other end of the branch.

'Shit!' He couldn't prevent the word from slipping out between his lips. His knee bore the brunt of the fall, as the palms of his hands slapped the soft, muddy surface.

The words echoed, as he pushed himself back up off the ground and reverted to Plan C – which was to run like hell in the opposite direction.

What Steffan didn't account for, was the other body changing course too, and he didn't see it in time. Not until Steffan's thirteen-stone, six-two body ploughed into theirs at full speed, knocking the wind out of both of them.

CHAPTER FIFTY-NINE

Gareth

'Steffan?' Gareth shuffled backwards from his sitting position. What was *he* doing here?

'Gareth,' said Steffan, a hint of confusion in his tone. 'I'm glad it's you.'

Steffan held out a hand as he walked towards Gareth, offering to help him up.

'Hold on, don't come any closer,' said Gareth. He was almost certain Bryn was the killer, but that was when Steffan was missing. With his return, Gareth began to question himself, and everything he had thought. 'What are you doing out here?'

'Same thing as you, I reckon,' replied Steffan, with a shrug. 'Trying to find a way out of this place.'

'How did you find me, though? Are you going to kill me?'

Gareth watched as Steffan frowned, squinting his eyes as though what he had just said had hurt his brain. 'I didn't find… hang on, kill you? I don't understand.'

'Well, I hate to ask this, but did you kill Benjamin? The others said it had to have been you, doing a runner like that.' He looked closely at Steffan's reaction, searching for a sign of guilt.

Steffan sighed. 'I didn't do a runner, not until a few minutes ago when Bryn fired that flipping shotgun at me. He must have been the one who killed Benjamin, all along. Him and that Ceri.'

Gareth was as conflicted as he had ever been. Was Steffan telling the truth? It matched his own thesis, but he felt a wariness, considering the risk of being alone with Steffan. There was a chance he could be wrong.

He pushed himself off the ground and back onto his feet, as he thought about what to do next. What to say.

'How do you know it was Bryn? And wait, Ceri's still here?'

'Yeah, still here, back, I don't know. But mate, they fucking locked me up, in one of their little sheds. My head's banging, they must have twatted me good and proper.'

'When you went looking for the mysterious person?'

'Aye, only it's not a mysterious person… it was obviously Ceri.'

'Why did they lock you up?'

'No idea, I didn't get chance to ask. I was too busy trying to get myself out of there.'

Gareth said nothing. It was a fair point. He felt relief that he was no longer alone – but he just hoped that what Steffan was saying was true.

'Shall we keep moving then?' asked Steffan.

Gareth nodded his head as he looked around. There were trees, trees and more trees, in every direction. He still had no idea which way they were heading. He hoped Steffan's army days had provided him with a more functional internal compass than Gareth possessed.

'You're lost as well, then,' smiled Steffan. 'No matter. It's not ideal, but with two of us, we might stand a chance.'

'Chance of what?' asked Gareth, although a pang of worry coursed through his chest as his heartbeat quickened. He knew exactly what Steffan meant.

'Getting the others out of that place,' was the confirmation he had feared.

‘We can’t go back,’ said Gareth. ‘I’m trying to get away from there. Aren’t you?’

‘Of course I am,’ said Steffan. ‘I was looking for the road, to find help. But now I’ve got you for that, and I’m not leaving the rest of the group behind.’

Gareth paused. ‘But isn’t it worth at least giving it another few minutes of looking for another way out… to get more help?’

‘Where do you suggest, mate? I’ve had no joy so far, and you obviously haven’t either.’

‘I don’t know.’

They both stood in silence. Gareth was completely out of ideas, but one thing was certain – he wanted to avoid that stupid fucking ‘wellness retreat’ for as long as he possibly could.

‘Tell you what,’ said Steffan. ‘There’s one more thing I think we could try.’

‘Go on…’

‘Follow me.’

Surprisingly, it didn’t take long before they could hear the rippling of the stream nearby. Steffan had suggested the possibility of it marking the outer boundary of the woods. If they could cross it, a road could well have been in touching distance, just on the other side.

‘Come on, let’s keep going,’ Steffan urged.

Gareth felt a surge of something building within him. Excitement? Relief? He wasn’t sure. Were they really going to get out of there? He certainly hoped so.

As quickly as he had allowed the sense of adrenaline and hopefulness to grow, his positivity waned rapidly. They were so close to the stream, so close to possibly making it out, finding help and bringing an end to the nightmare. It wasn’t the first step into the sludge that caught his attention, but after a couple more paces, the realisation set in.

The heaviness of the ground, sticking to their boots. Water pooling around them.

Their route to freedom was dashed.

'The stream's burst its banks,' said Steffan, looking down at his feet as he squelched the mud with his boots.

'So, there's no getting past it?' asked Gareth, though as he listened to the water – which had grown twice as deep – flowing at an even quicker speed than it had been earlier, he realised he already knew the answer. He didn't need Steffan to tell him.

Steffan gave him a sombre look. 'Sorry, Gaz. We're back to square one.'

CHAPTER SIXTY

Jodie

Unlike Jodie, Tara had finally managed to fall asleep. She had seemed to share some of the concern Jodie felt about Bryn, but there was an element of uncertainty in her responses, and it was clear she was not as worried by Jodie's hypothesis as she perhaps should have been, given her ability to doze afterwards.

Jodie didn't mind. In fact, she was pleased her friend couldn't see the signs. It was something of a blessing, her being more innocent and naïve when it came to the darker things in life. More than Jodie, at least. But that was good, and Jodie wished she could be as oblivious as her friend in such a situation. There would be less worry that way.

Tara wasn't stupid – if Jodie asked her to, she could create an Excel Spreadsheet at incredible speed, which could forecast profits and track past revenue, pulling in data from here, there and everywhere. And in the process, she would create and implement enough macros and formulas to make the average brain explode, just because she could. But, luckily for her, she had not been exposed to the things Jodie had, out in the real world.

It was those experiences which had caused Jodie so much worry – why she was worrying at *that moment*. As she lay there, with her eyes gazing towards the darkened ceiling, she felt light-headed and woozy, as the cogs in her mind worked overtime, trying to keep the flames of panic under control. She wanted to sleep, but she just couldn't allow herself the privilege.

It wasn't just Bryn's drunken aggression that reminded her of Phil. It was the control he had started to display. The *do as I say, or else* undertones to the way he had addressed them. The unspoken threat of consequences. It haunted her.

She thought back to the first time she had ever tried drugs. She hadn't wanted to.

He had forced her.

It had been a Friday night. Jodie had been at the local ice rink with her best friend, Lauren, and a few other mates from school. They went every week. It seemed as though every youth in the area did the same. It was allegedly an 'ice disco'; there was a DJ, lights and laughter. The place to be. Of course, there was a large proportion of kids who weren't there to skate. It was just about hanging out with your mates, getting drunk and enjoying yourself.

Out on the ice rink's car park, it was nearing the end of the night. People were waiting for their lifts home, or loitering until security – or the police – forced them to disperse. Jodie and Lauren were speaking to a boy known only to Jodie as Macca. He went to a different school, and from the things she had heard about him, he was a bit of a tearaway.

'Why don't you have some of this?' Macca had asked, unveiling what appeared to be a badly rolled joint.

Jodie was taken aback, as Lauren just gasped in wonder. 'Is that weed?'

'Yeah, you never tried it?' said Macca, smirking at her.

Jodie looked at Lauren, who stared back at her. After what appeared to be some reservation, Lauren nodded at Jodie, as if to encourage her to join in. But before Jodie had opportunity to either resist or succumb to peer pressure, she could sense his eyes burning into her. He was there.

She wasn't sure why at the time, but there was a distinct resemblance of jealousy to what Phil had done. He had ordered Jodie and Lauren to stay in the car, whilst he went for a 'chat' with Macca.

After he returned, they endured a silent car journey. Soon, they had dropped Lauren off at home, leaving just the two of them in the car. Alone.

As he pulled away from her friend's house, Phil nudged Jodie's knee. It made her flinch, and she recoiled like a scolded puppy.

'You mustn't take things from strangers,' he said. 'Do you understand?'

'I didn't take anything,' she replied.

'I know,' he said. Then he placed his hand on her thigh, squeezing it firmly before she had opportunity to move it away from him. 'You're a good girl.'

She wanted to throw up. Instead, her heart began racing as she realised he had pulled into a car park off the high street. It was dark and secluded. She looked around nervously. There was nobody else there.

'What are you doing? Why are we here?' she asked.

He smiled at her, before presenting the same sorry looking joint Macca had brandished earlier.

'He was very apologetic, that boy,' he said. 'Told me, no, promised me, he wouldn't come near you again.'

'What did you do to him?' she asked. In her mind, she could see Macca's face, bloodied and beaten – a result of Phil's evil hands. It was all her fault.

'Nothing, we just talked,' he insisted.

'Really?'

'Of course. What do you take me for? I'm not an animal. Anyway, do you have a lighter?'

She frowned. 'Why would I have a lighter?'

'I just thought…' he paused, before smiling. 'Never mind, I've got one… best not to tell your mum though, hey?'

He flicked his lighter, and Jodie watched as a flame glowed at the end of the joint, burning the paper gently. The car filled with pungent smoke, as Phil exhaled. He offered it to her, and she shook her head.

'Oh, go on,' he said. 'It's okay, I'm not a stranger.'

'I don't want to,' she said.

He sighed heavily, breathing more smoke after taking another drag. 'Okay, well, if there's something better you can think of doing, before we go home…'

She knew what he meant.

She didn't want to, but it was the lesser of two evils.

Against her better judgement, she took the joint.

The memory sent a chill down her spine. She glanced at Tara, who was still sleeping. Billy was too, and Jodie took some comfort in the fact his snoring had quietened. In fact, it had fallen into a kind of soothing rhythm – melodic and steady.

It took away from the silence which was otherwise surrounding her. A silence which was not so much peaceful, as an unnerving threat of what was yet to come.

CHAPTER SIXTY-ONE

Gareth

As Gareth and Steffan made their way back towards the light being cast from the cabins, Gareth told Steffan about the picture of Dafydd he had seen in Bryn's shed, what Bryn had told him about his nephew, and the story Francesca had told him about somebody with the same name, who had once worked for HomeHub.

'I guess they could be the same person,' mused Steffan. 'But I can see why the others weren't fully in tune with the idea. The only thing we can be sure of is who was behind tonight. Benjamin's death, locking me up… the whole shebang. The question is, why?'

Gareth pondered. 'They probably felt they had to do something about you, because you were a threat. I mean, none of us had the bollocks to go chasing shadows outside, did we? Except for you.'

'That's true,' agreed Steffan. 'Although, maybe I was just the only one *stupid* enough to do it.'

'You aren't stupid,' said Gareth. 'You managed to escape, after all.'

'Also true.'

'As for killing Benjamin, I genuinely believe the answer will lie with Dafydd.'

'Like I said, it's possible. But you said he got sacked from HomeHub, right? Caught on the take?'

Gareth nodded. 'That's what Fran said. Amongst some other stuff, but she didn't say what.'

'Seems like it'd be a bit of an overreaction for someone nicking a few bits out of the warehouse, but you don't think Benjamin offed him, do you? And he's somehow related to Bryn, and Bryn's finally got his revenge.'

Gareth did not reply. He pursed his lips and shrugged. What Steffan suggested was pretty much aligned with the explanation he had built in his mind, as unlikely as Benjamin killing someone was. But then, much of the evening had been spent deliberating on the culprit for Benjamin's own death, and there had been instances of surprising plausibility within their own group of colleagues. Without all the facts, it was impossible to know for sure.

The closer they grew to the camp, the more Gareth began to question the decision to go back. The seeds of doubt began to germinate. Bryn had already tried to shoot Steffan once, and with the dots slowly beginning to form an image of what may have happened earlier in the day, it seemed like a hopeless exercise. Probably even a death sentence of their own.

He looked at the determination in Steffan's face. His eyes fixated on what was in front of him. Committed to the cause. Gareth had no idea about life in the army, or what it was like to be a soldier, but from what he had learned about Steffan, he believed the forces had lost a real asset when he was given the boot.

One thing was for sure, there would be no chance of convincing him to leave the others, just for the two of them to save themselves.

'Do you think there's another way we can do this?' he asked.

'There doesn't seem to be many options to choose from,' replied Steffan. 'Or any, really.'

‘What about if we try and get some extra help – rather than it being just us two?’

Steffan laughed. ‘That’s kind of what I’m saying, bud. Where are we supposed to find help from? I tried to find a way out, and ended up barrelling into you instead.’

Gareth nodded. He knew Steffan was right.

‘Unless,’ continued Steffan, igniting the flame of hope inside Gareth. ‘I know it’s just as much of a risk, as it means going back to the camp anyway. But, we only know of one way out of here for sure, don’t we? Back out of the car park, hopefully climb over Billy’s car without much hassle, and then out onto the road. Maybe we could get lucky, flag someone down if they’re driving past. Get them to call the police.’

They would have to be really lucky, Gareth realised. There hadn’t been much of anything by the way of infrastructure on the road approaching the retreat. Short of coming to the retreat itself, he couldn’t imagine why anyone would include that road in their route anywhere. But he had no other ideas, and if it delayed the risk of Bryn blowing a hole through his chest, it had to be worth trying.

‘Let’s give that a go then,’ he agreed. ‘So… Ceri, did she say anything when you were tied up, in there with her?’

‘Other than “Get the fuck off me”, no, not really,’ said Steffan with a strained smile as he continued staring up ahead.

‘No, I mean, any indication of what they were doing with you, or were planning on doing with you?’

Steffan shook his head. ‘No, at least I don’t think so. It’s a bit of a blur, to be honest.’

As Gareth took his gaze away from Steffan and returned to face what was in front of them, he realised just how close they were to the camp. Naturally, their pace decreased and their shoulders hunched slightly, with both of them slowing to a watchful creep, consisting of measured and tentative steps.

'Can you see anything?' Gareth said.

Steffan lowered his stance and held a finger to his lips, before whispering 'come on' and darting to the left, behind a patch of overgrown brambles. Gareth followed, crouching down beside him.

'I think I heard someone talking,' said Steffan. 'I'm pretty sure it was Ceri. You stay down here for a second, and I'll move in closer, try to get a clearer picture of things.'

Gareth looked on as Steffan headed around the bush. His breathing became heavier as he imagined the sound of Bryn's shotgun being fired from just a few metres away, leaving Steffan in pieces, and him without a partner on the mission. He wouldn't stand a chance if he ended up going it alone. His self-doubt had awakened in Steffan's absence. It was mocking him again. He wondered whether he should follow Steffan – he didn't want to stay there, alone, just waiting to be found. He knew if he was tied up and held captive, there was no way he would make it out like Steffan did.

For a moment, he resisted his instincts, and stayed where he had been told to, but eventually his resolve was worn down by the voice inside his head. He followed the path Steffan had taken, hoping to find him safe and simply observing everything which lay ahead of them.

He skimmed along the side of the bush, as closely as possible without catching his jacket on the bristled twigs. As he rounded the same corner Steffan had taken, he felt a jolt in the pit of his stomach. He wasn't there. Gareth's eyes darted left and right, as he tried to pick out Steffan within the black cloak surrounding them. It was hopeless, he couldn't see him. He looked over towards the light of the cabins. There was no sign of Ceri. Her voice had vanished too.

Had she caught Steffan again? Surely Gareth would have heard something – shouts, a disturbance, anything.

Suddenly, Gareth felt pressure gripping onto his shoulder. A hand. It had to be. He couldn't bear to look back. He did not dare to ask who was there, for fear of the only response being blunt trauma to the back of his skull. Instead, he froze, staying as still as he possibly could, whilst attempting to regulate his breathing and fight his body's desperate urge to shiver.

'What are you doing?' asked the voice, quiet but so close he could feel their breath, warm against the skin of his neck. He turned around. 'I told you to stay where you were.' Steffan was looking at him with an expression of disbelief.

'Sorry,' replied Gareth. 'You were taking a while so I thought something may have happened.'

'Okay,' said Steffan.

'But hold on. How did you get behind me?'

'I'll show you,' said Steffan, patting Gareth on the back. 'Come on.'

Steffan took Gareth to the other side of the bramble and pointed out a small clearing at the base.

'I had to go in there,' he explained. 'I was completely exposed, just standing here. Ceri would have seen me, guaranteed.'

'But won't someone see us now?' asked Gareth.

'Nah, she buggered off – I just tunnelled my way back to be on the safe side. Plus, it's more of a shortcut.' He gestured his hand towards the row of cabins, which were less than one-hundred metres away. 'There's nobody out here. I couldn't even see Bryn anywhere. He must've gone inside or something.'

Gareth quickly scanned his surroundings and saw that Steffan was right. This may be their only chance to make their next move. 'So, let's go then.' He started walking forwards, towards the car park as Steffan grabbed his arm, pulling him back.

'Calm down, Jason Bourne,' Steffan grunted. 'You don't just run off on your own into battle, without knowing what the risks are.'

Gareth frowned. He knew full well what and *who* the risks were; a miserable old Welsh bloke with a shotgun, and some mentalist bitch who apparently had a fetish for tying up younger men. But they had gone, at least for now.

'We need to be careful,' continued Steffan. 'Someone could come back at any time, so we need a plan.'

'Okay,' said Gareth. 'What are you thinking?'

'We'll split up. That way, if one of us is spotted, the other still has a chance at getting away while they're distracted.' Steffan pointed at the space between themselves and finishing point. 'The biggest problem is that we'll run out of cover about halfway, see? Because of that, I think I should take the direct route, exposed and running like hell, but you go round a bit, where there's more cover, through the trees and come out from them straight into the car park. All right?'

Gareth's eyes narrowed. Steffan wanted him to go the *long* way? He wanted to get out of there as quickly as humanly possible, not delay it. 'I'll go the short way.'

Steffan sighed. 'You can if you want, like. But it's more exposed.'

'Like you said yourself, there's nobody around to spot me,' said Gareth. 'I want to get away, sooner the better.'

'Fine,' said Steffan. 'Let's move.'

Gareth watched Steffan as he began to move beneath the shield of the surrounding trees, whilst simultaneously preparing himself to make his own way back to the car park. One step closer to freedom and safety.

There was still no sign of anyone. Good news. *You can do this*, he thought to himself, despite something within him still trying to convince him otherwise. The side of his psyche which doubted him. It often convinced him he was worthless, and possessed a voice which sounded very much like Benjamin's. He closed his eyes, and took a final long, deep breath and counted himself down. *Three... two... one.*

He took off on queue, as though a starting pistol had fired to begin a race. The sound of his boots slapping the soft ground seemed to echo, ringing in his ears in unison with sharp panting, as his untrained lungs desperately struggled for more oxygen.

The last remaining cover dissipated at the halfway point. There was about fifty metres to go. This was it. The final stretch. He was going to make it.

Twenty metres. Ten.

He put the brakes on as he reached the gravel, not wanting to create any kind of audible disturbance, but his momentum wouldn't allow it.

Shit!

The crunch and scattering of small pieces of rock was short-lived but was not as quiet as he would have liked. He paused momentarily, listening for any indication of movement nearby, and flinched at the muted tone of voices. With a glance, he spotted his own car, parked where he had left it earlier, and darted towards it on his toes, keeping his steps as light as possible.

'What you doing out here, son?' said Bryn.

Gareth froze. The jig was up. As he had feared, Bryn was still wielding the shotgun he had fired at Steffan only a short while ago. He was waving it around, as though not in complete control.

He was drunk. In fact, looking at the unevenness of his feet as he staggered towards Gareth, it was more than that. He was well and truly inebriated.

'Bryn…' said Gareth, turning around with his hands held up as if to say *oh no, you caught me red handed.*

'I asked you a question,' grumbled Bryn. His speech was noticeably slurred.

'I'm… I'm so sorry,' said Gareth, trying to think. 'I know you said we were to go to bed, but I just needed to get something from my car.'

'Get what from your car?'

Gareth paused fractionally too long. 'Erm, medicine. To help me get to sleep – I suffer from insomnia.'

'Right,' huffed Bryn. 'But how did you get out? I locked the doors.'

Think quickly, Gareth.

'It was open, just now?'

Oh, you idiot, he thought. He could have kicked himself.

Bryn scowled. He clearly didn't believe him.

'I'm pretty sure I locked it, like,' said Bryn, but he didn't sound totally convinced.

'Oh,' shrugged Gareth. 'Weird.'

'Well, let's just get you back in there now then,' said Bryn, gesturing for Gareth to go with him.

Gareth simply could not go back into the cabin, to be locked inside and kept prisoner. Fuck the others, he was not going to join them.

'Bryn can we… can I have a quick drink? As I say, I'm a terrible sleeper, so a nightcap may do the trick.'

'A *drink*?' said Bryn, stumbling slightly as he turned around to look back at Gareth, who stood hopefully, smiling anxiously as he waited for permission to delay his entrapment.

'Yeah… please. Do you have any of your whiskey left?'

Bryn paused, as his miscalculating brain worked to compute what Gareth had asked. Then, he smiled.

'Aye, go on then. A drink.'

CHAPTER SIXTY-TWO

Steffan

Steffan could only watch in dismay, as Bryn led Gareth away from the car park and towards the camp. Why did Gareth have to be so foolish, as to insist on taking that route? It didn't matter that it was quicker if he was going to just get himself caught anyway. Steffan did feel some guilt for allowing Gareth to make the call, but they both knew the risks. It wasn't all on him.

A pang of dread gripped him as he waited for the sound of the shotgun, convinced its arrival was inevitable. But when it did not come, the sight of Bryn and Gareth walking away together left him wondering if his colleague had somehow managed to buy him some time, or if Bryn finding Gareth had just escalated whatever was supposed to happen next.

Even if it was the latter, he couldn't leave it to chance. There would be no excursion outside into the surrounding area, looking for help which may not have come. Steffan would have to do this alone.

He stepped from the dirt onto the gravel of the car park, leaving the shelter of the trees and grass, using the closest car to cloak his presence. With one more quick scan around, ensuring the coast was clear, he scurried diagonally to the car closest to the first cabin – the office he had been tied up in. Here, he whipped off Gareth's rucksack, which he had taken to allow Gareth's dash to freedom the best possible chance. *Fat lot of good that had done the lad*, he thought.

One at a time, Steffan removed every item, checking them methodically in hope that there would be something he could use. After several items of clothing, including what appeared – thankfully – to be unworn boxer shorts, Steffan had found a half empty packet of paracetamol tablets, a ball point pen and basic toiletries. It was a shame, he thought, that Gareth did not smoke. With a lighter, the can of aerosol deodorant would have combined to become a semi-useful flamethrower. Instead, he was forced to settle for the pen and a belt which he removed from a pair of jeans, before placing everything else back inside the bag and zipping it securely.

Undetected and somewhat armed, Steffan was as ready as he was ever going to be. It was time to move. He knew that he couldn't just follow the direction Bryn had taken Gareth, especially when he wasn't sure where exactly they had gone. Going around the back of the buildings was the safer option. The irony of it being the place he had earlier suffered a skull crunching blow to knock him unconscious was not lost on him. He held a hand to the sore wound beneath his buzzcut, massaging it gently. He would be ready this time.

CHAPTER SIXTY-THREE

Gareth

Bryn had grown more talkative after settling down with another drink. Not much of it was coherent, to Gareth at least, but for now he seemed calmer, and less agitated.

He had even put his bastard shotgun down. Gareth eyed it as he placed it down on the table nearest the door, before going in search of a tumbler to pour whiskey into.

'You're not saying much, lad,' said Bryn, pulling Gareth's attention back into the room. He wasn't sure where his mind had wandered to. But it was anywhere but there.

'Yeah, sorry,' he replied. 'I was miles away.'

Bryn gestured to the untouched drink sat in front of Gareth. 'Well, you best get that down you. I need to get you back to your bed.'

'Can I ask you a question?' asked Gareth.

'Aye, just the one,' said Bryn with a chuckle.

'Your nephew, Dafydd – how did he die?'

Gareth could feel the tension flooding into the room from the second Dafydd's name left his mouth. Bryn's eyes may have been glassy from the booze, but his stare lasered its way through the fog and into Gareth's own.

'Suicide,' growled Bryn.

Gareth's pulse grew quicker. He swallowed, before taking a prolonged breath.

'I'm sorry,' he said. 'But why – why did he do it?'

'I said you could ask one question,' said Bryn, shifting in his seat.

'Why are you locking us up? Why did you keep Steffan as a prisoner?'

Bryn shifted in his seat again, his hand reaching for the shotgun which he had carelessly left on the other side of the room. Gareth noticed his movement and reacted quickly, leaping out of the seat to step into his path, keeping him where he was.

'Back to bed for you,' snarled Bryn. 'Get out of my way now.'

'Why did he kill himself?' asked Gareth, pushing Bryn back, sending him crashing backwards onto his chair. 'What's the connection between him and Benjamin?'

Bryn tried once more to get up, clearly with the intention of getting past Gareth and to the gun, but Gareth pushed him again, stopping him from leaving the seat.

'There is a link, isn't there?' said Gareth, trying to sound empathetic whilst remaining stern enough that Bryn would know he wasn't messing around. 'He used to work for the same company as me, didn't he? He worked for Benjamin. What happened, Bryn?'

Bryn was shaking his head, as though he didn't want to hear a word Gareth was saying. Couldn't bear to. Suddenly, he looked broken. It was as though every dark moment that had happened in his life was being revealed, right before him. Laid out like cards on a poker table.

'Stop bloody talking, lad. Why are you asking me these things, for God's sake?' Bryn's hands covered his face. It was too much for him to bear, to relive what happened to Dafydd. 'It was all that stuck up posh boy's fault – his letter said so, you know, his note.'

'Who's fault, Benjamin's?'

'Yes, him. Dafydd said after everything he'd put him through – that's why he had to do it, why he had to… kill himself.'

Gareth had almost completed the jigsaw already. And whilst nobody else believed what he was thinking, he felt a strange sense of accomplishment. He had been right, but it was still difficult hearing Bryn confirm it. To see the pain caused by Benjamin, in the ones his victim had left behind. Because Dafydd was a victim – rightly or wrongly, whether he'd been a thief or anything else he had been sacked for. Whatever it was Benjamin had done, had pushed Dafydd to end his own life prematurely.

'Is that why you killed Benjamin?' he asked.

Bryn glared at him. 'I didn't kill him.'

'Listen, I understand,' said Gareth. 'To tell you the truth, I have never *really* admitted this to anyone, but I've been at the edge of that cliff – wanting to just give up, jump off into the darkness and never look back. Just like Dafydd. And I know these doctors and psychologists talk about chemical imbalances and what not, but Benjamin has made my life *hell* over the last couple of years.'

'That may well be true, but I promise you, I didn't kill the bastard. As much as I would have loved to, I couldn't bring myself to do it. It was never part of the plan.'

'But, if you weren't planning on doing anything to him, why would you have us here – the company of a man you purport to have pushed your nephew into killing himself?'

'We're skint!' shouted Bryn. 'We needed the money from the booking. And I didn't say we weren't going to do anything. We were going to confront him. Get him to admit what he had done. That was the plan, not killing him. Oh, God!'

'We? Wait, hold on – if you didn't kill him, who did? Ceri?'

Bryn didn't reply, instead leaving Gareth waiting for an answer as his attention was drawn towards the door.

'I think you've said enough, Bryn,' said Ceri.

Gareth turned to face the same direction as Bryn. Ceri had picked up the shotgun and was aiming it at his body.

'You've caused quite the disruption, young man,' she spat. She seemed worried, and was out of breath as she spoke. 'You and your friend. His mother must never have taught him not to hit a woman. Just wait until I find him.'

Gareth saw the grazes and cuts to her face. She looked such a mess. Steffan had well and truly given her a hiding. Then, he looked back at the shotgun, down the barrel – it was dark and deadly, and still pointed firmly in his direction.

'He's long gone,' Gareth said. 'We haven't seen him for ages.'

Ceri laughed mockingly, but her demeanour had become rabid. It was almost as though she had completely lost her mind. 'Oh, dear me. I thought Bryn would have told you how we'd captured him earlier, to stop him doing any more damage.'

'What do you mean?'

'Well, any more killings of course.'

'What do you mean? Steffan didn't kill anybody.'

'*Oh*? Well then, who did?'

Gareth looked at Bryn. He had denied it. If he was telling the truth, it had to be Ceri. His attention returned to her. To the gun she was holding. The gun she was aiming at him. He shrugged his shoulders.

'I don't know.'

'Exactly,' she said with a cold smirk. 'So yes, he's still out there somewhere. But he won't have made it far – there's…'

'Nothing else around for miles,' said Gareth, finishing Ceri's sentence with a sigh. 'I am aware.'

Ceri nodded, narrowing her eyes at him as though scrutinising his every move, every expression. ‘Exactly. So as I say, once I find him this can all be over and done with.’

‘No need,’ said Steffan. ‘I’m right behind you.’

CHAPTER SIXTY-FOUR

Steffan

Steffan took in the expressions of the three people. There was shock, horror and surprise, in no specific order. Partly in response to his sudden reappearance, undoubtedly. But he was certain the small matter of him holding his hostage around the throat was the largest factor.

He had suffered quite the shock himself, after he watched Ceri storming around to the front of the cabins as she hissed she was going to 'see where Bryn had got to', leaving a mysterious hooded accomplice to continue with the task at hand.

Once he had crept up behind the figure, jabbing the pen into their back as though it were the pointed end of a knife's blade, and instructing them to be silent – that was when he noticed it. The pile of empty fuel cans, and the smell of spilled petrol in the air. He always found it to be a familiar, somewhat pleasing smell – but not when it's been doused onto wooden structures filled with people.

In an instant, he had pushed the body into the wall and demanded an explanation. When the response telling him to 'get off' came from a female voice, he thrust the side of his body up against her, before grabbing the hood and yanking her face around in his direction.

Claire Roberts from HR. What the hell was she doing here? She struggled, her broad – almost masculine – shoulders jerking as he asked once more for an explanation.

She gave him a cold, hard stare. All she had said was 'you're all going to die, you know.'

He had kept the pen pressed firmly into her back, just next to the spine in the kidney area. There was no genuine danger of piercing the flesh, but she didn't need to know that. With the false threat of a fatal wounding and his continued grip, locking her throat in a chokehold, Steffan had instructed her to stay silent, and to make her way towards the front of the lodge.

It was at this point that he saw them. Bryn and Gareth, in the middle of the canteen, and Ceri, who was armed with Bryn's shotgun. She was pointing it straight at Gareth.

'Well, well… isn't this a lovely surprise,' sneered Ceri. 'I see you've found our dear Claire.'

'Claire?' exclaimed Gareth. 'What are you doing here?'

'Making a mess of everything,' hissed Ceri. 'We told her we had it covered, but she just couldn't help getting involved.'

'What do you mean?' asked Gareth.

'Put the gun down or I'll kill her,' said Steffan. 'You'll end up doing yourself as much damage as anyone else.'

'Please,' begged Claire. 'He's got a knife. I can feel it pressing into my back!'

Ceri laughed. 'Do you think I don't know how to use one of these things?'

'What I *think* is that you don't really want to use it,' he said, but he wasn't sure who he was trying to convince. At that moment, Ceri seemed as unhinged as he had ever seen someone – and that was no mean feat. 'But what *I know*, is how to break somebody's neck with my bare hands.'

He saw Ceri's eyes flicker at Claire, her guard slipping momentarily. A glimmer of something resembling fear, overshadowing the hateful darkness.

'The lad's right', said Bryn. 'Give it here.'

Ceri turned back to face the same direction as the gun. 'You can zip it. You've had to get two girls to do the heavy lifting tonight. You're a coward, Bryn. You always have been.'

'You daft cow,' he growled, pushing past Gareth and approaching Ceri. 'You know full well why I don't want to see this place go down.'

'We need the money, Bryn! This can help us. Think of the insurance… our problems will be solved!'

'I don't give a damn about the money, I never have,' shouted Bryn.

'Wait. Go down? Insurance?' said Gareth. 'What do you mean?'

'They're going to burn the place to the ground,' replied Steffan. 'They've doused the bastard place with fuel.'

'So that's why there was nothing for the tools before,' said Gareth, his eyes wide with realisation.

'No, this is nothing to do with me. I was telling the truth when I told you I had run out and was waiting for Ceri to pick some up,' said Bryn, 'now give me my bloody gun.' He placed a hand on the barrel and pulled whilst pushing Ceri with the other. She maintained her grip, refusing to let go. In the struggle, there was a blast from the muzzle.

Steffan ducked instinctively, and in doing so almost pulled himself and Claire to the ground. She fought against him once more, clearly seeing an opportunity to break away from his grasp, but he was too strong. He wasn't going to allow her to get away.

The room was clouded with the fog of dust. Thankfully, Steffan could make out the silhouette of Gareth's figure across the room, still standing. The shot must have gone up and into the ceiling, sending splinters from the wooden beams all over the room, and through the insulation.

As the air settled, Bryn emerged holding the shotgun. He was bright red with rage and practically foaming at the mouth. Ceri's hands were covering her face, and her entire body was shaking uncontrollably. Steffan wasn't surprised. She was no shooter, that was for sure, and she could quite easily have walked headfirst into the line of fire.

'What the hell are you thinking, you stupid bloody woman!?' screamed Bryn, inches away from Ceri's face. 'You know what? You win. I'm done. It looks like I'm going to have to fix this myself, after all. Gareth, let's go.'

Gareth looked at Steffan, as if he was willing him to do something to help, but Bryn began marshalling him towards the exit at gunpoint. Gareth said nothing. It was as though he had already admitted defeat.

'Bryn,' pleaded Steffan, as he continued to tighten his grip around Claire's throat. 'You don't have to do this.'

The old man just looked straight at him. Unblinking, possessed by his conscripted duty. 'I don't have a choice, soldier. And put that pen down. Unless you're planning on writing your flipping will.'

'What?' said Claire. 'You don't have a knife?'

Steffan grunted as he threw the pen at Bryn, before wrapping his other arm around Claire to immobilise her arms.

Bryn chuckled as he passed him, turning his back to them all as he and Gareth made their way outside. Seeing the opportunity, Steffan thrust the full weight of his being to shove Claire across the nearest table, and as he launched himself towards Bryn he heard her groan as she clattered into the row of plastic seats.

The sound alerted Bryn, and before Steffan could grab hold of him, he had turned and cracked the stock of his gun across Steffan's jaw in one movement.

'Looks like you're going to have to stay here,' yelled Bryn.

The pain was agonising, and by the time Steffan regained his senses and pushed himself back up onto his feet, Bryn was already gone. He looked around at the sound of Ceri screaming 'no!' and saw flames engulfing the door to the canteen and spreading across the wooden frame surrounding it.

They were trapped.

CHAPTER SIXTY-FIVE

Jodie

Against all the odds, Jodie must have somehow managed to doze off, because she jolted upright with a start at a sudden crashing noise. It was followed by frantic voices shouting over each other. In her disorientation, she couldn't decipher what was being said, but it sounded like an argument had broken out.

Tara grumbled and groaned, rubbing her eyes as the commotion – coupled with Jodie switching a light on – disturbed her too. 'What's going on?'

'I don't know, someone's kicking off though, I think,' replied Jodie.

'What? Who?'

'I don't know. Billy, are you awake?'

There was no response from the sleeping salesman.

'At least he's not snoring,' said Tara.

'He's probably faking it,' said Jodie. 'Oi, Billy!' She threw her pillow at him, but it had no effect. Climbing out of bed, she creeped over to him, nudging him in the back with her foot. 'Billy, stop pretending to be asleep. We need to see what's going on outside.'

Tara joined her standing over Billy's unmoved body. She tapped Jodie on the arm and smirked, before sucking on her little finger and sticking it into Billy's ear.

'Wet willy…' she said. 'Time to get up, little Billy.'

His arms flailed in retaliation to the saliva assault. 'Okay, okay, I'm up!'

'You're such a wimp, Billy,' scolded Jodie.

'Behave, I was sleeping!'

'Of course you were,' said Jodie, rolling her eyes. 'Come on, let's go.'

They opened the door – Billy being forced to go first, to see Bryn poking a retreating Gareth with his shotgun.

'What the fuck are you doing?' yelled Gareth. 'You're going to kill us all, you demented alcoholic prick!'

'Keep moving,' barked Bryn, continuing to nudge the gun into Gareth's chest.

'What's going on?' asked Tara.

Gareth faced them, there was a look in his eyes which Jodie hadn't seen from him before. Fear? Rage? She couldn't tell. This was new – beyond his default sullenness, Gareth rarely gave much away. He was a quiet, miserable person. Of course, there had been flashing glimmers of personality during that weekend, but even then, he had been relatively closed off.

'Oh, not much,' he shouted. 'Just Captain Caveman discovering fire – and deciding we're all going to fucking die!'

Jodie looked out of the window. She saw it. The shimmering orange, the flames engulfing the kitchen cabin just a few metres away. What was happening?

'Shut up, lad,' bellowed Bryn. 'The rest of you – in here, now!'

Francesca and Matthew had emerged from the end room, seemingly to investigate the same thing as Jodie, Tara and Billy. As Bryn herded everyone inside their bedroom, hysteria and confusion ensued amongst them all.

Jodie looked on as the words 'fire', 'die' and 'psychopath' flew around, bouncing off the walls like squash balls. A realisation struck her with full force; she didn't want to die.

'Quiet!' she screamed. Everyone, even Bryn, stopped immediately and all eyes were on her. She was breathing heavily. She could feel her heart thumping against her chest. 'Bryn… in the nicest possible way, what the actual fuck is going on – why are there cabins on fucking fire outside?'

'All you need to know,' he slurred, 'is that this was never meant to happen. He was supposed to pay. But not like this.' He began sobbing.

'Who was supposed to pay?' asked Jodie, exasperated. 'What are you talking about?'

'Benjamin,' said Gareth. 'And what now, Bryn? You're just going to sit in here and burn with us, are you?'

'A captain must go down with his ship,' declared Bryn emotionally. 'And if this ship is going to go down, I… I shall go down with her.'

'I've had enough of this bollocks,' said Billy, cutting him off. 'Bryn, are you going to let us out of this shithole or what?' he stood up and walked towards the door where Bryn was leaning against it, still choked up. 'Come on fella, out the way. Let us out.'

'You're staying here, all of you!' shouted Bryn, lashing out and pushing Billy backwards, sending him stumbling to the floor. Bryn proceeded to shoot a hole in the wall, as a warning to them all. It was a miracle nobody was hit, but it didn't prevent the screams.

In the melee, Jodie braved looking up from where she had thrown herself to the ground, as Gareth landed a right-hook on Bryn's eye socket. Beside her, Billy lay on top of Tara. He had tried to save Jodie's best friend. Perhaps he wasn't quite as much of a coward as she had thought. Although, from the confusion in his eyes, Billy may have been just as surprised by his heroics as she was.

As Gareth and Bryn wrestled, Matthew yelled at Francesca. Jodie turned to see him pushing her out of the window which had been obliterated by the shotgun blast. They were escaping. She prayed that she would escape too. She just needed to make it across the room.

The hope Jodie felt was soon overshadowed by the overwhelming smell of smoke, billowing in through the open window. Bryn was still occupied by Gareth, and Jodie held her breath as she watched them rolling around, blocking the doorway.

'Come on Jode,' shouted Tara. 'We need to get out now, before this whole place goes up!'

Jodie looked back at Tara, as her friend followed Billy to the window. She was right. The fire was coming. It was inevitable. And it was imminent.

But she couldn't. Not yet. She wasn't going to leave Benjamin to burn. She had vowed never to do that to anyone again, no matter what they had done. After all, there was still a part of her conscience that quietly consumed her, sustained in the back of her mind by the weight of her guilt.

She had ignored Phil's cry for help as he lay, trapped and helpless in the wreckage of the crash, and walked away as he awaited his fate. She would not, *could not*, do that again.

CHAPTER SIXTY-SIX

Steffan

After the latest blow to his head, Steffan felt groggier than ever. Whilst trying to absorb the situation before him, he struggled to stay on his feet and had to shift his weight, gripping onto a nearby chair for support. Ceri was flapping in panic at the sight of the fire, as it began to take hold of the outer frame of the building. Claire was just standing and watching it, as though her feet were nailed to the floor.

'Fire extinguishers!' Ceri shouted, rushing towards the kitchen.

Steffan rubbed his throbbing head. It would be futile to attempt killing the flames with a couple of domestic extinguishers at the rate they were spreading. They needed a way out.

'Claire, is there another door?' he shouted.

She looked at him with a scowl. 'How am I supposed to know?'

He wanted to throttle her. But there was no time. The smoke had begun to build within as the walls began burning through to the inside. He ran to the kitchen to find Ceri struggling with the weight of the red steel tank.

'Help me with it then,' she said, gesturing it towards him.

'Wet tea towels,' he shouted, pointing towards the sink.

After looking at him in confusion for a moment, she nodded her understanding and rushed over to douse some makeshift facemasks with tap water, as he took the extinguisher and headed for the doors.

'Steffan?' cried Claire, choking on her words.

He looked over in her direction and watched in horror as the ceiling above her glowed orange, the wooden beams smouldering as the blaze continued its journey of destruction.

'Shit!'

Steffan lifted the hose and pointed the nozzle towards the foot of the door, and began squeezing the stiff lever with desperate urgency. Ceri returned with a towel pressed to her mouth and nose, and handed one in turn to Claire and Steffan.

His eyes were streaming, as the smoke seeped into every blink. He was forced to wedge the towel between his face and shoulder, as he continued to spray foam all over the door. The struggling framework began creaking as the heat intensified. They were running out of time.

'This is hopeless… we can't wait any longer!' screamed Claire, rushing towards the exit and into the blanket of white, crashing through what was left of the door.

Ceri followed her, before Steffan – reaching the end of the tank's capacity – dropped the extinguisher and sprinted out and into the night air. He choked on the fresh air as it filled his lungs, his body battling the toxic cocktail of gases it had been subjected to. Through the clouds and confusion, he looked around; he had seen similar situations, lived through them, but none of this seemed real in the moment. The fire was spreading quickly, travelling towards the bedrooms which held the rest of his colleagues.

'Oh my god, Bryn's still in there,' cried Ceri.

'We need to get them out, now,' yelled Steffan. His gaze passed over the camp, as he tried to calculate a plan. Finally, it found the office cabin, which remained unscathed by the fire's touch. 'Ceri, those radios you and Bryn were using – where are they now? We need to call for help.'

She gave him a look of confusion, before shaking her head. 'They're just crappy cheap things; they won't be any use. Our proper two-ways are knackered.'

'Where are they now, in your office?'

'I don't know. Sorry.'

'Bullshit,' he shouted as he approached her, his face almost touching hers as he gritted his teeth and snarled. 'We need to see if they'll work. We need to do something. People are going to die... *Bryn* is going to die!'

'I'm sorry,' she said. 'I can't go to prison.'

'It's too late for that, and it's not what's important right now.' He remained just inches away from her, but still he screamed, pleading with her. 'Tell me where they fucking are!'

Her eyes widened in alarm. 'Okay! Yes, they're probably in the office in one of the drawers – but seriously, they're not working properly. It's no use.'

Steffan growled in frustration, before realisation struck him. 'Where's Claire?'

Ceri looked around them. 'She was here a minute ago. Claire! Claire, where are you!?'

'Bollocks,' he snapped, turning to run towards the office, before calling back. 'Go, now, try and reason with Bryn. Try and help the others. I'm going to get those radios.'

CHAPTER SIXTY-SEVEN

Gareth

Gareth wheezed and gurgled as Bryn's grip tightened around his throat. For an older bloke, he was strong. He really could handle himself. Though Gareth had never seen himself as much of a fighter. It was surprising just how good it had felt, as his knuckles connected with Bryn's face.

The strained sensation of his eyes bulging out of their sockets increased his panicked attempts to breathe. Wrestling his right arm free from beneath Bryn's knee, he spread his fingers, wrapping them across Bryn's face, gouging at his eyes with his middle and third fingers as though his head was a bowling ball.

But still, Bryn would not relent. As the old man squeezed tighter again, his thumbs adding more pressure to the larynx, Gareth knew it was now or never. Bryn screamed as his eyeballs were scratched at and pushed further into his head. Gareth snapped Bryn's neck back, pushing himself free as the ranger's grip lost its strength, before delivering a final jab to his falling enemy.

He gratefully sucked in as much air as he could, as Bryn writhed around with his hands to his face. Jodie charged over to the door, trying to force it open.

'Move, you fucking arsehole!' she screamed at Bryn, before picking up the shotgun from the ground nearby.

'Why haven't you gone out of the window?' asked Gareth, wincing as he pushed himself back to his feet. The adrenaline within him was dwindling, and his hands stung almost as much as his neck.

'We need to get Benjamin,' she said. She had a possessed look in her eyes. She appeared as mad as Gareth had ever seen anyone.

'We need to get out of here,' he said, raising his hands defensively. The way she was waving the shotgun around, there was no telling what she was capable of.

Pointing it at his chest, she took a step closer. 'You are going to help me, or I will use this thing and blow you to fucking pieces, have you got that!?'

Gareth gulped past the lump in his throat. Jodie was truly terrifying. He glanced down at the gun, which was still aimed at him, before looking back into Jodie's wide, unblinking eyes.

'Er, Bryn, mate. Any chance of you getting up and out the way?' he crouched down, patting Bryn, without taking his eyes off Jodie's for even a split second.

'You're going nowhere,' groaned Bryn, feebly reaching for Gareth. Jodie shoved the butt of Bryn's gun into the back of his head, knocking him back onto the ground. She pointed the gun back in Gareth's direction, and he instinctively grabbed Bryn by the ankles, dragging him away from the doorway.

'This is nuts,' he shouted as she opened the door.

'Shut up, let's go,' she screamed back.

'The fire could hit us any second!'

'So, hurry up, if you don't want to burn!'

CHAPTER SIXTY-EIGHT

Steffan

Despite the darkness within the office, the open doorway offered just enough visibility for Steffan to see inside. He looked for a light switch and flicked it on. The safe stood open on the opposite wall. Beside it stood a desk, with a storage cabinet positioned just behind it. The drawers were all pulled out, barely hanging on by their runners. He marched over to the unit and began rifling through each drawer, pulling things out and discarding them onto the floor behind him – paperwork, random charger cables and plugs, stationary… there was plenty of junk, but no sign of any two-way radios.

They were gone.

'Claire?' he called with a tone of desperation as he looked around. There was no sign of her. 'Where the hell are you?'

There was no reply. Instead, the door closed behind him with a sudden bang. He turned to face it as he heard the metallic click of the lock being turned.

'You stupid bitch!'

He hurried over to the door, before lifting his right foot and planting it sole-first against the wooden panel with the force of his rage. The door clattered open, breaking away from its hinges and tumbling across the gravel.

Looking from left to right, there was no sign of her, but the sound of footsteps slapping against the ground led him to the car park, where Claire was sprinting away.

'Get back here, Claire!' he yelled, beginning to take off after her, but it was pointless. She had soon climbed over the fallen tree and, save for a momentary glance back towards him, carried on until she vanished into the darkness.

Claire was gone, and with her, the only hope they had of calling for help. Steffan cursed her and turned back. It was down to him now.

The blackness of the night sky and smoke combined to create a vision of hell, with just the flickering light from the powerful inferno to illuminate his surroundings.

Up ahead, he could see Ceri was no longer alone in her watchful dismay. Steffan looked on in confusion, wondering if the trauma was causing him to hallucinate, as he saw Francesca pacing back and forth without any sign of the crippling twisted ankle she had suffered earlier in the day. Gareth hadn't mentioned anything about her making a miraculous recovery.

Somebody – Tara, he thought – had buried herself into Billy's embrace. A bizarre sight, indeed.

Matthew was the first member of the group to spot Steffan, and he began calling his name and pointing to alert the others.

'Did she have the radios?' asked Ceri as she took her eyes away from the sleeping cabin for a moment.

'Must have. Because she's gone, and they weren't there. Why the fuck would she take them?'

'Oh god, I'm guessing the money has gone, too,' she groaned.

'What, from the safe?' he asked.

'Hold on,' interrupted Francesca, pausing in her step. 'Who are we talking about? Who's *she*?'

'Claire,' said Steffan.

'Claire, as in, HR Claire? What was she doing here, why hasn't she got help? What the *actual* flip is going on?'

'Long story,' he said, his attention drawn back towards the proceedings before them. 'Is everyone else still in there?'

'Yes!' panicked Ceri. 'Bryn, he's still not come out!'

There was a deafening silence from the others, as they avoided making eye contact with him. He forced himself to bite his tongue at their cowardice.

'Well, we can't just stand around here doing nothing. I'm going in.'

He took a deep breath, gulping as much of the acrid scented air as he could take, before once again running blindly into the flaming danger ahead.

CHAPTER SIXTY-NINE

Jodie

'Come on, this is wasting too much time. We need to get out of here!'

Gareth's whinging was really getting on her last nerve. If she had the strength to carry Benjamin's body herself, she would have gladly whacked him over the head and left him and his miserable, pitiful face to burn.

'Just put some bloody effort in, Gareth, for once in your life!'

He gave her a cold, sullen glance, but he did as he was told. After placing a hand on each of Benjamin's ankles once more, he looked at her expectantly, awaiting her cue.

Whilst gripping at the other end, her hands wedged under Benjamin's armpits, she nodded in time to her count of 'one, two, three', before they both heaved him up and off the bed.

'Right, you go backwards,' she yelled, flicking her head upwards to direct Gareth back out of the door. She just hoped Bryn had seen sense and finally opened the main door out of the cabin, so that they didn't have to try and lift the deadweight of Benjamin through a shattered window.

Slowly, they made their way back to the room they had left Bryn in. The heat was intensifying by the second, and she squinted in frustration at the stinging in her eyes as sweat began to seep into them.

Bryn was no longer lying on the floor, as she looked through the building smoke, wisping hauntingly through the air. He was sat up with his back supported against a bed, motionless, staring blankly into the void, not even their return broke his wide-eyed stupor.

'Unlock the door and let us out of here, now!' she screamed.

He made no reply. He did not even flinch.

'Bryn,' groaned Gareth.

'No can do, I'm afraid,' said Bryn with a slur.

'Why are you doing this?' pleaded Jodie. 'You need to let us out of here now. Look around you!'

He returned to ignoring them, replying only with radio silence. Jodie looked on in horror as the wall beyond began to glow, smouldering from the outside. The smoke was only growing thicker, and it was becoming increasingly difficult to breathe. Benjamin's body jerked from the motion as Gareth stumbled slightly. He seemed to be struggling with the weight. Jodie was too.

'We'll have to go for the window, we're running out of time,' she called to Gareth, to which he nodded obediently, looking over his shoulder in its direction, before continuing backwards towards their exit.

CHAPTER SEVENTY

Steffan

After putting his boot through its second door of the night, Steffan lifted the neck of his sweater over his nose and mouth as he rushed into the cabin.

He opened the door to the first bedroom, and a translucent ball of heat almost knocked him backwards. The fire had taken hold in there, but as far as he could see there was nobody inside, and nobody calling for help. He closed the door again and moved along, desperately hoping that he found them quickly.

Hearing shouts, he finally discovered Jodie and Gareth, along with Bryn.

'Come on, you need to get out!' he shouted, watching in confusion as Gareth and Jodie attempted to force Benjamin's body through a window.

'How did you get in?' Jodie asked.

'The door's open. Come on!'

Gareth didn't move. As Steffan grew closer he could see just how laboured his breathing was. He was covered with bloodied cuts and scrapes across his face.

'Gareth, are you with us?' Steffan yelled, waving a hand across his friend's face. He sighed with relief as Gareth nodded, but the relief was short lived, as Gareth began choking violently before collapsing onto his knees.

Shit.

‘Gareth, get up, you need to help carry Benjamin!’ screamed Jodie, slapping him repeatedly.

‘Fucking stop,’ said Steffan, swatting her hand away. ‘He can barely fucking breathe.’

In one movement, Steffan threw Gareth over his shoulder, before wrapping Benjamin’s legs in his free arm. ‘Let’s go! Bryn, you need to move now!’

There was no reply.

‘Leave him, he said he wants to stay!’ wheezed Jodie.

He took one final look at Bryn who continued just sitting there, staring ahead blankly, and with a shake of his head Steffan continued trudging as purposefully as he could, beneath the burdensome weight of two men.

CHAPTER SEVENTY-ONE

Gareth

His head was spinning. He could see flickering light in a mesmerising blur, but he could not enjoy the sight as it hypnotised him. He could not breathe, despite his desperate attempts to find air. Instead, he was choking on the poison surrounding him. With every laboured breath he unwillingly exposed himself to more damage. It was so hot. The dryness of the air was cloaking his sweat ridden body, as though he were basted poultry, roasting in an oven.

The urge to succumb to his fate grew. *Just let go*, his conscience told him. The offer of rest was seductive. He wanted to sleep forever. Perhaps then would be able to breathe again.

CHAPTER SEVENTY-TWO

Jodie

Benjamin became heavier the longer Jodie held onto him. She was grateful Steffan arrived when he had. There was absolutely no way she could have managed to manoeuvre the body out of the window, after Gareth had decided to give up. She would not have left Benjamin, but she also knew it would have been incredibly difficult for her to leave Gareth behind, too, when it came to it. Despite how irritating she found him.

He was half the man of Steffan. She could see that in the way the ex-soldier had the other end of Benjamin's body in one arm, and Gareth's added weight over his shoulder on the other.

The coolness outside struck her immediately, and despite the overspill of smoke surrounding the area, somehow the fresh air began to dilute the smog in her lungs with every breath. It was over. They were out.

'Shit, is that Gareth?' said a worried voice as Steffan lowered himself down onto one knee and removed Gareth from over his shoulder with some difficulty.

'Where is he? Where's Bryn?' Ceri screeched at them. Jodie looked over her shoulder to see Ceri and her HomeHub colleagues watching on in concern.

'He's still inside,' said Jodie, a tight rasp to her voice. 'He said he wasn't coming out.'

‘What do you mean?’ gasped Ceri. There was genuine horror in her eyes. Horror and confusion. She started running towards the building, screaming Bryn’s name repeatedly. As Steffan released Benjamin’s legs, he tried to intercept Ceri, but she brushed past his outstretched hand and disappeared into the smoke.

‘Oh my god, what is she doing?’ exclaimed Francesca, the accompanying flapping of hands as dramatic as ever. Ordinarily, it would have irked Jodie, but she didn’t have the energy for annoyance or conflict. In the short space of a few hours, they had all seen and suffered enough to last a lifetime.

After gently placing Benjamin on the ground close to Gareth, she sat on the ground next to them and looked on as Steffan went after Ceri, pleading with her to stop, but with no success. It was a bizarre sight, watching people willingly rush towards a burning structure, but Jodie realised it was no different to her refusing to leave it without Benjamin. People ignore the chaos surrounding them, when their sole focus is a loved one.

‘Are you okay, Jode?’ asked Tara, sitting down beside her as Matthew and Billy attended to Gareth.

Jodie looked at her but said nothing. She couldn’t muster even a simple answer. Instead, she collapsed into her friend’s embrace and sobbed. Her energy, her capacity for anything else to go wrong was spent.

She felt Tara’s fingertips as they stroked her back gently, and in that moment, she felt as though maybe the nightmare was over. She just wanted to go home.

The group watched the building, encapsulated by the fire’s glow as if it were fresh charcoal on a barbecue, and for what felt like an eternity nothing happened. Nobody came out. Jodie began to wonder if it was too late for Steffan, Ceri and Bryn.

As though answering their silent urges for what came next, there was an explosion from within the cabin, which took Jodie completely by surprise.

'Oh my god!' squealed Francesca.

'What was that?' asked Billy.

Before anybody could suggest the cause of the latest big boom, the sound of sirens wailed in the distance. Jodie wondered if it was her imagination; after all, nobody had phone signal, so how could anyone have called for help?

'Claire,' mumbled Gareth, who was finally coming back around.

'What's that mate?' asked Matthew.

'Claire,' he repeated, before hacking from his chest. 'She must've called 999.'

If he was right, it was just another confusing incident in a weekend filled with them, but perhaps Claire had made the call. Perhaps she was the hero. Although, it didn't explain why the hell she had been there in the first place, and why she wasn't there now.

Jodie had so many questions.

The sirens grew louder, and the blue lights of police cars, fire engines and ambulances began bouncing off the leaves in time with the tune. Matthew and Francesca rushed off towards the car park, in order to meet the arrival, as somebody emerged from the cabin doorway.

Steffan.

He stumbled out of the door and onto the grass just as the remaining shell of the cabin began collapsing in on itself.

Matthew and Francesca ran back towards the others, returning with a white-helmeted firefighter just as Steffan, too, made it over to the group.

'It's going to take us a while to get everything past the fallen tree, to tackle the fire,' said the firefighter. 'Is anybody still inside?'

Everyone looked to Steffan, who shook his head. ‘No survivors, sir.’

CHAPTER SEVENTY-THREE

Gareth

Two Weeks Later

As Gareth sat in the driving seat of his Ford Focus, he allowed himself a sigh of relief. After spending the last couple of weeks resting, he had felt incapacitated at first, before his recovering consciousness smothered him with a sense of being lost and in search of purpose. He had no idea what was going to happen next, or what he was supposed to do. But now, the time to return to work had arrived.

He wasn't sure who he would speak to first, when he made it to the office. Theo, probably. That would be easiest. It was Theo who he had sent updates to during his time away. And Claire's, of course; without the HR manager there to keep tabs on him, it had been left to his line manager.

He had seen it plastered on news outlets and social media that the police had declared Claire as a person of interest, in relation to both the fire and the deaths of Benjamin, Bryn and Ceri. The cause of Benjamin's death had been confirmed as a stab wound to the back, with blunt force trauma to his head being contributory, but not fatal. In addition, the fire was quickly confirmed to have been an act of arson.

There were still so many unanswered questions about why she turned up at the retreat, and now that she was missing, it made it all seem even more suspicious.

He knew beyond Claire going AWOL, things would be different at HomeHub – in some ways, at least. Even a corporate Death Star like that place couldn't have emerged from the loss of Benjamin completely unscathed. The people who had been on the trip would have changed – something within him certainly had, and he found it impossible to believe any one of the surviving members of the group could have stayed exactly the same. They had all been through too much. But they *had* survived, and that was what they had to focus on.

Despite that, from what he had heard via Steffan's WhatsApp updates, it had quickly returned to a state of business as usual – or at least 'as usual' as it could have, in the circumstances. After a day of *company enforced* mourning for their late Managing Director, Benjamin's mother had swiftly stepped in to ensure the company continued to operate without any further interruption. Profit over everything – there were indeed some things that would *never* change. Gareth couldn't deny that it was what his old boss would have wanted.

That was why he was sure he had made the right decision.

The primary source of the place's toxicity had been taken away when Benjamin was murdered, but Gareth could not leave his future to chance. He could not simply 'wait and see' if things became better for him there. Because, what if they weren't? It had somehow taken the weekend from hell to realise it, but he had long been sleepwalking further and further into a dark place. Had it not been for the last fortnight, where he was forced to take a step back and contemplate *everything*, he possibly would not have found a way back out.

The tunnel was still shrouded in blackness, but he could see the faint light of freedom ahead of him. It would take some time to get there, and there would undoubtedly be some new obstacles and challenges to overcome on the journey. But he had to try.

The familiarity of the rush hour traffic no longer riled him, nor did he feel his heart begin to flutter and sweat begin to leak because of anxiety-fuelled flushes. Of course, he was nervous about returning there, even if it would be a quick in and out. But it was necessary – he needed to confront the place, to begin his healing process.

He coasted along the dual carriageway, not rushing. He would get there when he got there, and that was okay. After waking from a brief coma – two days of battling carbon monoxide poisoning – and being informed by the doctors he was lucky to have survived, he had been subjected to a fortnight of bedrest by them and his mother. During which, he spent a lot of time thinking and reflecting on what had happened, what it all meant, and what would happen next.

At long last, he had mustered the courage to speak to his loved ones, to tell them how he was feeling. How he had been feeling for as long as he could remember. To his surprise, they offered nothing but support. A visit to the GP confirmed that he was suffering from depression and anxiety. They were concerned about the likelihood of PTSD following the horrors he had encountered at the retreat, but in the meantime, he was provided with medication. A referral to receive therapy would be a long wait, he was advised, but being on the list was a start.

Finally, he was issued with a sick note, to follow the expiry of the one he had been given by the hospital. Of course, it relieved the pressure going back to work would have brought, but it was only delaying the inevitable. That was why he decided to close the door for good.

Whilst he was still unsure where the roads ahead would lead, he understood then, that the only way for him to reach his destination was to get himself better, and by asking for help in doing so, he would not continue to struggle alone, suppressing everything within himself.

The letter of resignation which sat beside him on the passenger seat was an ending, of course, but it was also the key to a new beginning.

CHAPTER SEVENTY-FOUR

Jodie

Two Months Later

The grave had been tired and neglected when she had arrived. The headstone was weathered, with signs of mud splash and old grass clippings from previous strimming by the cemetery's maintenance team. Dead flowers sat wilted and forgotten.

It stood to reason, Jodie thought. He had no family, or at least not one which cared about him. Her mother had never known the darkness behind Phil's façade. The darkness which had led him to their North Wales town in the first place, disowned by his family in Derbyshire, the allegations which he left in his wake as he started a new life. The new life which had started so brightly, before his darkness had seeped out through the cracks, resulting in his lonely demise.

* * *

On that night, in 2014, Phil had arrived at the White Horse pub instead of Jodie's mother. It had been another exhausting shift, with Jodie on her feet all night, serving punters and collecting dirty glasses, all for a crappy cash-in-hand pay packet. Even the tips did little to make it any more worthwhile.

Had it not been the middle of winter, she would have walked home instead of getting in the car with him. But, through spending so much time at school and working, he hadn't bothered her much, recently, so she collapsed into the passenger seat, taking the weight off her aching feet.

'Good evening, Jodie darling,' he said, stinking of beer and cigarettes.

'Where's mum?' she asked.

'At home,' he replied. 'Why, are you not happy to see me?'

'Don't fucking start,' she said, turning her body to face the opposite direction.

He laughed but said nothing as he drove out of the pub car park and onto the A-road towards home. Once The White Horse was well and truly behind them, he started to put his foot down. Jodie risked a look over her shoulder at him. He looked enraged. Ready to blow, like a grenade with its pin pulled out.

'You know what, Jodie,' he said, without taking his eyes off the road. 'I'm getting sick and tired of your mother.'

Jodie rolled her eyes. Did he really expect empathetic relationship advice from her? 'Oh yeah? What's she done now?'

'The usual,' he growled. 'Always picking at everything. "Why haven't you done this, Phil?", "Can you fix that, Phil?", "Have you even put fucking milk in this brew, Phil?", I've had it up to here!'

'Oh no, what a bitch,' replied Jodie sardonically.

'Exactly,' he exclaimed. 'Fucking bitch. Not like you,' he said as he reached his left hand from the gearstick over to graze her thigh. 'You've always been a good girl, haven't you?'

Jodie jerked her leg away. That wasn't happening again. She had wondered what her mum would say if she'd told her about everything her precious 'fiancée' had done to her over the past couple of years. But she had never dared tell her. What if she didn't believe her? What if she'd sided with him, and kicked her own daughter out onto the streets? That's what he'd said would happen.

It had always been easier to keep it to herself. But maybe she had been wrong.

'Oh, what's wrong with you, now?' he snarled. 'I thought we'd got past all of that nonsense.'

'There he is,' she said. 'The real Phil.'

'Shut it, you little slag, or I'll…'

'You'll do what? Rape me again? Call it harmless fun – nonsense? It's not nonsense, Phil. But you, you are a vile, pathetic little man.'

She had never used that word to describe what he had done before. *Rape*. But that was what it was. She had never wanted it, *any* of it, not really.

'You stop talking right now,' he yelled. The car accelerated more. Streetlights whizzed by in a blur. Jodie's stomach began to twist and tighten.

'Slow down, Phil,' she said, trying her best to remain firm and sound calm. He said nothing. The car sped past its turning and continued on the same road. He wasn't taking her home. 'Phil, stop now. Let me out!'

He ignored her still. She bunched her hands into fists and began ploughing them into his arm, but he was unmoved as his focus remained transfixed on the road. It was as though he had been possessed. As though he couldn't hear her. She screamed at him as she struck him, one futile blow after another, but he didn't flinch. He didn't slow down. He was going to kill them both, and there was nothing she could do to stop him.

Jodie opened her eyes again. The sheer terror she'd felt when bracing for the collision had forced them shut. What had just happened felt surreal. It was as though time had stopped, as the car began veering off the road and towards the fence and hedge and whatever else had been behind it. She realised the screams she had heard were her own. Now, there was silence.

She felt no pain as she blinked rapidly, scanning the car in a blur. Her hands fumbled at the seatbelt buckle as she tried to unclip it. The car was upright, which must have been a miracle. When she squeezed her eyes shut, bracing for the impact, she had been certain the car had been rolling, the ground tilting beneath her.

As she opened the door, she felt a hand taking hold of her arm.

'Jodie,' wheezed Phil. 'Help me, I'm stuck.'

She looked at him sitting there. His body was stiff. The door on his side of the car had caved inwards, trapping his leg. She didn't respond to him.

Outside she could smell fuel. There was smoke billowing out through the sides of the bonnet.

'Jodie, you fucking bitch,' he croaked after her, struggling to project his voice. 'Help me get out of here!'

She pulled her phone out of her pocket. Incredibly, the screen illuminated. It was cracked, but that had happened a while ago. There had been no further damage in the crash. She stared down with her thumb resting on the '9' key. She should call for help.

She looked up, back into the car where he sat – trapped, alone and vulnerable. The love of her mother's life, supposedly. The man who had made her feel so worthless, so disgusting, whilst he did those things to her.

Despite the smoke and fumes, she climbed back into the car and began digging around for her handbag which had that evening's wages and tips inside.

'What are you doing? You need to get help,' pleaded Phil.

Picking up the handbag, she dropped her phone into the back of the car, leaving it there. After one last look at him, long enough to take in the fear in his eyes, she climbed out of the car, and scurried away, allowing herself to distance herself before the car went up in in flames, the blaze illuminating the night sky in an instant.

A couple of passers-by had rushed to help Jodie, as she had moved away from the fire. She pretended to cry, telling them that Phil had been stuck inside and there had been nothing she could have done. All three emergency services attended, and after a quick once-over from the paramedics, to whom Jodie insisted she was fine, the police had taken her home.

Her mum had been devastated to discover what had happened to Phil that night. Eventually, Jodie had told her what kind of man he was, and to her relief, her mum believed everything. They were as close as they had ever been, for a while afterwards, until her mum found a new love, Tim. Jodie was happy for her, and whilst he did end up whisking her mum away to start a new life on the other side of the country, she knew this time, her mum had chosen a decent guy.

* * *

Phil didn't deserve her attention. Or even her thoughts. But after her sheer determination had ensured Benjamin's family would have a body to bury, an opportunity to say goodbye, she felt it was the least she could do. After all, she was the one who had walked away, leaving him to die alone on that fateful night.

Standing back, she looked with a sense of pride at her handiwork. A quick brush and a new bouquet – artificial, for longevity and a lack of required maintenance – of blue and white flowers, in recognition of his beloved Chesterfield Football Club, and Phil's final resting place showed some renewed dignity at last. It was ironic, really, given that

Jodie's own dignity was the very thing he had tried so hard to take away from her.

'You won't see me again,' she said. 'But I just wanted you to know, you didn't break me. Happy Birthday.'

Life had felt different without Benjamin. She went back to work as soon as it had reopened, despite being advised to rest. The doctors had completed all kinds of tests after the fire, and whilst she had suffered from a slight cough for a few days, there was no serious damage. Physically, at least.

At first, she had missed Benjamin. It seemed as though everyone did, but she couldn't help but feel her grief held more weight than theirs. Even more than Fran's, who had been far kinder to Jodie than she had ever been before. Jodie couldn't tell how much of that was down to the hormones; shortly after that fateful weekend, Fran had discovered she was three weeks pregnant. The identity of the father was unclear, but by all accounts, Matthew intended to stand by her whether it was biologically his or not.

Jodie wasn't sure if she would be motivated enough to keep up with the day to day of her job, knowing that she would never again hear his voice as he swaggered into the office. His absence had left a hole in the company as large as the one in her heart.

It was also tough to accept the way Claire had duped them all. Over the last few weeks, as more details had started to materialise about her real identity, her links to Bryn and Ceri – along with Dafydd, a former HomeHub employee – had come to light. It appeared she had been seeking revenge on the company and Benjamin from the very start of her time there.

But as the weeks passed, she began to adapt to the new normal. She and Tara had grown even closer, and they were even talking about the possibility of renting a home together. She felt immense pride at how their shared experience had awoken a new level of maturity in her friend, but Jodie would frequently check in on her and ask if she was okay. She did not want the effects of the trauma to tarnish Tara's innocence. But only time would tell if it had. She wasn't overly keen on the blossoming romance between her and Billy, though given he had saved her life, Jodie felt she owed him a chance at making Tara happy. She would be there to pull out the ice cream and tissues when it petered out.

As for her own love life, it didn't seem possible to get over Benjamin. He had been, as far as she was concerned, her soulmate. The instant connection she had felt when first casting her gaze over him, the flutters within her belly when he spoke to her. They were things that simply could not be replicated within a lifetime. But when the gorgeous new Managing Director, Jonathan Harrod, had been introduced to the Accounts Department last Monday, she was forced to question whether some people were lucky enough to be given a second chance at finding 'the one'; whether somehow, the Universe could decide to flick a *reset* switch for those people who deserved it.

People like *her*.

CHAPTER SEVENTY-FIVE

Steffan

Six Months Later

'Come on in, Steffan,' said Theo, inviting him into one of the warehouse offices.

Performance appraisals had soon come around, and Theo, having been promoted by Benjamin's mother and new MD, Jonathan, to serve as an Executive Director, was responsible for reviewing the performance of team leaders and department managers.

Steffan was somewhat confused by the situation. Whilst all of the other warehouse staff's appraisals had been and gone, he was yet to have his. Neither Rhodri, the warehouse manager, or his dickhead of a supervisor, Dan, had even mentioned it to him. Not wanting to appear pushy, he had decided not to chase it up with anybody.

'Take a seat,' instructed Theo, gesturing to the chair opposite his own. 'Don't look so worried!'

Steffan laughed nervously and gave a nod. He had never had much to do with Theo before, and couldn't quite get a read on his demeanour. He looked at the desk before him, scanning the performance report which lay on top of it. His name was at the top in bold, black ink.

'I'm doing my appraisal with yourself, am I?' he asked.

Theo cleared his throat. 'Er, yes. That was the plan.'

'Fair do's,' said Steffan. 'Thought it would've been with Dan or Rhodri, that's all.'

'Ordinarily, that would have been the case,' confirmed Theo. 'But, well... due to your performance and some restructuring across the business, we are pleased to offer you a new role as a shift leader.'

'So, a promotion?' asked Steffan.

'Precisely. There will of course be a pay increase, and new responsibilities etcetera, but we can go through everything like that in a moment. But yes, congratulations!'

Steffan did not know what to say. For the first time in a long time, he was being treated with respect – as though he was an important part of something. He had continued to work hard after the fire and had shown leadership and dedication. Obviously, despite the company's attempts to keep the full extent of the weekend quiet, word had got around and Steffan had earned the reputation of being something of a hero. If he was totally honest with himself, he deserved this, but after the last few years it still came as a shock to hear Theo's words... the company's words.

He was pleased he had stayed with HomeHub. It would have been just as easy to walk away after the teambuilding weekend. After the death of his boss – who was, he was sure, a bit of an arsehole, the emotional trauma of it all and even the injuries he suffered. Not to mention the sight of Bryn and Ceri, as she had tried to drag him out of the fire.

There were still reminders of what had happened, even now; Claire still hadn't been found, and although the police – and INTERPOL – had established she had left the country and made it to mainland Europe, they seemed to be struggling to find her trail. With that still going on, it was understandable that Gareth had taken the other option and resigned.

From speaking to him, Steffan knew he had needed to get away so that he could deal with everything he was going through. In the brief time they spent getting to know one another, he could tell Gareth was a decent enough guy. They had kept in touch after that weekend, Gareth kept him up to date with his recovery, and Steffan made sure he was in the loop with what was going on at work. Once Gareth resigned, Steffan didn't hear much from him anymore, but that was okay. They had made it through to the other side. And for now, maybe that was enough.

EPILOGUE

The term 'getting away with murder' is one which is normally used figuratively. Claire had uttered the words herself many times, in the workplace when discussing staff errors or wrongdoings, and even in observation of naughty children in public. But for the last twelve months, she had been 'getting away' with it in the most literal sense.

It hadn't been easy, but she was a survivor and always had been. After being born into a world made up of a combination of a piece-of-shit absent father and her good-for-nothing mother's issues with the law, Claire had floated in and out of the care system throughout her childhood. Because of this, she learned to toughen up from a young age.

From the things she would read as an adult, and news stories she'd heard about, she knew she had been lucky, in spite of her situation. The homes she had been placed in were fine. Not once had anyone raised a hand to her, locked her in a makeshift prison cell, or anything else untoward. But Ceri Evans had been different. She was the best foster parent bar none. The way she had treated her as though she was her own daughter, loved her even. She had given Claire the one thing she had never really known – the comfort and security of a real family.

Dafydd had been like a brother to her. After just weeks of her being taken in by his mother, that was how he began introducing himself to her friends. He was a softy, and she had lost count of the times she had fought his battles against school bullies, despite her being two years younger than him.

When she had heard about his passing, it broke her heart. In some ways, she blamed herself; she hadn't been there for him, after moving away to university in Leeds before eventually settling there after graduating. Her first job in Human Resources was for a large banking corporation at its UK headquarters. They would see each other at Christmas, and send each other messages on birthdays, but other than that, they had drifted apart. The news of his death sparked her guilt, and when she found out what he had written in his suicide note, she was flooded by a burning need to avenge him. She spotted the HR Manager position advertised at HomeHub, and she knew immediately that it was a sign.

When she had told Ceri and Ceri's brother, aka Uncle Bryn, of her new role, they were completely on board. It was the perfect opportunity to really find out the going's on of the place, about Benjamin, and gather enough dirt on him to obtain some kind of justice for Dafydd.

It was a challenge having to earn Benjamin's trust – towing the company line and pretending to agree with his outlandish management style – rather than giving in to the temptation to punch his smarmy, entitled face. The biggest issue, however, was that he was not stupid. He may have lacked anything which even slightly resembled a bedside manner, was as far away from PC as anyone else she had ever met and took direction from a defective moral compass, but in the entire time she worked with him, she failed to build any kind of criminal case against him, leaving Ceri and Bryn completely disheartened.

That was when one final opportunity sailed gently into her lap. It was as though it had floated down from Heaven itself. As part of an alleged new approach to boost employee satisfaction – but more of a photo opportunity to post on HomeHub's *Careers* page, and gaslight those on the outside looking in – Benjamin had suggested they organise team building trips, away from the office. A rare change from his micro-managing tendencies, he had surprised her in delegating the planning completely. It left the making of arrangements to her, and she brought Jodie in to 'help'. Claire had spotted Jodie's infatuation with their boss ages ago, so convincing her the isolation of a woodland retreat with Benjamin was a great idea was just too easy. The daft cow even took the credit for the suggestion when the boss met it with praise.

All that was left to do was for Bryn and Ceri to take a turn at trying to work Benjamin out – they had declined to manufacture an 'accident'. Instead, they decided they would put him through his paces in the wilderness, wear him down that way. The aim was to have him become lost and separated from the rest of the party, where they would interrogate him, pushing him to the point he accepted responsibility for Dafydd's suicide.

That was the plan, and after Ceri had told Claire of the financial difficulties the retreat had suffered during the pandemic, she was pleased the bookings would go some way to killing two birds with one stone.

But now, along with Dafydd, all three of them were dead. And she was to blame. Of course, none of this would have happened if Benjamin could have kept his dick in his pants. The entitled arsehole. If he hadn't phoned her up in a panic, begging her to come and fix the mess he had made by trying to shag Jodie, she wouldn't have been there. She wouldn't have killed him.

It was his fault. He shouldn't have mocked Gareth when she had raised her concerns about his mental health. He shouldn't have compared him to Dafydd, shouldn't have *said those things* about Dafydd. And then Steffan had spotted her outside, and the mess had grown more and more.

In the end, the truth of Benjamin's murder had died with her foster mother and uncle. She hated that Ceri and Bryn had died, and more so hated them being blamed for both Benjamin's murder and the 'tragic accident' which burned their livelihood to the ground.

She regretted taking their money, too. But perhaps that – and protecting her – was a price they would have been willing to pay, to be reunited with Dafydd. That was what she hoped.

Despite their death, she knew the police would still want to know about her involvement. She wasn't supposed to be there. So she ran. There was nothing left for her in North Wales anymore. She had to leave. After she fled the scene and reached safety, she tried the radios she had taken from the office. She may have been a killer, but she wasn't a monster. And besides, she needed to make sure Bryn and Ceri were safe. Frustrated that they hadn't turned on, she hammered one against her dashboard in a rage. Incredibly, it worked. Who said violence never solved anything?

With help on the way, she quickly sent a final email to HomeHub, resigning with immediate effect, citing 'personal reasons'. After that, she continued to drive, slipping away amongst the disarray the fire had wreaked upon the business. With the money she had taken from the safe, she had left the country the very next day, travelling on a ferry to France, to embark on her next journey. From there, she had kept a cautious eye on developments in the UK, and soon realised she needed to disappear completely.

* * *

Despite her guilt, and her freedom being under threat, the urge to avenge those who had wronged her, and her loved ones, remained alight. In fact, when she had watched the life drain from Benjamin's face, it had only grown stronger than ever before.

As soon as she stepped off the boat and onto Phuket Island, complete with her latest change of appearance and identity, she just knew it was where she needed to be. It would have been better had it not been the middle of monsoon season, but with rain came cheaper prices for her travel, so there was a silver lining to the scattered clouds above her.

The taxi from the pier to Phuket Town took just five minutes and cost around 250 baht. She had been advised by a friendly lady from Hong Kong to seek out the Songthaew Bus service for the best way to travel around. The lady had smiled in amusement as she described the 'blue buses', and as soon as Claire saw it, she understood why. More of a converted truck with wooden benches, rather than any bus she had seen back home, the trip to Patong took just over one bumpy hour to travel across the island.

For a fraction of the cost of the taxi, the Songthaew was just about worth it.

Despite the earlier rainfall, the sun was peering out over the beach. It was warm too. A few months ago, Claire may have complained, but she was well adjusted to the tropical climate of southeast Asia by now.

Walking along, she took in the endless streams of street vendors and Western takeaways on one side of the road, whilst to the other lay the long golden stretch of Patong Beach. She kept her eyes peeled on the signs and building, as she looked for the place. It didn't take long before she stumbled upon it. Taking a deep breath, she stepped in through the doorway, and glanced around, looking for him. It was surreal seeing him in the flesh, and as she approached him, her heart began beating faster and faster. She swallowed down her nervousness, as he looked up and made eye contact with her for the first time. His face was filled with confusion towards the stranger standing before him.

'Hello, father.'

AUTHOR'S NOTE

This book is a work of fiction. It is nothing more than a product of my imagination. That said, the story is set in North Wales, and there are references to genuine places. There are also a couple of fictional locations mentioned in the book, namely *Pontfechan*, which exists to allow me creative freedom in terms of geography, and the woodland which is home to 'Wellderness Adventure', *Pren y Glowr.*

The inspiration for 'The Miner's Wood' stems from a piece of Llangollen folklore which you may well already be aware of. I read about it some time ago, courtesy of Llangollen Museum (llangollenmuseum.org.uk). The tale relates to The Barber of Llangollen, who was executed at the top of a hill now known as *Moel y Barbwr*, or The Barber's Hill. The barber – and schoolmaster of the village – murdered his wife, not upon discovering her adultery, like the miner in my book, but over a dispute about *boiling or roasting a neck of mutton.*

On a less interesting note, the use of the brand names or products which are referenced in the book, is done so solely for the purpose of realism, and is neither an endorsement of, or an attempt to defame any of the companies mentioned.

ACKNOWLEDGEMENTS

Firstly, I would like to thank my wife, Emma for putting up with me. I can appreciate how frustrating it must be, if I'm 'in the zone' and typing away whilst mugs, glasses and plates mysteriously spawn and multiply around me. Thank you for taking a break from books about faeries to read *another* of my drafts… your initial thoughts and feedback genuinely help to shape my writing.

To Owen and Ella. You will both inspire a couple of interesting characters in a future novel, believe me. Also, Ella – keep reading (but not this book), and Owen – please just pick up a book (even if it's this book).

To Dad, aka Grandad Terry, I know that life has been flipped in an unimaginable way this year, but we love you.

If anybody was a bigger fan of my writing than Emma, it was my mum, Julie. I still cannot quite accept the cruelness of losing you so quickly, and I am so gutted that you never had chance to read this book… and complain there is too much swearing. I miss you every day.

Whilst I have done much of the work on this book alone, I don't think it would have reached this stage without the guidance of editor Abigail Fenton, who's wealth of experience and knowledge helped immeasurably. Thank you, Abi.

Thank you to Vikki for the excellent cover design.

Also, thank you to the many authors who have given me advice and encouragement during our bookshop's events, most notably Simon McCleave (for reading the book too!), Jenny Blackhurst and David Barnett.

If by chance you've made it this far… thank you, dear reader. I hope you liked it, and even if you didn't… a 5-star rating everywhere would be hugely appreciated!

www.ingramcontent.com/pod-product-compliance
Ingram Content Group UK Ltd.
Pitfield, Milton Keynes, MK11 3LW, UK
UKHW040108231025
8542UKWH00009B/114

9 781919 292809